THE BLACKBOARD CAVALIER

HOUSTON PUBLIC LIBRARY
HOUSTON, TEXAS

THE Blackboard Cavalier

BY JOHN MORRESSY

1966

DOUBLEDAY & COMPANY, INC., GARDEN CITY, NEW YORK

R01 0270 2307

All of the characters in this book are fictitious, and any resemblance to actual persons, living or dead, is purely coincidental.

Library of Congress Catalog Card Number 66–16934
Copyright © 1966 by John Morressy
All Rights Reserved
Printed in the United States of America
First Edition

66-59050

To Barbara

PART ONE

Things looked good.

Ernie didn't like to dwell on this, fearing that everything would go bad in a matter of minutes if he did; but he had to admit that so far, things really did look good. Well, pretty good. Not actually bad, anyway. Not yet.

At least he had reason to hope. Here it was June, and not a word had been said about letting him go at the end of the term. Of course, not a word had been said about keeping him on next year, either; but why be suspicious?

"Because you're dealing with Mikropoulous," Ernie promptly stated.

Mikropoulous. What the hell was going on in that swollen baroque monument Mikropoulous used for a head? He had been in to observe all the other new teachers three times this year, but he had seen Ernie only twice, and still not a word about coming in again.

That could mean that he considered Ernie satisfactory, and was going to keep him on.

"Or beyond redemption," Ernie snapped, "and he's going to dump you."

The thing to do was to face him, force him to answer one way or the other. But the tendency to let a sleeping dog lie was strong in Ernie, particularly when the dog was the chairman of his department. He decided to let things ride with Mikropoulous for a few days. There were too many other things to worry about. There was Doris. He had to do something about Doris, and soon. And then there was Europe. If he didn't let the people running the flight know his decision by next week, he could lose his deposit. But could he actually stay over there on the money he had? And what would Doris say when he told her? And what would he do if she said . . .

"It's got to be this week," Ernie said firmly. "This week or never."

"Don't say that," he replied quickly.

He was talking to himself again, but that didn't bother him any more. All things considered, it seemed the best way to occupy his time on the miserable thirty-five-minute bus ride that served as the opening movement of his day. Back in September, when this was all new to him, he had tried to read the newspaper, but that turned out to be impossible. The bus driver was a speed-happy sadist who turned the conveyance of his handful of passengers into a bone-shattering pilgrimage from pothole to pothole, hitting each one at top speed and making it a superhuman task merely to hold on to a newspaper, much less read it.

"No, I'm through fooling around," Ernie said. "I'll straighten out everything this week with Mikropoulous, and Doris, and everyone else."

"That's what you said last week," he pointed out. "And the week before, too."

After he had given up the newspaper, he had tried looking out the windows, but that was worse. First of all, they were too dirty. And if he got a clean one, all he saw was a row of empty store fronts, then the cemetery, then the apartment houses, more store fronts, more apartment houses, until he was ready to fall in a heap, sobbing. It was like looking at a festival of old John Garfield movies. All that was missing was Sylvia Sidney. No, that was out. Especially since the morning he had nearly dashed his brains out against the window when they went over the crater near the corner of Easthampton Street. Play it safe, he decided.

Ernie had toyed with the idea of talking to the other passengers then, but that idea didn't get past the toying stage. There were never more than three people on the bus at that hour of the morning, and none of them showed any signs of being a Samuel Johnson. The old woman who looked like Madame Maria Ouspenskaya left him with the uneasy feeling that she could, on very slight provocation, blast him with a curse that would turn him into something small and loathsome. At 7:20 in the morning he was already feeling small and loathsome enough without any outside help, and he saw no need to push his luck. The fellow who always got on at the Avenue, slumped into the seat behind the driver, and immediately went to sleep might have been a dark, embittered Conrad character, a hollow man straight from the heart of darkness. But he was probably just a bum. That let him out. It left only the big sweet-faced woman with the shape like a hassock. She looked nice enough, but she probably had a daughter Ernie's age with bad breath and lots of personality. No, thanks.

"But this time I mean it," he insisted. "I'll get the money together—"

"How?"

"Stop it. I'll get the money together, and I'll talk the whole thing over with Doris. She'll understand."

"Ha, ha!"

For a while, then, Ernie had tried making up little songs and singing them to himself. His first attempt, for sentimental reasons, was "Abercrombie and Fitch," sung to the tune of "Happy Birthday to You." He had always looked upon Abercrombie as one of the really great names, names like Rudolph Rassendyll, Wolfgang Amadeus Mozart, Rodion Romanovitch Raskolnikov, and Gwen Ffrangcon-Davies, names that conferred greatness on their bearer as surely as a noble lineage, names that made a name like Ernie Quinn sound pale and insignificant. He remembered, with rueful nostalgia, the day he had discovered Lascelles Abercrombie —here was a name to be reckoned with—and found his poems too long. Oh, well.

"Abercrombie and Fitch" was fun for a while, and then Ernie decided to be more practical and turn his little private recitals into study sessions by making up mnemonic songs. He was taking a course in Romantic literature at the time, so he began with

Wordsworth and Coleridge,
Wordsworth and Coleridge,
Wordsworth and Coleridge,
And Shelley and Keats,

sung to "The Ride of the Valkyries." He extended his coverage then, switching to the melody of "Yes, We Have No Bananas" for

*Words*worth, Coleridge, and Shelley;
Lord Byron, De Quincey, and Keats.

He was working on the "Largo al Factotum" aria from *The Barber of Seville,* which would have enabled him to fit in everyone, including the minor figures, as long as he wasn't too finicky about rhymes, when one day he forgot where he was and began to sing out loud. That was the end of the little songs.

"She *will* understand," he persisted. "She's that kind of a girl. She'll be willing to wait for me. We've been going out together for over four months now."

"Doesn't mean a thing. You're not engaged."

"But she's wearing my ring."

"So did Maureen. And Regina."

"And her father's probably going to offer me a job at the college," Ernie went on, ignoring that last bit. "He's never actually said so, but I think he is."

"But you don't like her father."

"I'm not going out with her father."

"But he comes with Doris, and so does her mother. Like trading stamps."

Why do things always happen like this? Ernie wondered. Last Christmas, it looked perfect. He was finally going to make it to Europe. Everything was great.

Then he met Doris.

Life is so nice and simple when you want one thing more than anything else in the world, but it's sheer hell when you want two, as Ernie was learning, painfully. He wanted Europe, and wanted it badly; but he wanted Doris, too, and he wanted her every bit as badly. So he had to figure out a way to get them both, to eat his cake and have it, too. It's not that hard, really, he kept telling himself; all you have to do is go out and get a hell of a big cake.

But what do you do when you don't have enough to buy one slice, let alone a whole cake? Especially when you're liable to lose your job on a few days' notice. Well, what *do* you do?

There was no answer. Fortunately, Ernie didn't have to think of one. After an arpeggio of jarring bounces that jellied his kidneys, the bus careened around a corner and headed down Glen Park Road at insane speed. The next stop was Ernie's.

Ernie Quinn felt that the seeds of greatness were within him. They were doing a pretty poor job of sprouting, it was true; but he refused to be discouraged. His was not to be an ordinary greatness, and perhaps, since it was an odd growth, it was the slow-starting variety. There were other possibilities, but he tried not to think of them.

Ernie wanted to be a book bum. If people could be tennis bums, ski bums, beach bums, or rodeo bums, then why, he reasoned, couldn't he be a book bum? He had originally thought of becoming a man of letters, but that didn't seem to be quite the right line of work. There were too many strings attached. A man of letters had to publish at least one book of Georgian nature poetry, and preferably during his undergraduate career. It was a little late for that now. He had to write long, angry letters to the *Times Literary Supplement*; he had to read Proust at least once a year; and although no one ever came out and said so, he had to have a hell of a lot of money; more than Ernie, anyway. A book bum, on the other hand, only had to read and travel around. He didn't really need much money, and best of all, he had no strings on his life. A book bum was a free man.

Ernie often dreamed of his future as a book bum. It was a good dream, even better than the C21 series, but C21 was taking up a lot more dreaming time lately. The best part of the book bum dream was the Grand Tour sequence, in which Ernie pedaled his way across Europe on a dusty, battered bicycle, a bag of books slung behind him, to become a welcome guest at peasant festivals, a reader of old, yellowed books by the light of a flickering candle, a thoughtful wanderer among picturesque ruins, a name to be quoted from Mayfair to Munich. He would become a legend in his own time, like Lawrence (either one), Wilde (but not quite so decadent), Byron, or Hemingway.

And when the wandering was over, he would return, an honored figure; students, scholars, and disciples would make the pilgrimage to his tiny but exquisite cottage somewhere in Vermont near the good skiing. His beautiful, devoted wife Doris would welcome them, and he would inspire them with his wisdom, his warmth, his never-failing kindness, humility, and understanding. He would knock the bastards cold.

But there were some rough edges to the dream. The reading, for instance: here he was, dreaming of a life as a book bum, and he hadn't read one book (one *real* book, not *Silas Marner* or *Giants in the Earth*) since September. It wasn't laziness that was stopping him, it was all the damn fool silly nonsense that he had to wrestle with because it was part of his job.

Things weren't supposed to be horrible, of course. They were supposed to be about as good as any man has a right to expect; at least, everyone kept telling Ernie so. Doris was awfully nice—the only nice part of the whole present set-up, as a matter of fact—and her father had dropped a few vague hints about something at his college as soon as Ernie finished work on his degree, and Glen Park High School wasn't a bad place to work in the meantime.

Well, no. Glen Park High School was sheer hell. It was a *good* school, and everyone knows what that means.

Students from Glen Park High School were always building satellites and cyclotrons, writing letters to the Pope and Bertrand Russell, and getting their pictures in the papers; they always won Glen Park more scholarships than any other school in the world, and had the highest percentage of everything that good students were supposed to have a high percentage of. Faculty members were regularly booted up the administrative ladder to positions where they faced "new challenges" (Ernie hated that term with a passion. The old challenges were bad enough, and Ernie had found that people who spoke eagerly of "new challenges" usually intended to dump them on someone else at the first opportunity), and the principal was always publishing editorial-page poems in stumbling Whitmanesque to celebrate the installation of a hot lunch program in the cafeteria, the painting of the auditorium, the reupholstering of the school bus seats, and other enterprises of great pith and moment. Alumni came to visit and to make an occasional speech in tearful tribute to the grand old members of the faculty and that wonderful principal who showed them what it really means, and so on. The emotional impact of their hosannas was diluted for Ernie by the aura of sleazy grandeur surrounding these specimens of the humbly successful man; there was an excessive sleekness to their wavy white locks, their silk lapels, their white-on-white shirts; the pinky ring was a bit too flashy, the shoes a bit too pointed, the tan a bit too deep. Ernie felt that all of Glen Park's alumni had become either used-car salesmen or Florida land speculators, and this made it impossible for him to be impressed by them.

No, Glen Park was sheer hell, and there was no avoiding the fact. Still, Ernie tried to console himself, two out of three isn't bad; and what else could he do? And no sooner had he said this to himself than he went wild and started making irrevocable decisions. He would get the money together . . . somehow. He would convince Doris that . . . well, he could concentrate on that after he got the money. He would work things out at Glen Park High School (or better still, level it to the ground with no survivors). He had to. He couldn't keep on the way he was now. It was too awful.

The bus pulled away with a great defiant expulsion of poisonous exhaust. It jolted its way down the road, rumbling and wheezing like an old asthmatic rhinoceros, and Ernie was left alone. Glen Park High School loomed up before him, two blocks away, beckoning. He lit a cigarette, bowed his head, and answered the summons.

It was an ugly, nasty day. There was a touch of summer in the morning air, the sun was bright in a sky like a Wedgwood bowl, and there was even a bird singing—not just another sparrow, or some damned pigeon, but a real bird, maybe even a robin. Ernie couldn't see it. But in spite of all these pastoral delights, it was still a rotten day; it was Monday. Not only that, it was five to eight on a Monday morning, and Ernie was about to begin another week of teaching. Sometimes there didn't seem to be any hope.

Arriving this early was something Ernie did less from enthusiasm than from desperation. The buses were not as crowded at this hour, the school was still relatively quiet and empty, and he could sort of ease himself into the day, instead of being flung in bodily. At times, though, sitting in his empty classroom waiting for the first bell, he felt like an early Christian martyr waiting for the show to start, or one of those lean, lonely figures in a di Chirico painting. Either way, he thought, I lose.

He reached the steps of the main entrance, where the early arrivals were loitering discreetly. Two girls called "Good morning, Mister Quinn," and he waved to them as he passed, marveling at their cheerfulness at this unspeakable hour. The very young, he thought, are different from you and me. From me, anyway.

The great bank of iron doors was as uninviting as ever, and he felt a tiny twinge of gratitude at not having to enter by way of the main portal (Somehow, "Doors" sounded insignificant when applied to things that looked as though they should have "*Abandon all hope, ye who enter here,*" or, as they say in Italy—and presumably in Hell—"*Lasciate ogni Speranza, voi ch'entrate,*" scrawled above them in letters of fire and a couple of three-headed puppies cavorting around front of them). He made his way around to the side entrance (Beggars, peddlers, delivery boys, and teachers), which was, as always, mysteriously unlocked, and entered. He had often wondered about that door; surely it was locked *some*times, but he had never found it so. Perhaps the janitor left a dish of porridge outside at night, and the good fairy hung around the area, making sure that no ogres or thieves entered until morning. Ernie really didn't give a damn, but thinking about it kept his mind off reality. Try as he might, reality kept intruding.

On this particular morning, reality intruded in its customary disastrous fashion. When Ernie had punched the time clock, he turned to check his letter box, and there, waiting for him, was reality in its ugliest form—a letter box crammed full of papers. Every damned one of them, Ernie knew in his heart, would be a notice, and they would all be urgent. He was able to milk some slight consolation from the sure knowledge that every damned one of them was going to be ignored, but that didn't make them disappear; it just postponed the suffering to a later date when it would return in intensified form. He could only hope that he would be stronger on that day.

The side door slammed, and Ernie heard the sound of slow, reluctant, Monday-morning footsteps approaching the time-clock room. He was not in a mood for cheerful greetings and sunny chitchat, so he pressed himself into a corner and did his best to be unobtrusive. Nothing was working right this morning.

"Hello, Quinn," the new arrival greeted him.

"Hello, Abe," Ernie replied. It was Abramowitz of the Chemistry Department, a small, slow-moving man with the expression one would imagine on the face of Job.

"Another Monday morning," Abe observed.

"Yeah. Sure is."

"Yeah."

Abramowitz turned to face his letter box, sighed mournfully at the confrontation, then began to pick slowly through its contents, emitting little grunts of curiosity and disgust.

"Another —— Monday morning," he said, half to himself, using a word that sounded Yiddish and, judging from its application, obscene.

"Huh? Oh, yeah," Ernie said.

"Well, there's not many left to go," Abe said, sounding as if he didn't believe it.

"No. That's true."

"No more meetings, anyway."

"That's something."

"How about that one on Friday? Did you ever see such a waste of time?"

"I wasn't there, Abe," Ernie said, then added furtively, "I cut out."

"You didn't miss much. Did anyone sign you in?"

"Yes. Bob Ferriss."

"Good," Abe said, nodding judiciously. "Got to make sure you're signed in. You miss a meeting around here, they go out of their minds."

"I know."

"Yeah. Well, off to battle."

"So long, Abe."

Abramowitz waved a sad farewell and trudged off down the hall toward the fragrant wing that housed the Chemistry Department. Ernie sighed and returned to the examination of his papers, accompanying his labors with a series of grimaces, winces, and exasperated mutters, a good deal of eye-rolling, and here and there an expletive. The top sheet began "Hi, teach! Your colleagues (that's us!!) are trying to—" and was flung viciously into the wastebasket without further perusal. If there was any proper time for coy drivel—and Ernie felt that that was a pretty shaky premise to begin with—it was not Monday morning. The second and third items to meet his eye were reminders of some fast-approaching deadline. They joined the first immediately. One useful thing Ernie had learned was that there was a great deal of crying "Wolf!" in administrative circles, and that a notice, regardless of its apparent urgency, could always be ignored without risk unless it was handed to you personally. Once they began giving them to you in person, though, it was time to shape up or start working on your résumé. The fourth surprise of the morning was the worst (the worst up to that point, that is; you could never be sure about how bad things would be in a few minutes). It was a curt, handwritten note—in tense, neurotic scratches of an old-fashioned steel pen—inquiring about Ernie's absence from Friday's faculty meeting and suggesting, in much the same manner as a holdup man suggests that one deliver his goods, that Ernie deliver his explanation personally to the assistant principal that afternoon during his free period. It was signed "*M. J. Grimm.*" When he had skulked out a side door the day of the meeting, Ernie's excuse—"It slipped my mind"—had seemed plausible. After all, he had never expected to have to use it; Ferriss was supposed to have signed him in. Apparently, Ferriss had defected. Now, when faced with the prospect of reciting his story in the presence of the Iron Maiden of Glen Park, Ernie found it assuming the consistency of damp tissue paper. A tissue of lies, he told himself, trying hard to be amused. But he was not the type for gallows humor.

There were still several notices to go, but Ernie's spirits were too low to face them just now. He decided to go up to his room and finish them there in the interval of blessed silence before the doors were opened and the halls began to ring with the merry laughter and colorful obscenities of the student body. Besides, there was always the chance that the world would end or he would break a leg or Miss Grimm would defect to Czechoslovakia in the next few minutes—a slim chance, perhaps, but one could still hope for the best. He walked to the end of the hall, passing, on his way, Sam Teller, the shop teacher, a tall, thin, expressionless man who reminded him of the mummified remains of a twelfth-century German saint. Ernie grunted a noncommittal greeting, and Sam responded with equal eloquence and vivacity.

He started up the stairs, trudging slowly across the hollow-sounding metal treads, glancing with minimal curiosity at the ribald graffiti and the runic mementos of withered loves that served as a frieze to inspire his ascent, and idly wondered what the hell the janitor did to earn his salary. He began to concoct a tale that the janitor, a shifty-eyed malcontent with all the driving energy of a ground sloth, was transcribing the wall-writings for the National Geographic Society and had vowed not to remove a single scribble until his work was completed. Ernie liked this one —it was a lot better than the thing about a tissue of lies—and he spent the remainder of his upward journey adding lavish embellishments to it. It was something to do.

He came to Room 318, entered, shut the door behind him, and

went to the desk. Overnight, he knew, great changes had taken place and great events had occurred: the ocean floor had heaved and shifted; stars had burst into being, suns had flickered into ashes, and the universe had whirled further on to its mysterious destination. But Room 318 was the same dreary, antiseptic side-pocket of existence it had been from the dawn of creation. If only Kafka could have visited Room 318, Ernie thought, it would have inspired a dozen novels, each one more depressing than the one before, and all of them limning the slow erosion of the soul of Ernie Quinn—or, more likely, Mr. Q.—who would wind up maddened by secret guilt or metamorphosed into a cockroach in every single one of them. He had the idea of turning into a gigantic cockroach and then visiting Miss Grimm with his excuse, but banished the thought immediately. She would only step on him, as she stepped on everyone. You didn't even have to go to the bother of turning into a cockroach. Miss Grimm was very accommodating.

That's enough of *that*, Ernie snapped, when he realized he was trying to sit at his desk as a cockroach would. He settled down, human-style, in his chair and began arranging the remainder of his notices before him. Here we go, he warned himself, clenching his viscera for the ordeal.

The top notice introduced an element of genuine, though unintentional, humor. It concerned nominations for the school honor society. Into the basket; on to the next: "All members of the faculty interested in forming a—"; next, please: "Just a note to remind you that *Windswept*, the student literary magazine, counts on—" Ernie was looking forward to the next issue of *Windswept*, but he had no intention of becoming a pitchman; into the basket. He was making good time now, coordinating his actions into a steady rhythm of glance, crumple, toss, glance, crumple, toss; then the blow fell. Insinuated among the harmless trivia was a viper, an asp among the figs, a serpent in the garden, a smiler with a knife under his cloak. It struck with deadly swiftness, and Ernie was doomed before he could raise a finger. On the day when all his energies ought to be devoted to dreaming up a tale that would excite a willing suspension of disbelief on the part of the Iron Maiden, Ernie had to prepare himself to be observed. The notice was written simply and unemotionally, like a death warrant; no ranting, no threats, no circumlocution; just a simple statement:

"*Dear Mr. Quinn, I will make my third and final visitation to your classes on Tuesday.*" That was it. Not the bleak, icy finality of "hanged by the neck until you are dead," but just as effective in its way. It was signed, in a single flamboyant arabesque two inches high, "*G.P.M.*" Gregory Peter Mikropoulous, the Sinon of Glen Park High School.

Ernie sat back in his chair and stared into space; in one blinding flash, it had been given to him to know and understand exactly how General George Armstrong Custer felt on that last morning. But at least Custer had a lot of soldiers and some guns. Ernie had only twenty-four hours' notice (He knew, but refused to admit it to himself, that if he had been a good boy and checked his letter box on Friday afternoon he would have had eighty-four hours' notice, not to mention a miserable weekend). He was tempted to fall on his knees, throw his arms wide, and beg Heaven to send just one small spare bolt of lightning down on him. Or better still, on Mikropoulous. None of that, he told himself quickly; you shouldn't think things like that. But he did, and frequently. It was just one more proof that they were getting to him, and Mikropoulous was leading the pack.

Mikropoulous was, in his own way, a giant among men; a sort of dwarfed Titan. He was intelligent, articulate, poised, and altogether charming at first acquaintance; and he was sly, treacherous, shifty, vengeful, and vindictive ever after. Or so he appeared to Ernie, who imputed to his chairman the pride of a young Spanish grandee, the cunning of a Borgia, the cruelty of a Cossack, the guile of a Hungarian gigolo, the conscience of a Romany gypsy, the single-minded fanaticism of a hashshashin, and the brooding malevolence of an injured Sicilian. In Ernie's book, ever since the day of the first observation, Mikropoulous had been heir to the triple crown bestowed on Silas Brown by Sherlock Holmes when he told Watson "a more perfect compound of the bully, coward, and sneak than Master Silas Brown I have seldom met with."

But even at the zenith of bitchiness, Mikropoulous was a pro, and no one could deny it. He had a bag of elocutionary tricks, for instance, that would impress a blood enemy (Ernie would have bet that he also had a bag of blood enemies), little mannerisms of intonation and gesture, ways of lifting up a word and holding it to the light so that it shone like a diamond. When he talked to younger teachers, he employed his specialty, the portentous pause, hesitating at just the right spots to give the impression that each phrase brought his listener to the brink of destruction, but Mikropoulous, out of benevolence and charity, was willing to spare him—until the next pause. It impressed Ernie deeply until, upon brooding over his conversation with Mikropoulous at a distance of a few days' time, he realized that although the man had talked at great length, and carried it off beautifully, he had not actually said anything important, only given the impression that he had. Ernie felt that he had been beautifully conned, as if he had been listening, enraptured, to a hauntingly familiar composition being played on the great Schnitger organ at Neuenfelde, and realized, days later, that he had heard a commercial jingle. After this, Ernie was on his guard, but Mikropoulous was still formidable.

Some people didn't mind being observed (or so they claimed; Ernie had his doubts about them), but they didn't have Ernie's record lurking in *their* background. A few minutes remained before the first bell was due to ring—plenty of time to work himself into a breakdown if he really tried—and Ernie decided to think about the last two observations and see if that would do the trick. At the very least, he ought to be able to get himself into a state in which he could gibber nonsense, and that was just what he needed for Miss Grimm. He knew that the students wouldn't mind at all. They were used to it.

He started off by going back to the first observation (how he despised that word; still, it was better than "visitation," which made him feel as though he ought to be on the lookout for clutching ectoplasmic fingers), when Mikropoulous had come in to watch him teaching *Macbeth* to a group of juniors, most of whom had not read it except in comic form. Some of them had read the real thing, to a background of television set and radio, and their version of Macbeth's last soliloquy sounded like something written down by Huck's friend the duke after he had polished off *Hamlet*. The only line they got straight was the part about "Lay on, Macduff," and that was only because it gave them the chance to say "damned," which they did with great joy and heavy emphasis. Ernie had accepted this philosophically. It was fortunate for him that they didn't cover this part of the play during Mikropoulous' visit, or he would have found a terse statement about the toleration of profane language seared across the observation report; others had already experienced this *coup de grâce* to their career, but Ernie was quite unaware of the danger. It just happened that on the day of the observation, in this one respect, luck was with him. Even Ernie couldn't lose them all.

The fact that one small chink in his armor had been inadvertently covered made little difference in the net results of Mikropoulous' visit. He was looking for weak spots and he found them. Some, of course, were justified. After all, Ernie had been teaching for less than three months, the observation took place in a class whose appreciation for Shakespeare was on a par with an eighty-five-year-old auld licht minister's fondness for teen-age dance fads, and the whole rotten business took place on a Monday morning. But on the other hand, some of Mikropoulous' objections bordered on the surrealistic; take the business of the simile.

Ernie was doing what educationists call a "medial summary" (one of the few educational terms that not only means something, but actually means what it appears to mean. It is a summary, and it comes at the midpoint of the material being covered). He was trying to put the contrast between Macbeth and Lady Macbeth into terms the students would understand, and he had developed what he thought was a good image: Lady Macbeth was like a fine crystal wineglass, richly engraved and delicately spun, ringing like a bell when tapped with a fingernail, but delicate, shattering to pieces when hard hit; Macbeth, on the other hand, was more like a beer stein, big and a bit clumsy, rough around the edges, not as clear and refined as the wineglass, but a lot tougher. When hit, he might chip a little, here and there, but he wouldn't shatter. Ernie used this comparison, and as far as he could tell, it worked. When he and Mikropoulous met that afternoon for the "post-observation conference," as the chairman grandly termed it, Ernie was looking forward to a compliment on this part of the lesson—not exactly expecting one, but ready to accept one without too much surprise; instead, he received a genteel, suave, civilized, perfectly executed psychological kick in the groin, Mikropoulous' personal specialty.

Mikropoulous had, of course, placed Ernie in the victim's chair, the one that faced directly into the sun glaring in the window over Mikropoulous' shoulder, so that Ernie could sit squinting and grimacing and looking as though he was ready to strike up a lively conversation with himself, highlighted by generous dribbling and lively gestures, while Mikropoulous, like something out of Blake's last drawings, peered darkly out of a nimbus of glaring light. Through some odd quirk of fate, the whole thing fell through on this particular day. The skies were overcast and there was no glare at all. Thinking it over later, Ernie almost convinced himself that this negligence on the part of the sun was the motive for Mikropoulous' irritation about the wineglass and the beer stein. He could almost hear the big Greek murmuring to himself, "All right—if God won't fix him, I will!" and then concocting some insane pettiness to harass poor, self-sacrificing, hard-working, noble, generous, kind, gentle, affectionate Ernest M. Quinn, whose true character would not be known until it was too late. And thank God for that.

So there he was, in the bad seat, knowing something unpleasant had to happen but not able to figure out what it would be or in what form it would make its appearance. Being an administrator, Mikropoulous had taken as his model, his guide, and his inspiration the inimitable Polonius, who never took the direct approach to anything if there was a devious route possible. This, Ernie had decided, was the way all educational administrators operated. If he passed his chairman in the hall one morning and Mikropoulous said, "Hello there, Ernie. How are you today, old man?", smiling sweetly all the while, Ernie was through. He probably wouldn't make it through the day without being fired, accused of some heinous crime, or struck down from behind as he entered the men's room. If, on the other hand, the principal were to accost him in the hall, knock him sprawling with a vicious backhand, and snarl, "Get out of my school, you lousy bastard, or I'll kill you," things were really looking up. He was probably in line for a promotion, at the very least. But every once in a while, just to keep people on their toes, the chairman would really mean it when he asked how Ernie was, and the principal would really mean it when he called him a lousy bastard. You could never tell. Fortified by these thoughts, Ernie awaited Mikropoulous' opening move.

Mikropoulous tried to dazzle him with stage business before

throwing out a single line. He leaned forward in his seat, took a pen from his onyx penholder (a *plastic* onyx penholder, Ernie later learned; just one more disillusionment), made two minor corrections on the paper in front of him, then raised his pen like some magic wand, meanwhile slithering forward over the desk toward Ernie, fixing him with his eye; if he had dropped about a hundred pounds and grown a long gray beard, he could have passed for the Ancient Mariner. Suddenly, like a lance coming to guard, the pen dropped to the horizontal, pointing directly at Ernie's heart and jiggling up and down. For one dreadful moment Ernie didn't know whether to clutch his throat and scream, disappear in a puff of smoke, turn into a toad, or just run like hell; he held his ground, and the moment passed.

"On the whole, Mr. Quinn . . . I found today's lesson . . . quite adequate. Quite adequate. In fact . . . taking into consideration your . . . short time in the field and your . . . lack of experience, I'd say it was a rather . . . good lesson."

"Thank you, Mr. Mikropoulous."

Silence for a time.

"There were, as I'm sure you understand, some features that . . . could stand improvement."

"Well, yes, I guess . . ."

"Now, you understand that . . . anything I say is intended as . . . sincere constructive criticism. I don't like to . . . pull my punches. If you do something magnificent, I'll call it magnificent . . . and if you do something asinine, I'll call it . . . asinine. But there's nothing personal in it. How's that—fair enough?"

"Fair enough for me. I like to know where I stand."

"Good. Good. That's one of the advantages of talking to . . . a man. I find that with the young ladies . . . one has a . . . problem of sensitivities. Any criticism, however objective and well-intentioned, is received with . . . tears. I know you're not going to start sniffling if I . . . point out a few areas where you might . . . improve your classroom performance."

Don't bet on it, Ernie thought, smiling a hail-fellow smile at Mikropoulous while his memory fumbled through dusty corners in search of the legend of the Spartan boy and the fox.

"Let's begin at the . . . beginning. You know the . . . policy of the department on . . . homework assignments. They're to be placed on the blackboard at the . . . beginning of the period."

"But the assignment *was* on the blackboard."

"Ah, no," Mikropoulous said with a fey smile that didn't quite come off, "let me read you what was on the blackboard, Mr. Quinn. You had written '48–59.' That's all. Now that's . . . hardly an assignment . . . is it?"

"I explained what it was all about before I wrote it on the board," Ernie said defensively.

"I'm sure you did. I'm not . . . accusing you of willfully confusing your students. But don't you see how much more . . . helpful it would have been to . . . identify the material on these pages? Essays, aren't they?"

"Yes, two essays on communications."

"Don't you agree that . . . there's more of a chance that the student will . . . recall the . . . titles and authors of these . . . essays if he sees them written on the blackboard and . . . copies them down for himself? And there's the . . . added advantage that if he loses his assignment book, there's a much better chance that he'll remember the . . . assignment without it."

The latter argument was unconvincing. If one wanted one of Ernie's students to remember an assignment, he was simply creating frustrations for himself. The best solution was an arrangement with the child's parents, whereby the assignment was written out in large block letters and pinned to the back of the student's jacket in some obvious but unreachable spot, to be removed only by the parent, who could then act as an overseer and make sure the work was done. Mikropoulous, who taught three classes of honor students, did not have this problem. His kids remembered their assignments. Ernie's kids often had trouble remembering that they were in a school. Ernie and Mikropoulous both knew this, and each of them knew that the other knew, but tact demanded silence.

The game was afoot now, and Mikropoulous pursued it, with much hallooing, through meadow and marsh. Too much reliance on notes, not enough class participation, questions too simple, answers too obvious, voice too low, overdependence on blackboard, and so on, and on, with too much of this and not enough of that, until Ernie began to wonder why he was being allowed to live at all. At this point, Mikropoulous cleverly dropped in a mild compliment, telling Ernie that he moved about the room gracefully (Ernie immediately had a picture of himself in a leotard, soaring through the door of Room 318 in a *grand jeté*). This was a way of letting the victim get his second wind before chopping him down for good, a tried and tested Mikropoulous' technique. Ernie didn't know this at the time, and was trying hard to be grateful for small favors when Mikropoulous made his final move.

"There's just . . . one last thing, Mr. Quinn," Mikropoulous said softly.

There was something familiar about the words, the way he said them, and the whole setting in which their little scene was being played, but it was weeks before Ernie was able to pin it down. When he did, he was stupefied at the sheer magnificent bitchiness it revealed in the man. It was as though he had found a hyena taking lessons in cowardice; it wasn't just gilding the lily, it was plating it. Mikropoulous was mean enough to begin with, but he actually hunted out little bits of business to refine and perfect his meanness. This particular one was a direct steal of Portia's line in *The Merchant of Venice*, where Shylock is all set to collect his pound of flesh, everything is going along smoothly, and then Portia sticks her nose in with her "Tarry a little; there is something else," and screws up everything. Ernie never had liked Portia, with all her damned nonsense about the three little boxes, and from this time on he liked her even less. What really killed him, though, was the way Mikropoulous worked the whole thing out so artistically. Here he was, criticizing a lesson in Shakespeare, and for his crucial moment—his confrontation scene, his final movement, his closing couplet—he chose a line from Shakespeare as a basis for his approach. The man was a mean, miserable bastard, but he was a real pro.

All these thoughts, though, came later. When Mikropoulous spoke, Ernie turned to him, all naïveté and sunny innocence, unaware that Mikropoulous, when shooting fish in a barrel, had a deadly aim.

"Yes, Mr. Mikropoulous?"

"The stein . . . and the wineglass," the big man said cryptically, losing Ernie completely for a few seconds.

"Oh, yes. The stein. And the wineglass. Oh, I used them for Macbeth and Lady Macbeth—is that what you mean?"

"That's what I mean, Mr. Quinn. Why did you happen to select those . . . particular items?"

"I thought something like that would make the contrast between the characters more vivid for the students. You know, more concrete."

"Yes, I understand your aim. I concur in it . . . wholeheartedly. But why . . . these particular objects? Why a beer stein and a . . . wineglass?"

"I wanted to use something familiar. Something the kids had all seen, possibly even handled."

"But why *these* things? Couldn't you have used . . . oh, a heavy fishing net . . . and a spider web? Or a hatpin and a . . . railroad spike?"

"I don't know. I think there's a better chance that our students have seen a wineglass and a beer stein than something like a fishing net or a railroad spike. I wanted to use something they'd probably all seen."

"Well, of course, Quinn, I didn't mean . . . specifically a fishing net or . . . any of those other things. I meant to suggest that when . . . dealing with adolescents, one can use . . . better imagery than . . . drinking implements."

"But I wasn't telling them to drink, I was just using the beer stein and the wineglass because I assumed that all the kids were familiar with them."

"You don't understand, Quinn. That's exactly my point. You're a teacher. You're not expected to . . . draw your illustrations from . . . the taproom. You know, it says a great deal about a man's . . . character and . . . background when he assumes that everyone he meets is familiar with the . . . trappings of the tavern. It's the sort of thing that can . . . reflect on one's . . . fitness for the profession."

Mikropoulous was leaning forward, hands clasped, a pious look of avuncular concern on his massive colonel-of-hussars face. The whole setup was rather disturbing to Ernie. Here Mikropoulous had practically come right out and said that Ernie Quinn was a reeling lush who lurched into school with his hat on backwards, and a loose, wet grin on his face, wound up puking all over himself by the fourth period, and saw wriggly green things by the seventh; yet the man looked genuinely concerned and deeply committed. Ernie began to fumble for an answer, but Mikropoulous had won and they both knew it. With a showy gathering together of papers, the chairman leaned back in his chair, beaming.

"Well, I think we've covered all the major points of this . . . observation, don't you, Quinn? If you don't have any questions"—he opened a drawer and put the papers into it—"or any remarks you'd like to make"—he pushed the chair back and began to rise—"I guess we can stop here. Now, I don't mean to rush you," he went on, taking his topcoat from the hanger, "but if there's nothing more, we may as well be going, eh? I'll have my remarks typed up and a copy placed in your letter box. Always those lessons to plan and papers to mark, you know." By this time he practically had his hand on the doorknob, and Ernie decided to flee and let the wounded shift for themselves. He had enough to worry about.

To first observation, then, had been bad. The second one was no better, but for just the opposite reasons. Ernie had made sure that the homework assignment was written out in full—it took nearly five minutes to do it and another five to explain the rich mosaic of names, vital dates, titles, subtitles, page numbers, and preliminary questions—and went to Mikropoulous' office confident that the Greek couldn't complain about a skimpy assignment this time. He was right. This time, Mikropoulous opened by noting the excessive time consumed in giving the assignment and the unnecessary amount of information incorporated into it. Thus he set the keynote for the second observation, the dominant theme of overreaction to the criticism of the first observation. This time, in addition to the comments on the assignment, it was insufficient use of notes and textbook, class control of the lesson, questions too difficult, answers too obscure, voice too loud, not enough use made of the blackboard, and so on, and on, with too much of this and not enough of that, until Ernie found himself wondering, a second time, why he was being allowed to live at all.

This morning he had learned the answer to that perplexing question. He was being spared, the note in his hand revealed, so that Mikropoulous could have the joy of observing him a third time, finding too much of this and not enough of that, until Ernie wondered why he was being allowed to live at all. This was known as "a career in teaching."

None of this should have come as a surprise or a shock to Ernie. Some months before, he had evolved, for his own diversion, an intricate, highly paranoid hypothesis which explained all the vicissitudes of his daily life in the bosom of Glen Park High School. It was not the sort of thing he mentioned to others—particularly Doris, who was majoring in psychology—but it served him nicely, covering all the angles, answering all the questions, plugging all the loopholes. All the torment and harassment visited upon him by the minions of the Board of Education was the work of a secret organization Ernie had christened MINUTCON—a bureaucratic acronym for the Ministry of Utter Confusion. MINUTCON was devoted to the destruction of all young men who wanted to be good teachers. Its weapons were red tape, absurd forms in quadruplicate, and observations. Its agents were numerous, highly skilled, and strategically placed. Mikropoulous, beyond a doubt, was one of the key operatives. There had been some room for doubt before, but this third observation was damning proof. Ernie withheld final judgment on Miss Grimm, whom he still regarded as an officious but unimportant functionary, like a German stationmaster. He was willing to believe that she was a dupe, but this afternoon would tell. They were closing in fast.

Like most of the things that befell Ernie, the creation of MINUTCON had been accidental and unpremeditated. One morning at the close of the second period he had picked up a paperback abandoned by one of his wards. Intrigued by the discovery that it was not a pornographic novel (or a "horny-porny," as one of his students called them), Ernie began to read it, and was introduced to the breath-taking adventures of Lancelot Savile, special agent of SCORPIO (Secret Commission on Rights, Peace, and International Order), and his never-ending battle with the international forces of evil, embodied in the wicked brotherhood of SADIST (Secretariat of Agitation, Demolition, Intrigue, Sabotage, and Terror) and its offshoots MAIM (Ministry of Anarchy, Insurrection, and Mayhem), SLASH (Specialists in Liquidation, Assassination, Slaughter, and Homicide), and CORRUPT (Council of Revolution, Riot, Unrest, and Political Terrorism). The complex web of plots, counterplots, and conspiracies impressed him at once with its similarity to his own one-man war against the nameless forces directing Mikropoulous, and before the day was over he had given these forces a local habitation (Glen Park High School) and a name (MINUTCON).

"So that's their game, is it?" Ernie said coolly, slipping into the role he had adopted to meet the MINUTCON threat. "Well, we shall see."

He had decided, at the very beginning, that if he was going to take refuge in fantasy it was going to be a good, fast-paced, action-packed fantasy or none at all; out of this decision was born an *alter ego*, Agent C21. To the world, Ernie was still Ernie Quinn, mild-mannered English teacher whose donnish charm and shy scholarly manner won him the warm affection of his colleagues, his pupils, and their parents. But beneath this diffident exterior smoldered Agent C21, nemesis of MINUTCON. A crack shot with his custom-made Settembrini .303, master of the garrote and dagger, expert at judo and karate, a remorseless killer with ice in his veins and fire in his eyes when dealing with the villainous minions of MINUTCON, he was nevertheless a man who, in his rare moments of leisure, wrote monographs on the breeding of Burmese cats, the elder Buxtehude, and Goliardic verse, and found true happiness only when he was reading Shelley to the one woman in his life, Doris, the little blind war orphan whom he had adopted. Agent C21 had a counter for every move MINUTCON could conceive; he was a match, and more than a match, for their most cunning and devious manipulators. Where Ernie Quinn would be confused and hesitant, C21 struck through the opposition and saved the day. Ernie had come to rely on him.

Fate, this particular morning, seemed to be on the side of MINUTCON. Before Agent C21 could devise a daring plan, something that would dispose of Mikropoulous, Miss Grimm, the janitor, and a few teachers who were neither MINUTCON agents, fellow travelers, nor dupes, but merely irritating people, the bell rang.

A bad day, precursor to a bad week, was about to begin. Ernie tucked Agent C21 into a handy pigeonhole of his mind, took a last deep breath, and settled back to await the morning's procession. The tumult and the shouting grew louder, and he thought once more of General Custer. Little Bighorn River, Montana, June 25, 1876. You are there, Ernie Quinn. And ten to one your rifle jams.

The students began to enter, one by one. Ernie watched the irregular procession of early entrants with the mild semidetached interest with which a vacationer in a hammock observes the busy and mysterious goings and comings of ants or bees. The daily parade reminded him of a panoramic reenactment of the rise of man; or perhaps his decline—it all depended on the order in which the students entered. Even then, there was not too much variation; Glen Park was a good school, and generally speaking, it had good students.

Certainly there was no poverty problem. No student at Glen Park High School came to school with ragged clothes and an empty belly; quite the contrary, there were many who might have benefited from a week or two on tea and crackers. When a Glen Park High School student used the words "poor," "hungry," or "underprivileged," he was referring to the natives of India or China, not to himself or his schoolfellows.

There were very few hard-core hoodlums at Glen Park High School. In that respect, the teachers were far better off than their comrades-in-arms who manned the embattled outposts of the Board of Education in less choice areas. Teachers at Glen Park were never stabbed and seldom cursed at—to their faces, at any rate—and violence among the students was usually restricted to isolated and unpremeditated punches exchanged in the heat of an intramural basketball game. Since there was no poverty, there was very little stealing; only a bit now and then, to keep the fingers supple. A sizable segment of the student body *tried* to look and act like hoodlums, thinking, apparently, that it was expected of them as teen-agers, but their hearts weren't in it. They followed the rules, but just couldn't get the hang of the game.

The few genuine hoods who made it to Glen Park High School tried to compensate for their numerical inferiority by a flair for attracting attention, employing such techniques as gaudiness and eccentricity of attire, loudness in the halls, and complete refusal to work. Unfortunately for them, once they had succeeded in attracting the attention, they were marked for elimination in the public interest, and it was only a matter of time before they were hurled headlong from the antiseptic halls of Glen Park High School. They comprised, at best, a small and transient segment of the student population.

By far the largest category of students was the one containing the "school-oriented," "socially mature," "well-adjusted," or even "gifted" youngsters; for Glen Park was, after all, a *good* school. These were the budding scholars, the loyal teammates, the devoted club members, the winners of awards, builders of projects, recipients of scholarships, writers of touching letters to great men and women, willing donors of time, effort, and energy to a score of enterprises that enhanced their education and the reputation of Glen Park High School.

There was a third category of students, whose existence was not so obvious as the first two. This was the privileged class, composed of the sons and daughters of school supervisors, principals, chairmen, and people of stature in the community. Ernie was unaware of their existence. Ignorance is bliss; but it can be dangerous.

On this portentous Monday, the first student to enter the class was Sidney. Sidney was actually *sui generis*, but if forced to generalize, Ernie would have grouped him with the good kids. Perhaps "lumped" him with the good kids is a better term, since that was the way things happened to Sidney.

Sidney was a victim, a soft, pale, fat boy who lumbered uncertainly through life in an aura of perspiration and anxiety. He was the poor soul who invariably lost his book the night before an examination, signed his name in the wrong place on applications, spilled ink on his compositions, and from time to time, for the sake of variety, broke his glasses or his arm. Sidney's approach was invariably the cue for a tale of woe, and when Ernie saw him waddling toward the desk on this, of all days, he was tempted to turn the tables and start pouring out his troubles to Sidney. It would serve no purpose, he knew; not only was Sidney helpless, but he really didn't give a damn about other people and their problems, and never listened when anyone tried to tell of them. As far as Sidney was concerned, *his* problems were the only meaningful issues facing society today, and all mankind existed only to solve them. Sidney's parents backed him to the hilt. The thought of retribution was tempting nonetheless, but Ernie held back and listened to Sidney's latest crisis.

"Mr. Quinn, I got to go to the Lost and Found. My trig book is gone."

"Are you sure you didn't leave it home, Sidney?"

"I'm positive, Mr. Quinn. I remember when I left here Friday I couldn't find it and I needed it for the homework so I was going to borrow Robert's but then I thought it must be home someplace because we had that big test last week and I know I had the book home to study for it so I figured it was still there and I didn't bother borrowing Robert's book but then when I got home and looked I couldn't find it and now I need it to do my homework so I got to go to the Lost and Found."

"Yes," Ernie said thoughtfully. "Well, you go ahead down to the Lost and Found, then."

"And Mr. Quinn, if nobody turned it in can I go to the bookstore and see if I can get one there, 'cause I need it for this homework that I got to get in today or I'll be failing and then I need it to study for the finals 'cause I got to get a good mark to keep up my average and maybe I lost my book or it was stolen so I won't have any?"

"Yes, that's right, Sidney," Ernie said brightly.

"Then I can go?" Sidney asked, uncertain.

"Go where?"

"To the bookstore if nobody turned my book in to the Lost and Found 'cause if I don't do this homework and turn it in today—"

"Right, Sidney," Ernie assured him. "You try the Lost and Found, and then go to the bookstore if you have to."

"Yeah, okay, Mr. Quinn."

"And Sidney—why don't you try the math office, too? And Miss Grimm's office? Someone might have turned it in there, you know. Better hurry, now, so you'll miss the rush."

Sidney fled, leaving Ernie with the thought that a junior MINUTCON was a distinct possibility; but he filed this away for future consideration.

While Ernie was occupied with Sidney, the room had been filling out around the edges. In the front, near the window, reading a French review book, was Elaine, a quiet girl and rather plain, but with the hauteur of a czarina; at the opposite corner of the room, back near the rear door, sat Shaggy McLoughlin, looking as huge, raw, and formless as an unlicked bear cub, wearing his perpetual oblivious grin; a few seats in front of Shaggy was Randall, a thin, clinical boy who wore dark suits and resembled the young Calvin Coolidge. Randall was reading, with great interest and apparent understanding, the latest issue of *Scientific*

American. Randall was frightening. A few seats ahead of him, in the seat nearest the door, an ideal spot for those who wish to see and be seen, was Cindy, a girl with the pale, tranquil beauty of the princess in a fairy tale, exquisite taste in dress, and a brain about equal to a sparrow's. Not a very bright sparrow's, either. But Cindy didn't really need brains. She got along fine. Sitting in splendid isolation in the rear of the room was Steve Hirsch, wearing a trim sport jacket, crisply pressed trousers (which he kept from bagging by keeping his legs straight out in the aisles), a neat white shirt, striped tie, and a snotty expression. Steve was the sort of boy who makes a great first impression—particularly on mothers—and then ruins it by being himself. He had not passed a test since mid-term, and had given up all pretense of doing homework. Ernie's warnings, and the three letters he had sent to Steve's parents, had been ignored. Steve was going to be Ernie's best-dressed failure of the year, and a great deal of the credit, Ernie thought righteously, could go to the parents who had helped him become an irresponsible bum.

Ernie noticed the students only subliminally. His mind was on other things, so many other things that he hardly knew where to begin worrying. At least he was prepared for all today's classes. Thank God for that. It freed hours of time for worry about those other things: things like Miss Grimm, for instance.

That could probably be settled at lunchtime. Aaron would know something. Before he stopped giving a damn, Aaron had known and played all the angles, and he still remembered them. And if he couldn't think of something, Fred Millard could. Between the two of them, they could solve the problem of his confrontation with the Iron Maiden. All right; one down.

Next was the observation tomorrow. Aaron could help a lot on this, too, but he'd take coaxing. He hadn't been observed in years and he got nasty when anyone even mentioned the subject, so he'd probably be better as a last resort. Millard wouldn't be much help, either. He had just published an article in some half-assed educational journal, so he was safe for at least three more years. He could come in to an observation blind drunk, with a giggling bimbo on his arm, regale the class with lurid stories, and throw a punch at Mikropoulous for a finale, and the observation report would praise him for vivid teaching. He didn't have to give a damn any more than Aaron, and he didn't.

There was always Mrs. Ramsay, but she was dangerous. Ernie knew, from agonizing experience, that any conversation with Mrs. Ramsay ended up in a monologue on her wonderful daughter, whose name—Heaven help us all—was Rowena, and who was single; but not for long, if Mrs. Ramsay had anything to say about it. And Mrs. Ramsay had a hell of a lot to say about it, most of it directed at Ernie, who had the misfortune to be the newest bachelor on the faculty.

This Rowena business scared him. He had come to picture Rowena as inexorable. If he met her, he was through, and his own feelings would have nothing to do with it. The whole subject gave him an uncomfortable Greek-tragedy sensation, and he only made it worse by imagining what Rowena—ye gods, *Rowena*—must look like: a sincere, myopic, pillow-chested Girl Guide with a face like a dissertation and a figure like a bran muffin; a girl with an affinity for tweeds, sensible shoes, and neutral lipstick, whose sole passions in life were Tennyson and the recorder. True, he had never seen the girl; but her mother, a marathon talker with a tongue of fool's gold, had limned her attributes on a dozen awkward occasions. Ernie had sketched her out mentally on the basis of these talks, as police artists construct a suspect's appearance from the description of witnesses, and he found her wanting—wanting *him*, if her mother was any indication. It terrified him.

He decided not to ask Mrs. Ramsay for any help. After thinking the matter over for a few seconds more, he decided to avoid all contact with her for the rest of the term. That would be the safest thing. This duly noted and resolved, he was free to return to the main artery of worry, the observation.

So far, he had eliminated Aaron, Fred, and Mrs. Ramsay. Trying to narrow his list to those whom he could be fairly certain of seeing at lunchtime left him with only two more names, Miss Rose and Miss Payseley, neither of whom, he knew, would be much help. Besides, they were not really people, they were delicate, fragile creations of dried butterfly wings and pressed flowers, and it was he who should be protecting them, and not vice versa. He eliminated Miss Rose and Miss Payseley in a flush of manly pride, and then realized that that left him with no one. Now I am alone, he thought, and wished that he could come up with as good a soliloquy as Hamlet did with similar provocation. But Ernie was not Prince Hamlet, nor was he meant to be. All things considered, it was probably just as well.

Ernie emerged from his musings to cast a proprietary glance around the room, which by this time was almost full. He looked up at the clock on the rear wall: three minutes to zero. Agent C21 stirred fitfully in the back of his mind, bringing images of hideous destructive mechanisms set to explode in the key cities of the West at the stroke of 8:30, a scant three minutes away, while he lay bound and gagged and heavily drugged in some archfiend's hideaway—but there was no time for that now. Besides, Ernie felt that he would be needing C21 later in the day, and didn't want to tire him out. He dismissed the guardian of democracy and began looking for his grammar book.

He dug it out of his bag, opened it on the desk, and arranged his seating chart and lesson plan beside it. Sidney, meanwhile, came galumphing in, brandishing a bedraggled trig book as if it were the Golden Fleece, and settled in his seat to await his next catastrophe. The class was all in place now with the exception of the two star performers, who made a habitual late entrance, today as always. Just before the bell, Maxine and Shirley came twitching into the room, eliciting leers and muttered exchanges of lewd dialogue among the males. If appearances were any indication, Maxine and Shirley were going to spend their lives standing under streetlamps, one hand on the hip and the other swinging a small mesh bag, soliciting the attentions of drunken conventioneers and lonely servicemen. Regardless of the season, their attire was unvarying: skirts and sweaters that fit like a coat of paint, mad rococo hairdos in varied hues, and emphatic make-up reminiscent of La Goulue in her decline.

Then the class bell rang and the day began. As always, the burden of the first period fell on Ernie, who explained, illustrated, coaxed, and cajoled his somnolent and puffy-eyed scholars with a minimum of interruption. A terse statement by Elaine, a penetrating question by Randall, an insane observation delivered *a propos* of nothing by Shaggy, and a spasm of sweaty confusion in verbal form by Sidney constituted the class' participation for the first period. Ernie preferred it this way, but he knew that it boded ill for observations, and if Mikropoulous happened to choose the first period to strike tomorrow, he could milk the business of low class participation for at least a page of unfavorable comment on his report. The odds were in Ernie's favor in this instance; Mikropoulous himself was as puffy-eyed and somnolent as any man living until he had finished his morning coffee during the third period. Just to play it safe, Ernie assigned a cluster of thirty questions from the end of the chapter to be prepared for an oral quiz tomorrow. That would arouse some signs of life. Maybe.

He drifted into the second period with a light heart. This was his duty period. Every teacher had to have one duty period, and the potential was hellish, but Ernie had been lucky. He was assigned to cover a study period. This in itself was no prize, for some of the study periods at Glen Park High School were like nothing more civilized than Saturday night on the Barbary Coast, but Ernie's luck consisted in having a second period study, which meant that the class, besides being sleepy, was small—only fourteen in it, and at least three of them were in the Dean of Boys' office on any given day. Ernie had even improved on his good fortune by making arrangements for "independent study." This meant that on Mondays and Thursdays he brought the class to the library, where they did their homework, or defaced library books, while he read *Punch*, which by some miracle was one of the mainstays of the library's periodicals shelf.

The second period was no problem at all, but when the bell rang to end it, Ernie was daily plunged into the Slough of Despond, where he remained until the end of the fourth period, one hundred and four agonizing minutes later. After the second period came the Home Room period, when the roving scholars met in their official class to be bombarded with notices, announcements, warnings, and nasal renditions of inspirational verse by their leader, Dr. Shefin, over the bitch box. The Home Room period lasted only fifteen minutes, but it could be an eternity of pain. This was clerical and collection time. First of all, Ernie had to take the roll, check absences and latenesses, collect notes from Friday's absentees and verify the parental signatures before filing them away carefully in exact chronological order. Then came the announcements: tell Mommy and Daddy of the approaching PTA meeting, or remember the approaching essay contest, art exhibit, science fair, sports day, visit by dignitaries, dance, immunization program, pep rally, or fund drive. Then the collections: national charities, local charities, school publications, General Organization dues, a special showing of a movie, a required review book, and anything else under the sun that might occur to Shefin, Grimm, Mikropoulous, or any teacher on the make who felt like initiating some elaborate undertaking that required the time and effort of the entire faculty and made him look like a born leader. The Home Room period would have been bad enough if the class had been organized, but a custom prevailed among older faculty members and administrators which brought confusion close to the absolute point attainable. If any student had to be called to the office, confer with the Dean of Boys or the Dean of Girls, or report to a teacher, the notice—effective immediately—was sent during the Home Room period. On some days the room resembled the retreat from Caporetto.

In the midst of the clerical duties, the announcements, the collections, and the urgent summonses came the voice from beyond: a cheery hello from the principal, Dr. Norman Shefin, who then led the students in the pledge to the flag and followed with a few lines of verse of the type found in *The Hardware Dealers' Monthly* or *Bowling News*. Ernie had not given much thought to the subject of the tone proper to disembodied voices, but if pressed, he would have come out against cheerfulness. On the one occasion when Ernie had heard Shefin read a poem written by a fully accredited poet (poetess, really, since it was Edna St. Vincent Millay), Shefin had managed to garble the last line, rendering himself, Miss Millay, and the cause of English literature in Glen Park High School ridiculous. It was said that Shefin had been a gym teacher before beginning his ascent into the upper strata of the educational world, and Ernie believed it. The man certainly read poetry like a gym teacher.

Another, and far more exotic, possibility that had occurred to Ernie was that Dr. Norman Shefin did not exist, and that his lines were read by an anonymous derelict who stumbled into the office every morning and was given fifty cents and a piece of stale Danish pastry to read the day's message. If someone had told Ernie this, he would have believed it. He had never seen Shefin, and had no proof of his existence aside from the daily bray from the bitch box. Perhaps Shefin was as unreal as the

Wizard of Oz; perhaps he was really Frank Morgan. It was something to think about. But not during Home Room period.

The students were not connoisseurs of the spoken word, but they knew a pretentious ass when they heard one. Shefin's cheery "Good morning, boys and girls of Glen Park High School! Good morning, teachers! Welcome to another day of learning adventure!" was invariably greeted with a muttered counterpoint of scurrility and snickering from the back of the room. Professional ethics demanded that Ernie frown on the perpetrators, but in his heart of hearts he was with them to the end.

On occasions when school events of special significance were in the offing—roughly three times a week—Shefin's one-man show was augmented by an appeal from some student leader. Apparently the students were carefully screened to weed out anyone who might, by means of originality, intelligibility, or forensic skill, put the principal in an unfavorable light. They all spoke in the same apathetic and narcotizing monotone, and every message ended with a feeble "We've all put lots of time and work into this, so come on, gang—let's pull together and make it a big success!" delivered in a tone that betrayed the speaker's resignation to ignominious failure. It might have been mike fright, but Ernie doubted this. As far as he could judge, fright in any form was alien to Glen Park High School students.

When the Home Room period ended—which, thank God, it always had, so far—Ernie had three minutes in which to gather his papers and gird his loins for a dash down the hall to Room 337, where he met his next two classes. It was not much of a trip as far as distance was concerned, but the obstacles to a speedy passage were formidable. Home Room being what it was, Ernie was never ready to leave at the bell, and so every day he had to buck the maelstrom of rushing students eddying around classroom doors bidding touching adieus to their lovers and exchanging homework or test answers with their fellows, and fight, like a salmon leaping upstream to spawn, against the current surging toward the staircase. He arrived in a state of disarray, ready for nothing more challenging than a refreshing half-hour's nap. Instead, he was faced with a mob of thirty-five restive adolescents for whom the English period was an unwelcome interruption between the free play of Home Room and the pandemonium of lunch. Their prevailing attitude was one of surly resentment. After forty minutes of intellectual guerrilla fighting with these Yahoos, Ernie had just three minutes to fill his lungs with pure sweet air to fortify himself for his fourth-period class, a group of seniors who came to Room 337 directly from their gym period, bringing the heady atmosphere of the locker room along in their wake. He had christened this class "The Sweatshop." It was an ideal setting for reading aloud from the poetry of Sandburg or Stephen Duck, but it was no place for a gerund or a participle, and even an infinitive would find it rough going. Ernie did his best, strengthened by the thought that this was the nadir of the day, and that things always looked much better when the fourth period was behind him.

The bell rang, and the students debouched into the tumult of the halls, leaving Ernie alone. Room 337 was not in use during the fifth period, so he was able to gather his accoutrements at leisure and go to the lunchroom through empty halls. This was the first good time of the day, the first time he was free and on his own, and he always celebrated by stopping off to wash, comb, and praise himself, saluting his image in the men's room mirror with a cheerful "You're looking great, boy," or "You're halfway home, sport—hang on!" and a conspiratorial wink. Sometimes it worked.

Then it was on to the lunchroom.

There were two entrances to the faculty lunchroom. One of them led through a dingy back-of-the-boiler-room corridor populated by roving herds of great black beetles, past a row of pungent refuse cans, up a narrow, poorly lighted staircase, then down another, even darker corridor and through the back door of the kitchen. The other led down wide, clean, well-lighted stairs from which one could see the park that gave the school its name, then through a spacious corridor into the student lunchroom, from which one entered the main door of the faculty dining room. Ernie had used the latter path for the first three weeks, and it reminded him more and more of the infiltration course at basic training camp. When, in the fourth week of the term, Aaron had offered to act as guide down the secret passage—as he called it—Ernie accepted eagerly. His first trip was filled with misgivings; when they finally reached the lunchroom door, Ernie half expected to find an opium den on the other side. The sight of the kitchen was anticlimactic. The secret passage left much to be desired in the way of scenic beauty, but it eliminated the walk through the students' lunchroom and that was good enough for Ernie. Then, too, on bad days he could always be Agent C21 making a hair-raising escape from—or a secret one-man raid on—the headquarters of MINUTCON. All things considered, it was the only way to travel to the lunchroom.

As he walked through the kitchen door, he nodded to the head dietician, a weathered blonde who traveled under a heavy coat of make-up, reminding Ernie of a 1938 Packard with a jazzy new two-tone paint job, and he exchanged a few lines of rigidly formalized dialogue with her. They had been performing this ceremony since shortly after Ernie's first entrance, and long practice had lent it the dignity of a medieval antiphon.

"Hello, Mrs. Lummis. How are you today?"

"I'm fine, Mr. Quinn. And yourself?"

"Ready for a good meal. What's the special today?"

"A nice meat loaf, whipped potatoes, and creamed carrots. Choice of beverage and dessert," Mrs. Lummis recited. This portion of their litany varied minutely from day to day in content, but not in delivery.

"Oh. That sounds delicious," Ernie said, manfully stifling the automatic impulse to gag at the memory of whipped potatoes à la Glen Park. "Sounds just fine."

"I'm glad to hear that. You know, some people around here are always complaining about the menus."

"Oh?"

"Yes, and they don't come to *me*, they run to Dr. Shefin, or Miss Grimm. You wouldn't believe it, Mr. Quinn, but there are some real troublemakers on our faculty."

Ernie believed it fervently, but could hardly say so. He contented himself with the observation that one meets people like that everywhere. Mrs. Lummis sighed and nodded. Their revels were ended. Ernie pressed on to the lunchroom.

The scene that greeted him was familiar, and even, in an inexplicable way, comforting. In the corner, at the good table, were four battle-hardened old-timers exchanging lurid stories of their early teaching assignments in Depression days. Their conversation was a rich tapestry woven of mysterious allusions and unknown names, like a symbolist poem recited in a foreign tongue.

"You think *that* was a tough school? Hah! You should have been at Thomas A. Edison when Mulvehill was principal, back in '36. He ran that damn' school like Marine boot camp."

"Look who he had with him, Eddie. Garson and Kantrowitz for Deans; they were two tough cookies. And then—"

"*Everybody* at Thomas A. Edison was a tough cookie. They didn't fool around in those days. Kid opened his mouth, you knocked him on his ass."

"That's what they need here. Make men out of these little punks. They're all spoiled rotten."

"Damn' right. A good licking never hurt a kid yet. Straightened out a lot of them."

There was a general truculent murmur of assent, and a pause while all mentally enumerated the scores of latent public enemies who had been transformed, by the simple expedient of repeatedly being knocked on their individual asses, into doctors, lawyers, scholars, judges, senators, bank presidents, or even dentists.They overlooked the students who had, as a result of the same pedagogical approach, become ward heelers, barflies, con men, winos, and panhandlers. No need to consider *that* side of the picture. They were probably bums to begin with anyway.

"Kantrowitz and Garson were something, weren't they? If a kid looked at them cross-eyed, they'd put him through the wall."

"That's what they need around here. Too much of this damn' child psychology around this place, if you ask me."

"Kantrowitz got in a lot of trouble over some kid he slugged, didn't he?"

"Yeah, but not at Thomas A. Edison. That was later, when he was coaching at Pulaski."

"No, you're wrong, Max. Garson went to Pulaski in '38, that's what you're thinking of. Kantrowitz was made head coach at Thomas A. Edison then. He stayed there until he retired in '48."

"It was '50, Sam. He retired with Podnak, remember?"

"Harry Podnak? Who could forget Harry Podnak?"

They all chuckled softly to themselves, savoring the memory of the golden days of Harry Podnak; days that would never return, not with these snotnoses and their teachers' college crap ruining the schools. It was often hard, these days, to tell the younger teachers from the students. Boys doing a man's job, that's what it was. No wonder the kids all took dope and stabbed each other. Not like the old days. They all sighed deeply, almost in unison.

"Podnak never got the chairman's job, did he?"

"No. There were a lot of stories about that, but I never believed them. It was all politics."

"Didn't Podnak get himself into a lot of trouble when he slugged some kid?"

"No, that was Kantrowitz, when he was at Thomas A. Edison."

"Thomas A. Edison! What a hell of a place that was back around '36! Remember Mulvehill, Max? He ran that place like Marine . . ."

And so it went.

The table next to the veterans' convention was unoccupied, primarily for acoustical reasons, and the one next to that was unoccupied because it was piled high with the debris of the fourth period. At the table next to this lunchroom midden, looking like two aged Cordelias flanking a reupholstered Lady Macbeth, were Miss Rose, Miss Payseley, and Mrs. Ramsay, all of them cooing and clucking and sighing shrill little sighs of genteel dismay. They made a tableau that would have warmed the heart of Helen Hokinson. The only jarring note was an emanation of get-up-and-go from Mrs. Ramsay.

The Misses Rose and Payseley might have passed, in their youth, for Snow White and Rose Red. Miss Rose, whose hair still showed some traces of auburn, was a thing of pastels and morning mist o'er the lea. She resembled a minor poetess—any minor poetess—of the late nineteenth century, the sort of woman who dies a spinster at ninety-four and leaves behind her endless volumes of lyrics celebrating leaves, dew, and kittens in a style compounded of sublimity and contractions, all transcribed in a fine, spidery hand. Ernie knew the type well, for he had created just such a poetess. Her name was Lydia Lark Flingstock, and she was due to make her first appearance in print in a very short time.

Miss Payseley, the thinner and more ethereal of the two, was a sweetly demented old soul whose real role was as the aging mother in a Williams play, in which she could run distracted through gauzy scenery in a Georgian ball gown and ramble on about her handsome beaux, all of whom are now either corpulent Rotarians or dead. Miss Rose may have looked the poetess, but Miss Payseley had the equipment, a bottomless well of sentiments of the sort gleaned from get-well cards. She had a way of speaking that made everything sound like a mystical experience. Those members of the faculty who had no taste for the wistful called her "The Old Lady Who Lived in a Fog." To these two fey creatures, anything less Arcadian than a Boucher or a Fragonard was sordid naturalism.

Mrs. Ramsay sat with them, but she was not of their world. Mrs. Ramsay had a figure like a jelly doughnut, a face like a kewpie, and a mind like Fu Manchu. She could smile and smile and be a bitch; and she did, and she was.

Ernie nodded to the ladies without slackening his pace. He was headed for the table where Aaron and Fred were sitting in cocoons of silent post-prandial peevishness, looking disdainfully at their empty plates.

"Well, did you enjoy your meat loaf, whipped potatoes, creamed carrots, and choice of beverage and dessert?" Ernie asked brightly as he set his bag on an empty chair.

"Delicious. I haven't eaten so well since I was in the Army," Aaron said bitterly.

"I don't know about that, Aaron," Fred said with great gravity. "I don't think the meal was in a class with cold sausage patties and ice cream."

"You must have been an officer. In my outfit, sausage patties were a delicacy. Most of the time we got boiled shoetops. We didn't start eating decently until we were captured by the Japanese."

"Your cook stayed on after the war," Ernie chimed in. "We got a lot of boiled shoetops, too. It was his specialty."

"They're not that bad, you know? Chewy, but nourishing. The secret is the sauce."

"Now that I've worked up a good appetite," Ernie said, "I'm going in for my ration. Can I get anyone another coffee?"

"None for me, Ernie," Millard said, and Aaron shook his head emphatically.

When Ernie returned with his tray, coming by the great circle route which took him around the far side of the room from Mrs. Ramsay, the conversation had turned from war stories to more serious matters; in fact, to the most serious matter ever discussed at the lunch tables, in the faculty room, and along the corridors of Glen Park High School. Aaron and Fred were talking about money. Ernie let them go on uninterrupted, for he had heard all of it before, nearly every day, and he had nothing to add. Besides, he didn't want to get involved, start arguing, and let his lunch get cold. It was bad enough hot. He listened, finding the dialogue a comfortable background to his meal, like a new arrangement of an old familiar tune.

"Now you, you have nothing to complain about, Millard. You have your apartment, your car, your trip to Europe every other summer—"

"Hold it, hold it, Aaron. You saw my apartment. It's no presidential suite."

"Is mine? Try living in a four-room apartment with three kids sometime."

"All right, then, we're both miserable. But remember, I'm paying off a loan on the car, and I only go to Europe by working on the summers I'm here."

"I'm still not touched. *You* work summers so you can go to Paris and sit in a sidewalk café and leer. *I* work summers so I can eat winters."

"You know your trouble, Aaron—you're jealous because I'm single. You probably have fantasies about beautiful girls coming in white Bentleys to pick me up, and whisking me off to Majorca for the weekend in Daddy's private jet."

"Like hell I do. In my fantasies, they whisk *me* off for the weekend. You go get your own fantasies."

"Say what you like, Aaron. I know how you married men feel about bachelors."

"I'm against you all," Aaron began. "You're a drain on the economy. A blight on the landscape. You buy all these luxury items like shoes and underwear and force up the prices for us canaille who have families to pamper. Don't side with him, Quinn," he said, turning to Ernie. "There's still hope for you. Some nice girl will come along and rescue you from solvency. Why don't you go talk to Mrs. Ramsay?"

"Nummum," Ernie said, caught at a disadvantage. His mouth was full of whipped potatoes.

"I knew you'd say that," Aaron said triumphantly. "See, Millard? Everybody knows you for the scandalous wastrel you are."

"Actually, Aaron, it's all a façade. I'm carrying the torch for the Iron Maiden, and she won't give me a tumble."

At the mention of his current bête noire, Ernie gulped down the last morsel of meat loaf and burst into the conversation.

"The Iron Maiden, Fred—I need some help with her."

"You got a rival, Millard," Aaron said happily. "Try sending her flowers, Quinn. Then take her to a nice restaurant, a gypsy restaurant, maybe, with violins."

"This is serious, Aaron. She wants me to explain about the faculty meeting Friday."

"Doesn't she know what Shefin was talking about, either? That's encouraging," Aaron beamed. "I thought I was getting senile."

"She wants to know why I wasn't there."

"Why don't you just tell her?" Millard said with a little Cheshire-cat smile.

"Oh, sure. I'll just go in and say I had better things to do."

"Someone ought to do it, Ernie," Millard said solemnly, laying a brotherly hand on Ernie's arm in encouragement. "This isn't a time to be selfish. We'll all cherish your memory."

"You can talk, both of you," Ernie said petulantly. "You've got tenure. I don't even know whether I'll be back next year yet."

"You don't? Oh, the dirty bastards!" Aaron said feelingly, serious for a brief moment. "If they don't keep you on, what the hell are you supposed to do this late in the term? You ought to pin Mikropoulous down right away."

"I don't even want to think about Mikropoulous. I'll have time to worry about him tomorrow. Right now I want a story for Miss Grimm."

"Do you have any kind of an excuse at all?"

"No, I just cut out. I couldn't stand listening to Shefin blither for an—"

"Listen to Shefin *what?*" Aaron broke in.

"Blither."

"He doesn't blither, he gibbers. Doesn't he, Millard?"

"I don't think he actually gibbers. Jabbers, maybe. Or maunders. I'd say maunders."

"He blithers," Ernie insisted. "You know, like a blithering idiot."

"He's not an idiot, Ernie. He has a long way to go before he makes idiot. Don't try to curry favor."

"All right," Ernie said quietly and patiently. "Whatever he

does, I couldn't stand listening to him do it on a Friday afternoon. Besides, I had to go someplace and I didn't have much time."

"I bet he had a date," Aaron said, winking broadly at Fred. "Was she pretty? Come on, tell us about it."

"That's it, keep fooling around. I come to you for help, and you want to play games. It's times like these that show you who your friends are."

"I hate to see a teacher cry," Millard said tenderly. "Tell me, Ernie, what can I do for you? Don't ask Aaron. He's all wrapped up in his selfish little world of greed and resentment."

"I want a good, convincing excuse for missing the faculty meeting last Friday, that's all. It doesn't have to be dramatic, or original, or anything but convincing."

"We'll think of something," Millard assured him.

"I need it this afternoon."

"Don't worry," Aaron assured him, too.

The three fell silent for a time, like two specialists and a worried patient all pondering the same malevolent disease from their varying personal viewpoints, busily framing questions, evasions, accusations, denials, recriminations, and mutual denunciations. Aaron abruptly turned on Ernie with the hot blaze of inspiration in his eyes.

"What did you use in the Army?"

"What do you mean, what did I use in the Army?"

"In the Army, when you were in the Army—you *were* in the Army, weren't you?"

"Sure, but what are you talking about?"

"Well, what did you do when there was a long hike, or a bivouac, or a field problem?"

"I went on them."

"A zealot," Aaron said to Millard, who shook his head sadly.

"You're not helping us very much, Ernie. Didn't you ever malinger?"

"A little, in basic training. I didn't *have* to malinger. I was at Headquarters."

"That's where you separate the men from the boys. Anyone can malinger in a line company; it takes a master to malinger on a nice soft office job. I bet I was the only radio interviewer in the Pacific with a bayonet wound in his foot," Millard said with nostalgic pride.

"How the hell do radio interviewers get bayonet wounds?" Aaron demanded.

"That's just the point: they don't. They get laryngitis, the damn' fools, and then when they get out of the hospital they find they've been assigned to a rifle company. But a bayonet wound is a real combat wound. Nobody touches a man with a bayonet wound."

"I didn't know you were in combat, Millard. What did you do, interview Japs?"

"Of course not. I stepped on a bayonet in the barracks one night. This idiot in the next bunk was using it to clean the dirt out of the cracks in the floor, and I jumped out of my sack barefoot and landed right on the damned thing. It wasn't serious, but they had to take me to the hospital to remove it, so I was on record as having a bayonet wound. After that, whenever I felt like a rest I'd start limping and wincing and they'd put me in for observation. It didn't look like malingering because I'd do a little interviewing while I was in the hospital. Sometimes I'd emcee a USO show."

"Very creative," Aaron said approvingly. "You put me to shame. The best I could manage was dizzy spells."

"Dizzy spells weren't bad, if you could make them believe you," Millard said generously.

"Oh, they believed me. I complained once or twice and the first sergeant wouldn't let me go on sick call, so I fell down a flight of stairs. Then he believed me."

"That was good," Millard said. "If you keep falling down on soft things they'll never listen to you, but a flight of stairs is a real clincher."

"It did the trick."

"I had a hernia when I was in basic," Ernie ventured, "but they fixed it."

"They'll fix anything if you let them," Aaron said disdainfully. "Damn' busybodies."

"Was that all?" Millard asked.

"Was what all?"

"The hernia. Was that all the malingering you ever did?"

"My knee swelled up a few times," Ernie said, trying his best.

They looked at him, then at each other, shook their heads, and sighed.

"It's a good thing you came to us, Ernie," Millard said.

"I don't think it's so damn' good. The period's nearly over and all you've done is tell war stories."

"We're creating a mood," Aaron assured him.

"Right," Millard seconded. "We'll come up with something in a minute."

Aaron brightened.

"Did Grimm see you at all on Friday?" he demanded.

"No."

"All right, then. You had a cold."

"That'll never work, Aaron," Ernie protested. "I don't sound as if I have a cold, and she'll never believe me if I say I got rid of it over the weekend."

"Yes, she will. Stick your fingers in your nose and pull one of the hairs."

"One of the front ones," Millard added.

"Right. Well, go ahead, do it."

Ernie tried it, hesitantly at first, then, urged on by his mentors, with verve and vigor. Seconds later he was sneezing, his eyes were watering, and his nose was running. It was perfect. Aaron, looking as proud as Pygmalion, rose grandly from the table.

"Just try it at one-hour intervals, and give yourself one last good yank before you go into Grimm's office. If there's any difficulty, check with my assistant, Dr. Millard. I have to leave now and make my house calls."

"He'll make a great superintendent of schools someday," Millard said drily as Aaron trudged out of the room.

"He sure will. I think I'd rather have him as a professor of Education, though. He knows all the things you have to know, but nobody ever teaches you."

Millard nodded. They lit cigarettes and smoked in silence, appreciating Aaron, for a minute or two. Then Ernie realized that he had solved only one of his problems.

"Oh, damn!" he moaned.

"What's the matter now?" Millard said, sounding only mildly curious.

"I forgot to ask Aaron about observations!"

"Don't even mention observations. They're not the sort of thing civilized people want to talk about," Millard said frostily.

"Mikropoulous wants to talk about them."

"*That* certainly doesn't disprove my statement."

"He's going to observe me tomorrow, Fred, and I have to knock him cold. This is the last one, and the other two were bad. Awful."

"That's unfortunate."

"Can you suggest anything?"

Millard took a deep drag on his cigarette and blew the smoke out in a thin stream between his pursed lips. Watching him, Ernie was impressed anew by something that had struck him the first time he saw Millard, and had been reinforced in every one of their talks, after Aaron had made his customary early exit from the lunchroom: the obvious fact that Millard had been born at least two centuries after his proper time. Millard would have been perfectly at home in Will's, The Grecian, or White's Chocolate House. He could have mingled with the crowd at Drury Lane, strolled in Hyde Park, and gambled away a fortune at Bath, and it all would have suited him much better than sitting in the faculty lunchroom at Glen Park High School, bitching about salary and swapping war stories. Fred Millard was the spiritual descendant of Joseph Addison; he even bore a superficial resemblance to him. And it was in his character, too, perhaps even more than in his appearance. He seldom indulged it, but Millard had the dry, penetrating wit of Mister Spectator in abundance, and even more of the poised, aloof, cool self-discipline. And, like Addison and many of his contemporaries, he was conscientious about everything but his duty.

Millard was a good teacher, and he could have been a great teacher, but his heart wasn't in it. His heart was in everything else. If you were thinking about a trip to Europe and asked him, quite casually, "Fred, what's the best way to get from Perugia to Bologna?" he would greet you the next day bearing a portfolio of bus schedules, railroad timetables, cyclists' tours, auto maps, a complete itinerary of northern Italy, a personal list of inexpensive pensions and restaurants, two English-Italian dictionaries, passport application forms, and the name of a reliable travel agent. If you mentioned that you were going to take in a show, he could tell you the best seats in the theater in every price range, and where and how to get them, give you the addresses of the six nicest French restaurants near the theater and the names of their headwaiters, and personally arrange all reservations. On the briefest of notices he could supply a list of wet towns in southern Maine complete with the names of the places where you could get a really good martini, or the ten places not to go in San Francisco, or the only three Italian restaurants in Nebraska, Greta Garbo's leading men, FM stations that specialized in Spanish drama, reliable harpsichord tuners, winners of the Gran Prix de Monaco, and good wines from small, obscure, German vineyards. He could be enormously helpful and cheerfully cooperative on any subject under the sun, as long as it had nothing to do with teaching or schools. Ask him about anything touching on his profession, though, and he closed up like a morning glory at sunset. He played the game, and played it well. He was, Ernie believed, way ahead of the game. But he never lost sight of the fact that it was a game.

"Well, make sure you have a good, complete lesson plan," Fred advised hesitantly.

"I'll work on them tonight."

"And ask plenty of questions. Keep the kids talking."

"Anything else?"

"I can't think of anything at the moment, Ernie."

"Any tips? Any angles? Any clever diversions?" Ernie pressed him. "I really have to do a great job this time, Fred, or I think Mikropoulous will let me go."

"Oh, don't worry about *that*," Millard said confidently. "Whether or not you're a good teacher has nothing to do with your job here."

"What does, then?"

"All the things that shouldn't count at all. Having a lot to say at faculty meetings—and making sure you *go* to them, too; getting your classes to build things, or put out a class newspaper; getting all the forms in early; not failing anyone you shouldn't fail, or, better still, not failing anyone; being seen around the school after hours giving the kids extra help; volunteering to do anything the office suggests, no matter how absurd it is; buying coffee for Mikropoulous and Shefin; lending Mikropoulous new books that he mentions and never asking for them back . . ."

Ernie began to wonder if he hadn't made a mistake about Millard. He had the right century, but he was no longer so sure about the identity. Millard was sounding more and more like Fielding, or even Swift.

"That might fool Mikropoulous, but it will never fool the kids. They'd know."

"Who cares about the kids? Oh, I know, everyone here likes to talk as if they do, but they don't. They don't give a damn for anyone but themselves, Ernie. Once you realize that, you're home free."

"It sounds too easy, Fred. Rotten, but easy."

"It isn't easy at all, Ernie," Millard said, dropping the tiny stub of his cigarette into the dregs of his coffee and studying the results bemusedly. "It's not easy at all. It's damned hard."

"Yes. I see what you mean."

"I don't think you do. You will in a few more years, but you don't now. Don't let it worry you, though. Try your best tomorrow, but work on the other things. Get your grades in on time and play the game, and you'll be safe. Butter Mikropoulous up a little. It won't hurt. He won't be here forever, anyway. You'll have time to soothe your pride when you get tenure."

"Okay. I'll try."

The bell rang. Lunch was over. It was back to the grind for Ernie and Fred. Ernie had a fairly decent sixth-period class, and they were winding up the semester on poetry in this and his eighth period, which made for a pleasant afternoon. And his seventh period was a preparation period, which was glorious. There was always Miss Grimm, hovering like Nemesis over the end of the day, but maybe something would happen to save him. He felt that he was over the hill; for today, at least.

Fred, who was inured to the cacophony of the students' cafeteria, bid goodbye and headed for the door. Ernie watched him leave, still pondering over his last words, and suddenly things fell into place. There was no doubt now about Millard's true spiritual identity. It wasn't Fielding or Swift at all. It wasn't Addison, either, but that was close. It was Lord Chesterfield.

Ernie started out of the lunchroom, and as he passed the old girls' table he saw, out of the corner of his eye, a brisk commanding wave of Mrs. Ramsay's hand. He marched doggedly on, ignoring her shrill "Oh, Ernest!", knowing that once he made it to the kitchen he was safe. She had the weight and experience, but youth and speed were on his side. He slipped through the back door and hurried down the passage.

He had to run up the stairs and down the corridor to Room

318, where he spent his sixth and eighth periods, so he was out of breath when he arrived. Since many of his students also enjoyed fifth-period lunches, they were out of breath along with him, and for the first ten minutes, the classroom sounded like time out at an octogenarians' basketball game.

His sixth-period class was a pretty good class; not perfect, of course—there was Arnold, who never spoke, and Judy, who never shut up—but on the whole, it was a pleasant group, and Ernie enjoyed teaching them. He didn't teach them much this particular day because he was working out his lines for Miss Grimm, who would sit—heavily—in judgment upon him in less than an hour, but ordinarily Ernie and his sixth-period class worked well together.

Today he contented himself with giving them definitions. This helped them to fill up their notebooks, giving them a sense of accomplishment, and gave Ernie a chance to declaim some of his favorite lines, a harmless amusement which bored the class only a trifle more than one of his standard lessons. He assigned a group of Shakespeare's sonnets for homework—read and be prepared to explain or paraphrase (and then he had to explain what he meant by "paraphrase." Oh, well), and managed to end a sentence just as the bell rang, which seemed to be a good omen. Regardless of their fate, the little victims scampered merrily from the room, leaving the world to Ernie and Miss Grimm.

On the way to her office, Ernie ducked into the men's room to try Aaron's technique again. He yanked hard at his nostril hair, and sure enough, it worked. He was going to blow his nose, but decided to sniffle instead. It lent verisimilitude to his performance. He looked into the mirror, and was pleased at what he saw: the watery eyes were perfect, and the little twitch of the nose as he sniffled added the final touch. Greatly encouraged, he sniffed, blinked, and twitched the rest of the way to her office with bold self-assurance.

He needed every bit of it. Miss Grimm's office was designed to demoralize all who entered, distilling them to a tepid jelly of guilt and insecurity. It combined the worst features of a dentist's waiting room, an induction center, a bus station late at night, and a strange bar in a bad neighborhood. The ceiling was high, the walls were bare, the floor creaked, the lights glared, and by some strange quirk of acoustics every sound from the dutiful pattering of a typewriter to the rumble-and-thud of a file cabinet drawer was turned into a grating rasp that set the nerves to jangling. The furniture might have been repossessed from the loan department of a small, resentful bank located in the heart of the Dust Bowl. A long, agonizing bench, all right angles and sharp edges, flanked each side of the entrance. Straight ahead of the doorway on which they stood guard was a wooden rail with a creaking gate, guarded by a succession of old women who had sworn to model themselves on Horatio and imitate, at their tiny and insignificant post, his brave deed at the bridge. And beyond the battered and many-splintered desk that served as their sentry box lay judgment, in the person of Miss Grimm.

Miss Grimm was ramrod-straight, rock-hard, an iron fist in an iron glove. She dressed in severe, unornamented black, wore her hair in a bun, and sported—if such a word can be applied to a perfect combination of the Puritan and the martinet—steel-rimmed glasses, which suited her perfectly. She was a smallish, angry woman with an eye like a gunsight and a forefinger like a dwarf harpoon. She seemed to hold the present company at any given moment directly responsible for the world's ills and her own, and fixing her victim with a bright accusing eye, she battered him with irrelevant recriminations, enforcing her charges with frequent thrusts of the forefinger. Miss Grimm always gave Ernie the feeling that *she* knew what he was up to, even when he wasn't up to anything in particular. She might have been the daughter of Carry Nation and Erich von Stroheim; among her ancestors one would be sure to find Oliver Cromwell, the first Earl of Shaftesbury, Caligula, the Marquis de Sade, Judge Hathorne, William Clarke Quantrill, and Wackford Squeers, and on the distaff side Medea, Bloody Mary, Ilse Koch, Goneril and Regan, Mrs. Danvers, and the old lady in "American Gothic." At least it seemed that way to Ernie, who discerned a touch of all of them in her air and manner, especially when she was dealing with a younger teacher; him, for instance.

As assistant principal, Miss Grimm was in charge of discipline. In most schools, this would mean that Miss Grimm was the arbiter of student conduct and no more, but in Glen Park High School, thanks to the functional non-existence of Dr. Norman

Shefin, beloved principal, Miss Grimm's area of responsibility had been extended—by Miss Grimm—to include faculty discipline as well. Her qualifications for this position were, as Ernie saw them, simple and obvious: she had a deep-seated resentment of youth, young people, and young ideas and a firm conviction that everyone under sixty ought to be put in his place and kept there. Even those *over* sixty were expected to watch their step. It was Miss Grimm who descended like the Furies on the teacher who clocked in a minute late or clocked out a minute early; who, if male, dressed too casually and if female, too attractively; who turned in a day late one of the myriad forms issued in shrill urgency by some pettifogging minion; or who dared miss a faculty meeting. This last infraction was a capital crime in Miss Grimm's small, piercing eyes; it smacked of insubordination, insolence, disloyalty, dereliction of duty, insurrection, inciting to riot, anarchy, and general snottiness, and was treated fittingly. The offender was brusquely summoned to her office, made to wait interminably on the ugly, uncomfortable benches, subjected to a fifteen-minute barrage of sarcasm, innuendo, and humiliation, and then released, with the promise that this incident would appear on his records and haunt him to his dying day. There was no excuse short of death—preferably painful and lingering—that could satisfy Miss Grimm.

No one, as far as Ernie knew, had ever dared to miss two faculty meetings, so he had no idea what punishment was meted out to second offenders. He assumed that one was left alone in a room with a loaded pistol and instructions to do the only honorable thing a man could do under the circumstances. If this were the case, there would be no problem. He would shoot Miss Grimm and run like hell.

Actually, there was no real need for him to worry yet. As far as Miss Grimm knew—unless Bob Ferriss was an informer—this was the first faculty meeting Ernie had missed. Bob had covered for him the first three times, signing his name on the faculty attendance roster (the honor system, as applied to the faculty of Glen Park High School), and Ernie had reciprocated by signing Bob's name whenever the need arose. Somehow or other they had gotten their signals crossed on Friday, which probably explained why Bob wasn't in today. On thinking it over, Ernie recalled that Bob hadn't been in on Friday, either; at least he hadn't seen him. The dirty sneak, Ernie thought; he's probably off somewhere dying and he didn't even let me know. He wished that he had a few minutes to spare, to think up nasty complications to visit upon his accomplice, but there was no time for that now. The door to Miss Grimm's office loomed before him. Courage, man, he told himself weakly. He paused for one more pull at his nostril hair and entered, sneezing violently.

Covering his approach with a heavy barrage of wet, messy sneezes, Ernie went to the gateway of the inner sanctum where one of the weird sisters was always on duty. He looked down, expecting to recoil at the sight of a wizened crone gumming maledictions, and received a shock, the only nice shock of the day so far, possibly of the entire week. Where there should have been a Gorgon there was a Venus. She was young, she was fair—not gorgeous, maybe, but a definite improvement over anyone Ernie had ever seen stationed at the post before. She had green eyes, a nice little snub nose, short blond hair, and miracle of miracles, a smile—a real, honest-to-God, glad-to-see-you smile that lit up Miss Grimm's gloomy keep like a Van Gogh in a mortuary. This was definitely a good sign.

"May I help you?" she asked, in a voice that suited her perfectly. Ernie savored it, not answering immediately, and she repeated her question.

"Oh, yes. I'm Mr. Quinn. I'm supposed to see Miss Grimm this period."

"She's expecting you, then?"

"I guess so. She sent me a note."

"Do you mind waiting a minute? I'll see if she's free."

Ernie nodded obligingly and watched as she rose and went to the great door. She disappeared for a brief time, then emerged and came back to her desk. She moved nicely. She was tall, slim, lithe—lissome was the word Ernie was digging for, and he finally located it. He was glad she was just *that* tall and no taller. Not taller than he was, anyway. Ernie liked tall girls, but he always had the feeling that they looked upon him as a lecherous dwarf, despite the fact that he was close to 5′11″ on those occasions when he was neither slumping, ducking, nor cringing—*rare* occasions, these days.

"Miss Grimm will see you in a few minutes. You can sit down over there," she said, indicating the hideous benches.

"Yes. Okay. Sure," Ernie said; then, abruptly, he asked, "What's your name? I haven't seen you here before."

"I'm Lynn Rogers. I just came here last week. Mrs. Rubin had to have an operation."

"How did you get this job?" Ernie asked, genuinely curious. "I thought you had to be ninety-five years old and ugly to work in Miss Grimm's office."

Lynn assumed a furtive expression and cast a narrow glance around the room. "Well, if you promise not to tell—I lied about my age."

Ernie laughed. "I won't say a word."

She smiled back at him, and things looked good. He blessed Miss Grimm, Mrs. Rubin, Bob Ferriss, Glen Park High School, faculty meetings, and all who had had a hand in bringing him here this afternoon. He loved, and blessed, every living thing. If there had been a bunch of water snakes wriggling around on the floor, he would have blessed them, unawares. He withdrew his blessing from Miss Grimm seconds later when she called Lynn into her office, leaving Ernie alone, once more, with his thoughts.

He drifted toward the benches, thinking about Lynn Rogers. It was a nice name; another good sign. All too often, when he met a pretty girl, she had a name like Frieda Moldschlagger, or worse. Feeling as he did about names, Ernie had never really accepted the idea of a rose by any other name smelling just as sweet. He was certain that given time, he could come up with half a dozen names for a rose that would have gardeners running in all directions, gagging and holding their noses; it was enough to make him skeptical.

That reminded him; he yanked savagely at his nostril hair, and delivered three Gargantuan sneezes, spraying the area generously. Then back to Lynn Rogers.

Lynn made Ernie think of all the tall, tawny beauties who lope across the advertising pages in polo coats or ski pants, being courted by anonymous young men with sports cars and neatly combed hair. A girl like Lynn seemed to make real all the misty moonshine Ernie had spun around the idea of courtship ever since the momentous day he learned that girls were more than just targets for taunts and snowballs: Sunday afternoons at Lime Rock; dinners at the country club; lean, tanned arms and tennis rackets; camel's-hair coats and autumn foliage; stunning après-ski outfits and fresh moonlit snow; beach picnics and driftwood fires; all the things that people do in *New Yorker* ads and O'Hara novels.

But it wasn't working out that way.

Damn it all, Ernie thought bitterly, why can't things ever go right? Doris and I could have all that, and even better, but we never do; there's always something coming up, something getting in the way, messing up all the good times. And when we do get together, there's always somebody around, and it's usually her father. She must think he's the greatest man alive, the way she's always letting him stick his nose in. She probably hopes that someday I'll see the error of my ways and decide to become just like him. Fat chance.

If only it could be just the two of us, just Doris and me, Ernie thought, even for a little while, we could work out everything. But it was never just the two of them. The courtship of Doris was seeing Ibsen played by the drama club at her father's college, and then going backstage with the Professor (ye gods, the *Professor!*) to congratulate the cast, when what you really wanted to do was bombard them with dead cats and rotten fruit; it was visiting with close family friends, all of whom had been bosom companions since grammar school days and had a fund of little private jokes and cute names that made Ernie feel like the man without a wedding garment; going on group tours of museums and acting interested in what the Professor said, even when he didn't know what the hell he was talking about; seeing movies he recommended and talking about them afterward, too seriously and stuffily; all the things that Ernie just didn't want. He wanted Doris, not a way of life, but he was getting a way of life, and it was the Professor's way, not Doris', or Ernie's, or anyone else's.

It was a bad way to start things off, and a bad way to continue. Ernie knew it would be hard to change, and if he let things go, they would just get worse. He would become a pale copy of the Professor, and his life with Doris would become just the sort of thing her parents would consider desirable. He could picture it, and frequently did, to his dismay. As Ernie and Doris grew older, they would become solid pillars of the community, staunch members of the PTA, singers of old songs around the piano, wearers of funny aprons at backyard cookouts and funny hats at their three-drinks-and-you're-out New Year's Eve parties. As life ripened, rewardingly, their great moments would arrive: Doris would become president of the Woman's Club and an inspired, inspiring volunteer worker for painless and respectable charities; Ernie would be interviewed for the local paper and his book, *The Beloved Professor*, a glowing tribute to Doris' father, would be warmly received and remaindered almost immediately; their picture, posed with the stupefying monotony of all presentation pictures, would appear on the home news page under a caption telling how Professor and Mrs. Ernest Quinn, "Ernie and Dodie to their many friends," were overwhelmed to receive the Harvey Mumblebaum Memorial Plaque for their many services to the community; they would make that trip to Europe, along with a dozen other equally reputable couples, and would return with reel upon reel of moving pictures which Ernie would show to all their friends, accompanying his show with witty patter and funny mispronunciations; and eventually they would die, and, departing, leave behind them a little brass plate in the visitors' bathroom of the local hospital. Ernie felt like crying.

And then he realized how foolish he was. He had been going out with Doris for a long time now, nearly five months, and he hadn't found anything wrong with her (with her *parents*, but not her).

There had always been something wrong, something he just couldn't make himself like about the others. Some of them laughed too loud, or in the wrong place. Others had an odd way of smoking, or ordered strange, expensive drinks that made them sick, or else the turned out to be demanding, or snotty, or just plain dull.

But not Doris. Doris was just right. Tall enough to wear flats without looking like a pygmy, but small enough to wear heels without towering over Ernie. Five-four; maybe five-five. Shiny golden-brown hair, just shoulder length; when she wore it loose she looked like the archetypal co-ed, and when, for some special occasion, she wore it up or pulled back, she put on poise and grace and sophistication as easily as she would insert a hairpin. Bright, sky-blue eyes that were always fresh and new-looking, full of appreciation and interest when Ernie looked at her. And never any funny stuff with the hair or eyes or make-up to make herself look like a high-priced hooker, or any strange clothes that made her look as though she had no bust, or no waist, or a neck like a giraffe. She had taste. She had polish. She was . . . just right, that's all.

Ernie enjoyed thinking about Doris, but it made him nervous. He knew that he liked her a lot, and sometimes—especially when they were together—he was pretty sure he loved her. When he thought about *that* later he got terrified and almost went all the way back to where he didn't even like her any more.

Loving someone was so damned permanent. Loving someone meant getting involved, and getting involved meant giving up more and more of yourself and accepting things you didn't want, and shouldn't accept, and wouldn't accept if you weren't in love. When he relaxed, and let his imagination off the leash to go sniffing around in corners and digging up all sorts of dreary prospects, Ernie could imagine a future life with Doris that held everything, down to the tiniest detail, that would make his life miserable. But as long as it included Doris, he felt that he could take it; was, as a matter of fact, dying for it. Maybe that's love, he pondered uncomfortably. If it is, it's sheer hell; chocolate-covered, candy-coated hell; the honey on the razor blade, the thorn on the rose, the kick in the ass with the satin slipper.

He had even tried to ease himself out of Doris' life, but it didn't work at all. The course in Romantic lit gave him a wonderful excuse: between his teaching and his courses, he could hardly have time to see Doris regularly; anyone could understand that. And the teacher was a maniac, a brand-new Ph.D. who felt that he had to "prove himself" by making the course impossible.

When they got to Byron, and Ernie had to read all of *Don Juan*, he stayed home to work over the weekend, and didn't see Doris, and it nearly killed him. He called her up the following Tuesday, and when he found that she had no plans for the evening, he ran to her like a whippet and nearly splintered her ribs when she opened the door. And when she squeezed back just as hard and nearly broke *his* ribs, he didn't mind it a bit.

Doris was sweet. Not artificial sweet, like a relative or a salesgirl, but lovable sweet. A friend, only softer. Doris was the kind of a person who made Ernie feel that she really did give a damn, about everything (which was okay, but he could take it or leave it alone), but especially about him (which was great).

But there's always a hitch. That's life. Doris had a family, and

Ernie just couldn't get himself to like them. It was like having in-law trouble without even being married.

Ernie knew their type. In moments of sober reflection he could see just how they would behave toward him. They would plan his capture with the thorough cunning of desperation, tying him down slowly but surely with a succession of gossamer bands: family dinners, little gifts, private jokes, evenings *en famille* playing Scrabble in French, or working out insanely complicated variations of Ghost; just like the Lilliputians immobilizing Gulliver in his sleep. Then, when their long, deep planning came to fruition and he and Doris were irrevocably one, all smiles would stop together and Doris' parents would begin to treat Ernie as if he had ridden down upon them like a Hun, snatched up their daughter at full gallop, and left them behind to weep and tear their hair while he, great hairy drunken brute that he was, had his wicked way with their fair innocent. How did I ever get involved with them? Ernie asked himself helplessly. And, even more to the point, how can I get uninvolved? And if I do, can I manage it without getting uninvolved with Doris, too? What the hell would I do if I screwed up everything between Doris and me just because I don't like her parents? And then there was Mrs. Ramsay. If she ever thought that Ernie was free and unattached, she would have Rowena (Ye gods, *Rowena!*) jumping for the rebound like a seven-foot pro center. It called for a cool head.

Ernie's troubled speculations on affairs of the heart were interrupted by the sound of Miss Grimm's private door opening and closing. He returned to the problems of the immediate present with a sickening thud. The sight of Lynn assuaged his anguish somewhat, especially since she whispered across the rail to him in a conspiratorial, you-and-me-against-the-world way.

"She's on the phone now. I think she'll see you as soon as she's through."

"Thanks. Is she in a good mood?"

Lynn pondered for a moment. "Well, she's not in a *bad* mood."

"Umm. She will be when she sees me."

"Don't worry. She's not bad, really. If you have any time afterward, why don't you come downstairs and have coffee? You can tell me all about it. I'm good at consoling teachers."

"Consolation is just what I need. As if things weren't bad enough, I'm going to be observed tomorrow."

"By Miss Grimm?"

"No! Mikropoulous. He's bad enough."

"Well, then, try to come downstairs, all right?"

"The faculty lunchroom?"

"That's right. I stop in for coffee every day around this time. I'm usually alone. 'Bye now," she said, with a smile and a little wave that made Ernie cringe inwardly.

There. He knew it would happen, and it did. Lynn was pretty, and probably loads of fun and a great consoler, but she was too pushy. She wasn't like Doris, who made him feel like a man, not a victim.

Of course, having coffee with Lynn would still be a lot better than spending the seventh period in the odious little pen on the third floor that was used for a faculty lounge, smoking too many cigarettes and counting his grievances like Silas fondling his gold. Doris probably wouldn't mind *that*. Even when you're on a diet, you can still look at the menu. Better think it over, he decided. Later, not now.

Ernie looked up at the clock. Less than fifteen minutes of the period left, and the Iron Maiden was still busy. He had his routine down pretty well, and he didn't want to think about his other problems any more—not for a while, anyway—so he decided to let Agent C21 stretch his legs a bit. It was a good spot for him. Ernie leaned back on the hard, uncomfortable bench.

Agent C21 could feel the hard, uncomfortable bench pressing through his trenchcoat. He shifted his weight, flexing his broad shoulders, and six submachine guns jerked up on a line with his chest.

"Don't move, you! Don't move, do you hear?" cried the captain of the guard in terror, edging away from his captive.

"Relax, old man, relax," C21 said with a charming smile, "I wouldn't miss this meeting for the world."

"You vill soon be singing a different tune," said one of his captors in a cruel, guttural voice.

The others exchanged knowing glances and grinned down fiercely at C21. One of them snickered.

"Haff you neffer heard of Hässlich Von Grimm?" the guttural one demanded.

"I've heard a great deal, none of it very good," C21 *replied coolly.*

"Schwein! I vill show you!" the guttural one snarled, lunging at C21 *with the heavy, metal-plated butt of the submachine gun.*

It was over in a split second; a swift karate smash and the hulking brute's neck was broken. Before the stupefied guards could act, C21 *had snatched the submachine gun from his limp victim and fired five quick shots, swinging the weapon in a smooth, deadly arc across the room. He rose, stepped over the corpses, and tapped with the smoking muzzle on Von Grimm's black door.*

"I'm coming in, Von Grimm," he said. "This is the showdown."

"Indeed it is," said a cold voice from behind the door.

With a single kick at the doorknob, C21 *smashed his way into the room. One look at the sight that greeted him and he let the submachine gun clatter to the floor. A frightened girl was standing before Von Grimm's blood-red desk. Behind her sat a woman in black, with steel-rimmed glasses and her hair in a bun. She was ramrod-straight, rock-hard, an iron fist in an iron glove. She was Hässlich Von Grimm, the Iron Maiden of MINUTCON, and she was aiming a Luger at the girl's temple.*

"I thought you'd be in Istanbul by now, Doris," C21 *said to his terrified ward.*

"They shot the plane down over the Adriatic," she answered dully.

"What about Rassendyll and Ffrangcon-Davies?"

She shook her head.

"They were my friends, Von Grimm. You'll pay for this," C21 *said evenly. "You and your whole rotten organization."*

"We shall see—"

"—see you now," Miss Grimm said sharply from the doorway of her office.

Ernie was brought back with a jolt. He rose to his feet bravely and began the slow march to the black door and whatever lay beyond. As he walked, confused thoughts tumbled through his mind, as they do, according to tradition, in the plight of a drowning man. (Ernie had noticed these symptoms in himself before, and from his conversations with other young teachers he had learned that they, too, suffered with them. He had decided that it was evidence of an unnamed but endemic professional disease, something on the order of painters' colic, mule-spinners' cancer, potters' asthma, grinders' rot, twisters' cramp, clergymen's sore throat, and miners' nystagmus. He had christened it "teachers' twitch"). Could he remember his lines? *No.* Even if he could, would she believe a single word of them? *No.* Quick, something else—faint, and then lie there moaning, foaming a little around the corners of the mouth; or adopt a hideous, lurching, twisting, limp, and mumble something about the slippery stairs in Glen Park High School and Workmen's Compensation; or vomit—but they wouldn't work, any of them, and he knew it; he was being foolish and trying to think of everything in the world but what he ought to be thinking of. Face up to it, lad, he told himself, boldly, but not very convincingly. At the door, he took one last vicious yank at his nostril hair, nearly tearing his nose off but bringing on a series of sharp, barking sneezes that left him feeling —and, he hoped, looking—moist and flushed.

"Well, Mr. Quinn," Miss Grimm said frigidly.

Ernie was not sure what to do. Her manner suggested that the only course open to him was to throw himself to his knees, grovel piteously, and blubber "Mercy! Mercy!" but he rejected that. He decided to sniff.

"You *might* use your handkerchief."

"Yes. Thank you," Ernie said, drawing a sodden grayish mass from his pocket and mopping his nose and adjacent portions of his face.

"You were absent from the faculty meeting last Friday afternoon, Mr. Quinn. Will you tell me why?"

"I had this cold."

"Really, Mr. Quinn. A lot of us have gone to faculty meetings suffering from colds, and worse things than colds. Is that the only excuse you can offer me?"

"Yes."

"It's not a very good one, I must say. It doesn't indicate a very conscientious attitude." Her lips were growing thinner by the second.

"It seemed to be the best thing, under the circumstances," Ernie said lamely; then, moved by a sudden inspiration, he added, "My nose was bleeding pretty badly. I thought I might distract people. You know, sitting there with my head back, and blood, and everything." Aaron would love that.

"You have a point there, Mr. Quinn," she said reluctantly, "but of course you should have notified me immediately. I'm the one who excuses people from attendance at meetings, you know."

"Yes, I know. I guess I didn't think it was necessary," Ernie said, and realized immediately that he should not have said that, of all things, to Miss Grimm, of all people.

"There is a right way and a wrong way of doing things, Mr. Quinn," she answered him, enunciating each word with care. "I'm not saying you did the wrong thing in absenting yourself from Friday's meeting; but you certainly did not go about it properly. In future, I hope you'll consider it necessary to consult with me before you do anything of this kind."

"I will."

"I hate to see this attitude of disregard for the right way of doing things on the part of you younger people. I don't mind telling you, Mr. Quinn, there's going to be a crackdown on the attendance at faculty meetings in future," she said, warming to her favorite topic. "I've been getting some bad reports from the clerks, too, about people coming in late and leaving early, and the librarian has had some requests for outrageous books, all of them from you younger people . . ."

The librarian, a mumbling antiquity, was thrown into paroxysms of pharisaical outrage at the mention of any author racier than Dickens. Ernie had nearly precipitated a book-burning festival last fall by submitting a book-request form for the complete works of Henry Miller and signing it "*M. J. Grimm.*" The wound still rankled, if Miss Grimm's roster of fixations could be taken as any indication.

". . . coming to class late, setting a very bad example for the students, and then just taking a day off whenever you please, whenever you have the sniffles or a headache or you just don't feel like doing a day's work—"

"I've never missed a day, Miss Grimm," Ernie broke in, trying hard to keep the rage in his voice from showing.

"I beg your pardon?"

"I said I've never missed a day of teaching," Ernie said, more evenly.

"Well, I didn't say *you* had. I was talking about all the other young teachers around here who think they can come and go as they please. Your friend Mr. Ferriss has been out for two days."

"Maybe he's sick," Ernie said, making a mental note, marking it "Urgent!" to call Bob immediately after school and warn him.

"I certainly hope he is," Miss Grimm said tartly; then, realizing her unhappy choice of phrase, she added, "That is, I hope he's genuinely sick, for *his* sake, and not just taking a premature vacation."

This addition seemed to strike her as an unusually clever turn of phrase. She looked up at Ernie, awaiting his appreciative smile, which he decided not to give her. He was too busy being resentful and inwardly irate to waste any time being diplomatic, and besides, he thought, the mean, sarcastic, backbiting old bitch didn't deserve it. He wasn't going to chuckle on cue for *her*.

"Well, Mr. Quinn," she snapped, with a busy shuffling of papers and an exaggerated glance at her watch, "the period is almost over, and I don't think there's anything more for us to discuss. I wouldn't want to make you late for your eighth period." She straightened her glasses angrily. Ernie thought immediately of the Hollywood bit in which the plain girl is transformed into a mad, wanton vision of loveliness merely by shaking her hair out of a bun and removing her glasses. It would never work for Miss Grimm, he decided. She'd still be a mean, ugly old broad, only her hair would be a mess and she'd be half blind.

"Thank you. Goodbye."

"Good day, Mr. Quinn."

Ernie walked out of her office with an unaccustomed feeling of confidence. He had not really won a victory, but he had not been reduced to a sodden, emasculated heap blubbering abject apologies, and against Miss Grimm that was practically a victory.

He passed Lynn's desk, and as he did he remembered her mentioning that she would be in the faculty lunchroom. He checked the clock and mumbled angrily when he saw that the period was all but over. He would have been willing to let his eighth-period class run amok through the halls while he sat and passed the time of day with Lynn—just this once, for consolation—but it wasn't as simple as that. After all, he had a job to do. Damn it.

He left the office and was practically to the stairs when he heard someone calling his name. Without thinking, he turned. It was Mrs. Ramsay, and she was all a-flutter, like a giant dish of custard.

"Ernest Quinn, I thought I'd *never* catch you!" she said, trying hard to be coquettish, even though she was out of breath.

"Oh. Well, here I am."

"I have such a surprise for you, Ernest. You'll never guess!"

She hit the nail right on the head that time, Ernie thought. At that moment the bell rang, ending the seventh period, but not Mrs. Ramsay. She rambled on, but the bell, directly over their heads, drowned her words in its ear-splitting tocsin.

"—to the school!" she concluded. "Won't that be fun?"

"It sounds grand," Ernie said neutrally, moving slowly up the stairs away from her.

"Now don't you dare let her know I told you," Mrs. Ramsay said, waving a plump forefinger cutely, like a comic German butcher.

"No. No, I won't. I have to run now, Mrs. Ramsay, really. I have a class."

He was halfway down the corridor to Room 318 when he realized what Mrs. Ramsay must have said: Rowena was coming to the school! Things were closing in, fast.

He entered Room 318, and the customary eighth-period turmoil subsided. Teaching was out of the question. He assigned an extempore composition on the topic "Woman versus Man" and sat back to brood. The thought of Lynn, Rowena, and Miss Grimm pursuing him with carnivorous intent was disturbing. He began to wonder if there could possibly be such a thing as an Orpheus complex. He worked on that for the next thirty-seven minutes, and by the end of the period, he was convinced that there was. There had to be, because Ernie could feel himself coming down with a classic case of it.

When the eighth period ended, Ernie fled to the time-clock room, snatched the contents of his letter box and crammed it into his bag in a single sweeping motion, punched himself out, and disappeared through the side door mercifully unseen by Ramsays, Grimms, or Mikropoulouses. He knew that if he ran like hell he could catch the last safe bus; after this time, the buses were filled with students, and students were the last people he wanted to see right now. Well, fourth from last. So he ran like hell, caught the almost-empty bus, and sat back to gather his thoughts. He still had big things to do today.

He rummaged through the dross that he had ripped from his letter box, finding, at first glance, little of value or interest in the wadded clump of papers. There were two urgent forms, two reminders, another notice about *Windswept*—after countless delays, it would appear on Friday—a message from the principal, and two envelopes with his name on them. The plot was thickening; Ernie's interest was aroused.

One envelope was unmistakably from Mikropoulous. The other was in an unfamiliar script, possibly a feminine hand. Ernie tore open the second envelope, and when he started to read the contents he wanted to jump to his feet and shout to the world in general, "I told you so! I *told* you she was pushy!" It was from Lynn: "*Seventh period tomorrow? I'm dying to hear your story. Yours, Lynn.*" *Yours!* Ye gods, he thought frantically, at least wait until I ask! He could feel things closing in all around him. And since he was on the bus, he soon found himself in a heated exchange with his built-in devil's advocate.

"You don't know what the hell you want, do you, you silly bastard?" he said contemptuously.

"Yes, I do," Ernie retorted. "I want to go to Europe, and I want Doris."

"Sure. And an hour ago you were mooning over Lynn. *Clown.*"

"I wasn't *mooning* over Lynn. And even if I was, it was only a momentary aberration. Lynn is pretty, but she's like all the others. She's not like Doris."

"Then marry Doris."

"But I might have to give up Europe!"

"Then go to Europe."

"But I might lose Doris!"

"Then marry Doris and go to Europe."

"We'd starve!"

"Then don't do anything. Keep putting things off until Doris gets fed up and you're too old to care about Europe and you've wasted your whole life and wound up a two-bit Prufrock. You may be out of a job soon, if you're not careful. That means no Europe, no Doris, nothing."

"Oh, shut up," Ernie snapped, disgusted at the way he could destroy a good mood in a matter of seconds with a few well-chosen words based on clear, objective facts. He was getting to loathe clear, objective facts. He wasn't too keen on his devil's advocate, either. A troublemaker, that's what he was.

There was still the other envelope to look at. Desperate for any form of distraction, even a threatening letter from Mikropoulous, Ernie assaulted the second envelope and wrested loose a brief typewritten notice. "*Dear Mr. Quinn,*" it read, "*I shall make my observation during Tuesday's sixth-period class.*" It was signed with the dreaded Mikropoulous cartouche.

It wasn't so bad, really. If the choice had been up to Ernie, he would probably have named the sixth period himself. Of course, there was always the chance that it was a devilish ruse and that Mikropoulous was counting on Ernie's concentrating his preparation on the sixth period and was going to drop in on one of his other classes in hope of finding him unprepared. That was the sort of thing one could always expect from Gregory Peter Mikropoulous, guide, philosopher, and friend of no one on earth but Gregory Peter Mikropoulous. The more Ernie thought about it, the more likely it seemed. After all, if Mikropoulous saw him do a really good job he wouldn't have much justification for firing him; and judging from the curtain of silence surrounding the question of Ernie's continuance next year, there wasn't exactly a grassroots movement to sweep him into a permanent position at Glen Park High School. But if Mikropoulous really pearled his harbor and slipped in on, say, the first period, he could have Ernie flat on his behind in the street, jobless and unreferenced, in a matter of minutes, and all because Ernie wasn't prepared. There didn't seem to be much left for Ernie to do but to concoct a real knockout lesson for each of his classes. Being a new experience, it might even turn out to be pleasant, he told himself, grasping at the first straw that passed, but missing it. He knew, but chose to ignore, the fact that Mikropoulous needed no justification for dropping him. He could teach a lesson that drew a standing ovation from the entire student body and faculty, and still wind up flat on his behind in the street. That's education for you: the next-to-last refuge of the scoundrel, Ernie thought unhappily.

By concentrating on ideas for tomorrow's lessons—none of them very good—Ernie was able to keep from facing up to any more unpleasant truths for the rest of the ride home. He arrived home shortly after three o'clock. The house sounded empty, which was all right as far as he was concerned. He was always glad to avoid the daily ritual which began with his mother's, "Well, how was everything at school today?"—a question that had not varied in phraseology or intonation for the past twenty years, ever since the day when little Ernie Quinn, in short pants and long stockings, first stuck his shining morning face inside a classroom, and had it hit almost immediately, and a question which he had never answered honestly and never intended to—and ended in a Joycean flow of reminiscence from his grandfather, who remembered when lads Ernie's age could compose poems in Latin and Greek, and did so, on the few occasions when they were not slipping bombs into His Majesty's mailboxes or throwing grenades at passing lorries.

Ernie went straight to the kitchen to look for news. Clan Quinn dwelt in an old house of ten or eleven rooms (opinions differed, and no one bothered to count the rooms and settle the matter, preferring to retain a central theme of argument for use when all other topics had lost their savor), but the nerve center was the kitchen. In the kitchen, on a typical night, Grandfather sat chewing on sips of whiskey-and-water and cursing the Black-and-Tans, Father read the newspaper and muttered dark mutters about the coalition of foreigners and Republicans who were ruining the country, and Mother moved stolidly about in pursuit of many tedious, steamy, and apparently pointless tasks. Ernie often wondered, when he compared his kin with the toothsome, seemingly interchangeable, family groups in television commercials, whether the Quinns had not skipped a generation somewhere; in a sense, he knew they had. Both his father and his grandfather had married late in life, and the span of the three generations of Quinns would have done for four, or perhaps even five, married-in-their-teens generations of normal television Americans—the kind who worry about perspiration, cigarette filters, and the whiteness of their towels and their neighborhood.

Ernie picked up the note he found leaning against the sugar bowl. This was getting to be quite a day for notes, he reflected as he read the latest communiqué: "*We're visiting Auntie, staying for supper, come if you can make it, don't be late, we're eating at six sharp, Mother."*

Ernie's mother was living proof that one could lead a long, happy life, raise a fine son, and be a good neighbor, without caring too much about formal punctuation. Ernie and his mother lived in different worlds, and they knew and accepted this fact. Ernie was not quite able to move about freely in his parents' world, which consisted chiefly of innumerable relatives, most of whom he had never met, and local political crises, which bored him to madness. His grandfather explained the apathy by saying scornfully, "He's not a Quinn, that one," and his father ignored him completely, but his mother played the diplomat and tried hard to give him a way out. She was not exactly overwhelmed by his decision to become a teacher, but—except in the mornings, when she hammered away with a vengeance—she was willing to live and let live, a rare trait among the Quinns. Tonight, for instance: she knew what "supper at Auntie's" meant to Ernie, so she inserted the escape clause that had become a standard feature of all family-gathering invitations. In the midst of the interminable gloomy discussions of dead relatives, dying neighbors, and Machiavellian power struggles in the local Democratic club, someone would say, "Where's the lad?" Grandfather would reply, "Oh, himself is too busy with Shakespeare and Milton and all the other Jews and atheists to bother with his own flesh and blood," and his mother, without looking up, would say, "The lad's busy, he works hard at his job, he's not like some of the Quinns I could name," and there would be an argument and Ernie would be forgotten. God bless her for understanding, he thought, and especially at a time like this, when he had a million things to do. Well, three.

He made himself a cup of coffee, lit a cigarette, and sat down to check his worries. He had to call Bob and tip him off about the Iron Maiden. Then there was the business of lesson plans. Then Doris. It was going to be a busy afternoon, and an even busier night.

First came the phone call to Bob. It was more a debt of honor than a gesture of friendship; it was, in Ernie's eyes, a kind of lend-lease commitment to be fulfilled. He and Bob were not actually friends, certainly not friends in the Damon and Pythias, Roland and Oliver, Hamlet and Horatio sense. They were allies, co-belligerents united against a common enemy. Bound by a chain forged of resentments, frustrations, and feeble defiances all directed against the power elite of the Board of Education and Glen Park High School, they substituted a conspiratorial sharing of grievances and petty sabotage for a true meeting of the minds.

They were completely different in attitude. Ernie was content to fight and win his battles in the labyrinthine ways of his own imagination, but Bob was a born denouncer. He would have made a magnificent Bolshevik or—if he could learn to handle a sword—a good Scaramouche. Ernie had seen that the first time they met.

Ernie was sitting in the third floor faculty lounge, a squalid little cell that resembled the setting of a George Price cartoon, a place of peeling paint and naked light bulbs, of groaning springs, sagging cushions, and frayed edges on furniture that looked like something washed up by the Johnstown flood, when Ferriss stalked into the room. Ernie gave him a quick appraisal, and returned immediately to the adventures of Agent C21, who was, at the moment, trapped in a burning faculty room with no apparent avenue of escape. At first glance, Ferriss was not particularly striking: square face, crewcut, intense accusing eyes glaring out from behind emphatic black glasses; a typical young hot-shot teacher trying to look dedicated; like all the rest, Ernie thought smugly. Then Ferriss began his entrance speech.

"The swine! The dirty, treacherous swine!" he snarled, pale, trembling with rage, his jaw working.

"Who?" Ernie asked, his interest shifting to the newcomer. C21 could hold out for a while.

"Dirty, low, skulking vermin! Traitors!" Ferriss explained.

"Who? What happened? Was it a sneak observation?" Ernie demanded in sudden panic.

"Look at this! Look!" Ferriss howled, waving aloft a badly crumpled newspaper. "They cut the appropriation! They cut it in half, the swine!"

"What appropriation? Who cut it?" Ernie cried, caught up in the wave of demagogic fury emanating from this angry stranger. "What are you talking about?"

"Look. Right here, right at the top of the page. See?"

Ernie looked, and in the upper corner of the page found a ten- or fifteen-line release about some appropriation for a conservation project that had been cut in half by a congressional committee.

"Is this important?" Ernie asked innocently.

"In itself, no. It's a simple question of principle. These swindlers are lining their pockets under the pretext of serving the people. Scum!"

Ernie couldn't see how people could line their pockets by cutting appropriations, but he let that pass. Ferriss then went on to explain, in profuse detail, how the fate of the republic had been all but sealed by this particular act of skulduggery. He named names unfamiliar to Ernie, quoted articles from obscure magazines, and cited at least four similar cases that Ernie had never heard of. Ernie, having nothing else to do at the time, gave Ferriss the impression of being a good listener; Ferriss, who was fast running out of listeners, bound him to his heart with hoops of steel. In ensuing weeks, he allowed Ernie to read carbon copies of the ornate, incoherent letters he fired off daily to congressmen and newspaper editors, and lent him copies of *Foreign Affairs*, *National Review*, and *The Nation*. Some of these journals were rather difficult to read, since they had been torn in half in a fit of outraged disagreement and then painstakingly reassembled with mending tape; but, then, Ernie wasn't very much of a political man to begin with. On four successive occasions within a period of less than two months, Ferriss described the United Nations to Ernie as (1) a Fascist superstate; (2) a tool of Communist aggression; (3) the noblest achievement of twentieth-century man; and (4) a front for Afro-Asian imperialism. Ernie found Ferriss' views confusing, but never boring. Bob Ferriss might not have been too clear as to just what he believed, but he believed it at the top of his voice.

Ernie drained his coffee, fixed himself another cup, laid his cigarettes and matches and an ashtray neatly before him, and turned his chair toward the telephone. In the Quinn household, the telephone was, perforce, in the kitchen. He dialed, then leaned back and lit a cigarette, awkwardly, while he waited for someone to answer the telephone.

"Hello? Who's this?" a woman's voice said defensively. That would be Bob's mother.

"Hello, Mrs. Ferriss. This is Ernie Quinn."

"Who? Who is it?"

"Ernie Quinn, Mrs. Ferriss. I work with Bob."

"Oh, yes. Ernie Quinn. You work with Bob. You were here once, I remember. Yes . . ." she said, her voice trailing off and growing fainter, as if she were slowly backing away from the receiver.

"May I speak to Bob, Mrs. Ferriss?"

"Bob isn't feeling well, Ernie. He's up in his room. I don't know . . ." she said *poco a poco diminuendo*, as was her wont. This was her standard reaction to any situation calling for a decision. Ernie knew that if he had the time and the inclination he could hold the line for an hour, not saying a word, and she would still be on the other end, patiently awaiting a direct order.

Ernie's first meeting with Mrs. Ferriss had shaken his faith in the laws of heredity. Judging from her explosively *engagé* son, Ernie had expected her to be a great bosomy madame chairwoman of the type found at charity bazaars, a woman beside whom Joan of Arc would seem timid and apologetic. Instead, she turned out to be a woman with an invisible personality. Apparently, Bob had inherited his fiery activism and his flair for outrage from his father. Ernie could not check this conclusion firsthand. Bob's father, like many other American fathers living and dead, was dead.

At the moment, not having either the time or the inclination to hold the phone for an hour, Ernie acted decisively.

"It's pretty important, Mrs. Ferriss. I think you'd better let me speak to him."

"He's upstairs. He has laryngitis."

"He doesn't have to say anything, Mrs. Ferriss, he can just listen. Will you get him, please?"

"Well . . ." she said faintly, and then Ernie's eardrum was nearly shattered by the ringing whack of the receiver being put down sharply on a hard surface. There was an interval, during which Ernie began to wonder if she had just wandered off somewhere and drowned, like Ophelia, and finally there came a harsh, raspy sound something like "Ernie?"

"Is that you, Bob?"

"Yes. Can't talk. Laryngitis. What's up?"

"It's that faculty meeting last Friday. Grimm called me in to explain about it. She must have checked over her attendance roster and found me missing."

"Sorry," Ferriss croaked. "Forgot to warn you."

"It's okay, Bob. I got out of it. I had to give her a big story, but it turned out all right. You may be in for some trouble, though. I told her all about how you were supposed to sign me in but you punked out on me and—"

"Swine!"

"Don't talk, Bob, you have laryngitis," Ernie said brusquely. "We chatted for a while about how lousy it is to put all your faith in someone and then have them betray you. She was very sympathetic."

"Vermin!"

"Speak up, Bob. I can hardly hear you," Ernie said, suddenly drunk with power. It was the first time in all their acquaintance that he had talked and Bob listened, and he liked it this way. Bob favored him with a few strangled epithets, and he listened, grinning, until he began to feel a little ashamed of himself. It was kind of mean to do this to Bob; he didn't have much of a sense of humor even when he was well. Ernie decided to reassure him.

"Take it easy, Bob. I was just fooling. I told Grimm I had a cold and a bad nosebleed Friday, and she believed me. I *think* she believed me. She didn't give me the big routine she's supposed to give people for missing faculty meetings, anyway, so she didn't *not* believe me. But she went off on her 'irresponsible younger teachers' speech—"

"Petty bureaucratic tactics!"

"—and she mentioned you. You've been out two consecutive days, so she's convinced you're holed up somewhere with the d.t.s or something. I wanted to warn you, so you can make sure you're covered. You could make this into a pretty good thing, you know? Why don't you go in the first day you're back and breathe on her?"

He couldn't make out Bob's reply.

"Well, take care of yourself. Don't hurry back. Grimm can stew for a while. Just make sure you cover yourself."

"Thanks, Ernie."

"It's okay. Can I do anything for you? Get you something to read?"

"No. I'm all set."

"You're sure?" Ernie pressed him, feeling that he ought to do something.

"Honest, Ernie. Thanks, anyway."

"We have to stick together. We're badly outnumbered."

"Yes. Thanks for calling."

"So long, Bob," Ernie said, wanting to stop the embarrassing flow of gratitude.

He hung up the receiver, leaned back, and lit another cigarette. One down. All right; now it was time to work on the lesson plans. He looked up at the kitchen clock. It said 3:39, which meant that it was actually 3:34 because the kitchen clock, like all the other clocks in the house, was kept five minutes fast, for reasons known only to Grandfather and God.

Three thirty-four. Ernie would have enjoyed a nap, but he knew it was a luxury he couldn't afford, not with five superlative lesson plans to complete by seven o'clock. Well, by eight. Maybe 8:30. Doris would understand.

It was time to get down to work. No naps, no fooling around, no Agent C21; just steady work. He stood up and squared his shoulders, setting his jaw in a firm, determined line. He had to pass through the living room on the way to his room, and there was the sofa, all plumped up, looking comfortable.

It was nearly 5:30 when Ernie awoke from his nap. He felt damply warm, puffy, and slow, like a man who falls asleep on a commuter train, and he had to lie still until he was up to working again, so it was nearly six when he finally got to his room.

He got out his books, opened his assignment pad, and dug out a handful of the blurrily mimeographed lesson plan forms provided by Glen Park High School in order to stifle any vestige of imagination or originality on the part of its teachers. He filled in the class and date on the top of one, then sat back to rest.

He knew it was dangerous, but he couldn't keep from looking at his voluntary bookcase; looking at it meant thinking about it, and thinking about it meant getting angry and not being able to work well, so it was not the thing to be doing now. He decided that since he was going to do it sooner or later anyway, it would probably be just as well to get angry now and get it all over with, instead of letting it build up.

The voluntary bookcase wasn't originally intended to make him angry; he had thought it would make him a little happier. When Ernie went out on a book-buying spree he put the new ones in his voluntary bookcase, the one that contained only wanted books, not required ones (they went into the drudge bookcase). At first, it provided him with a certain amount of harmless amusement. He arranged the books in order of priority, and whenever he bought a few new ones he went through the whole batch, setting up new priorities and establishing a new reading order for himself. He was quite pleased with the arrangement until it dawned on him that all he was doing was fooling around with a lot of books that he wasn't reading. At last count he had a hundred and twelve unread books neatly arranged in order of unreading: tight, clean little paperbacks; dignified hardbacks with bright dust jackets; even a few special editions, some in leather and some in slipcases, with strange, exotic bindings. They looked great, but they were supposed to be read, not admired as if they were monuments or historic sites.

But a teacher, Ernie learned, doesn't just go out and buy a book he wants to read and sit down and read it. There's always something closing in and catching up fast. There's a course you have to take, which means books you have to read—books that under ordinary circumstances you wouldn't even use to housebreak a puppy—and papers you have to write. Or else there are tests to make up, or tests to correct, or papers to mark, or forms to fill out, or grades to hand in, or reports to compile, or meetings to attend, or excuses to dream up for not having done any of these things. He began to feel righteously and defiantly glad that he hadn't gone to Friday's meeting, and sorry only that he hadn't had the nerve to tell Miss Grimm his real reasons for not being there. That got him thinking about Miss Grimm. And Mikropoulous. And Shefin, and Mrs. Ramsay, and the Professor, from the top of the system to the bottom and on both sides, all of them working like hell to get him involved in things he didn't want to be involved in and shouldn't *have* to be involved in. Ernie knew what he wanted to be: a book bum. He was willing to teach until he could be a book bum. He was willing to be a good teacher, too, and a conscientious one, but that wasn't enough. He knew that he ought to be reading. But they always thought of something. They always found a new way of leaning on you, he thought, nibbling away at those precious hours, snapping great chunks out of the weekend, even figuring out new requirements to eat into your summer. And when they weren't doing that, they were plotting and scheming to get a mortgage on your life or a lien on your soul. Why is it so damned hard to be what you want to be? Ernie asked himself desperately. Why won't they let a man alone? They never let a man alone.

This wasn't getting him anywhere. He went out to the kitchen, fixed himself another cup of coffee, and brought it back to the room to drink as he worked. He managed, after a bit of a struggle, to get his resentment quieted down and set to work, sticking to it doggedly with a minimum of interruption. He left the room only twice: once for another cup of coffee, and once to make himself a thick, heavily salted-and-ketchuped cold roast beef sandwich and open a bottle of beer. He accomplished a lot; not as much as he had hoped, but far more than he had expected. It was nearly nine o'clock when he finished—not so much finished, actually, as just stopped cold, fed up to the teeth with motivations, medial summaries, pivotal questions, aims, and purposes—and slumped back triumphantly in his chair. There were five completed lesson plans before him, and while they might not be classics of their kind, they were finished, and right now that was all that mattered.

Two down, and it wasn't even nine o'clock yet; not bad. Ernie dug out a sweater and started on his way to face down worry number three. He had a quick picture of himself striding down a dusty street, two fresh notches in his .44, toward a small, dark, distant figure; but there was no time for that now, and he dismissed it.

He headed for the train. Doris' house was a half-hour away by train or bus, and the bus was a lot more convenient, but he had been taking the train ever since he sold his car for Europe money. The money was almost all gone by now, and Ernie still wasn't in Europe, but he assured himself, in his sober, reflective moments, that it was just as well not to be driving a car at this time, when he was so often under the influence of Agent C21, who spent much of his time roaring down back roads in a custom-made, bulletproof, Krafft-Ebing DV-8 with a concealed battery of ground-to-ground missiles in the trunk. The bus was associated, in Ernie's mind, with Glen Park High School, and he disliked anything associated, however remotely, with Glen Park High School. Besides, on the bus he always got into arguments with himself, and right now he didn't want to hear what he knew he would say if he got the chance. On the train he could use Agent C21. He had worked out a few good scenarios centering around secret papers and hired assassins on the Orient Express, and they just didn't work out right on a bus.

He arrived at Doris' house at about 9:40. In view of the hour, he was prepared for a slightly brisk reception, and so he was pleasantly surprised when Doris burst out the door, dewy-eyed and bright, and said, "Oh, Ernie, I'm so glad you're here! I have the most wonderful news!"

Her last words set off alarms deep inside his nervous system; all his defense mechanisms swung into action. Doris' idea of wonderful news could be something like a one-day sale of wedding rings, a manufacturer's closeout of French Provincial bedroom sets with twin night tables, or a scholarly article by her father arguing that all young teachers should marry immediately, especially ones named Ernie Quinn, and should never, under any circumstances, dream of visiting Europe. He fought down a strong urge to run off into the night. Not too strong, really; it wasn't easy to run away from Doris.

"Oh? What is it, Doris?"

"It's just wonderful, Ernie. Come on inside. I want the Professor to tell you himself."

Doris' father, a professor of Education at the local college, was known affectionately as the "Professor" to everyone, including his wife and daughter. Ernie had his opinion of this little idiosyncrasy, but kept it to himself.

"Do we have to go right inside?" Ernie asked, closing in.

"Well . . . practically."

When distant sounds of curiosity began to come from inside the house, Ernie relaxed his hold.

"What's the news, Doris? Is it something to do with your father?"

"Yes—but that's all I'll tell you. Come on," she said, taking his hand and bringing him inside. She was cute as hell when she was like this, and Ernie would have preferred to stay on the porch for the rest of the evening; but cute or not, she was also unswerving. He was drawn inexorably inside. Doris' mother, looking exquisitely bored, loomed out of the family room.

"Hello, Mrs. Flecker," Ernie said.

"Ernest, dear, how are you?" she said cheerfully but ritually. "Has Doris told—"

"No!" Doris cried. "Ernie's going to hear it from the Professor personally. Where is he?"

"He's on the telephone, dear. I do wish he'd let *me* at it," she soliloquized to the world at large. "I don't know *how* I'll get the word to everybody before *dawn* at *this* rate. Will you have something, Ernest? Get the poor boy something to drink, dear."

"Beer will be fine, Doris," the poor boy said.

"Certainly not! As soon as the Professor tells you the good news we're all going to have a drink of cognac—is that all right, Mother?"

"Charming thought, my dear. I could use it right now."

"I'll get the things. Why don't you go inside and sit down, Ernie? I won't be a minute."

Ernie wandered into the family room, feeling vaguely displaced, wishing everyone would stop running around like people in a situation comedy, give him something to drink, and tell him what was going on. He never trusted surprises—they were usually disappointing. He was, of course, curious. He could not imagine what great *coup* Doris' father had scored, and he wished they would stop dragging the damned thing out. Anything less than appointment to the College of Cardinals was going to be an anticlimax if they didn't tell him soon.

He was moping about the room looking for something to read when Doris came in with the tray bearing a magnificent smoky-green old-looking bottle and four fat little glasses. She put the tray down and turned to him—she certainly did look cute when she was like this—and he took her around the waist and pulled her down on the couch beside him.

"Ernie, you're terrible," she said cozily as soon as she could. "Suppose my parents walked in?"

"They wouldn't interest me, Doris. They're nice enough, but you're nicer. Come here."

"You behave, now," she purred, settling down against his shoulder.

They broke clean at the sound of footsteps in the hall, and Ernie had managed to transfer most of the lipstick to the sleeve of his sweater by the time Doris' father entered in a flourish of tweeds, trailing clouds of pipe smoke as he came.

Doris' father wore a pipe. On special occasions, such as tonight promised to be, he actually smoked it, but as a rule he wore it. He posed with it, holding it stolidly in one hand and cupping his elbow in the other. He rubbed it against his chin or the side of his nose while he weighed a remark. He used it as a prop to point a moral or adorn a tale. It was his rod and his staff, his Excalibur, his talisman, and from it he drew wisdom and strength and poise. But the pipe was not his only tool. Ernie had noted that Doris' father was a man of varied abilities. He could beam, when he was happy, or wanted to appear happy. He could chuckle, when he was amused, or wanted to sound amused. He could even twinkle, under the proper circumstances and in the proper company. And this beaming, chuckling, twinkling Turveydrop was the father of the girl Ernie loved and intended, eventually, to marry. And if you get Doris, he told himself, you get the Professor; dump the Professor, and you dump Doris. That's the way it is.

Ernie felt thwarted. The old familiar feeling that they were catching up fast and closing in on him returned. He felt like someone out of a Greek myth, one of those poor bastards like Oedipus or Sisyphus or Tantalus, who just couldn't win. Then again, he cautioned himself, it could be plain old paranoia; but damn it, they *were* catching up fast and closing in!

"Well, Ernest my boy, you've come at a pretty lively time," the Professor said, beaming and smiling a kindly old smile that made his eyes crinkle up at the corners—I bet *that* took a lot of practice, Ernie thought peevishly—and placing his hands on his wife's and Doris' shoulders in a warm gesture he had probably picked up from a Norman Rockwell illustration, "a pretty lively time indeed. I don't mean to sound pretentious, but I think I can call this the peak of my career."

There was a great deal of warm, cozy beaming on all sides, in which Ernie joined, for Doris' sake. A sudden thought came to him that perhaps the Professor was going to take a sabbatical somewhere far away, or join the Peace Corps, or do *something* that would keep him away for a few years. He beamed and smiled on the Fleckers with genuine feeling.

"Will you end the suspense for me, Professor?" he asked.

"Gladly, Ernest. I'm going to be made chairman of the Department of Education at the college. Actually, it's been in the air for a few weeks, but today it became official."

"Congratulations," Ernie said, really meaning it. Hell, the Professor looked so happy he couldn't dislike him now—later, maybe, but not now. "I bet you're all pretty happy."

"We certainly are, Ernest. Oh, it will mean a lot of work, but it's the kind of work I like. Fortunately, I've got a good department to work with." He paused dramatically, and gave Ernie an enigmatic smile. "And I hope to get a few more good men very soon."

"Well, I certainly wish you luck," Ernie said, hoping he was noncommittal in gesture and intonation. That last little bit, with the pause and the Giaconda smile, made him feel certain that there was a job offer in the near future. Armageddon was just around the corner.

"Thank you. I'll need it," the Professor said humbly. "Now, why don't we all have a drink to celebrate?"

"I thought you'd *never* say that, dear," Mrs. Flecker said with grand ennui. "Heavens, what a day. And tomorrow's going to be worse." She hurled herself upon the couch, giving Ernie the momentary feeling that she was going to go into the death scene from *Camille*; but she only sighed, tragically.

"And Friday," Doris said, encouraging her.

"Don't even *mention* Friday. It will be absolute *chaos*, I *know* it will. Hurry with that drink, will you, dear? I have a *thousand* calls to make, and it's getting late."

"You'll be able to come Friday, won't you, Ernest?" the Professor said, interrupting his pouring and posing with the cognac bottle. "We'll be having a little celebration."

"Little!" Mrs. Flecker said in anguish, rolling her eyes heavenward. "We're having the Congress of Vienna!"

Ernie had a quick vision of the little celebration, a kind of festival of tweeds, Scotch, and academic whimsey; but what the hell, there would be Doris. And it would be kind of mean to say no.

"I'll be glad to come. Thanks."

"Glad to have you. Any friend of Doris, you know," the Professor said archly.

Doris smiled shyly and took Ernie's hand. He squeezed her hand, felt his ring on it, and remembered what he had been thinking in Miss Grimm's office that afternoon. He felt like a bastard. By all his standards, things were closing in with terrifying speed and completeness, but with Doris by his side he really didn't care. Even the Professor wasn't so bad. Maybe he'd change, now that he was a chairman; although, if one were to judge all chairmen by Mikropoulous, the change could be on the order of Dr. Jekyll's. Ernie wondered idly if the family would stop calling him the "Professor" and begin referring to him as the "Chairman." It was something to think about. Later, though.

There was a small fuss as the Professor passed the glasses around. He proposed a crisp toast to the future, all sipped, then the four of them sat back and began to dig through the pockets of their minds for some small change to toss into the conversation. Doris made the first sally.

"I'm glad you could come tonight, Ernie. When you didn't call, I knew you were coming, but for a while I was worried that you'd miss the good news."

"I'm sorry I was so late, Doris. I was working on my lessons for tomorrow. They had to be especially good," he explained to the company, "because I'm going to be observed."

"Oh, you poor thing!" Doris said, looking at him as a mother looks at her consumptive child.

"Bad time to be observed, isn't it, this late in the term?" the Professor said. "School's practically over."

"Yes. I guess I was overlooked."

"Tell me, Ernest, what do you think of observations?"

That question, from a newly appointed Chairman of Education, was like the Pope asking a young novice how he felt about sin. Ernie took another sip of cognac, made a great deal out of lighting a cigarette, and answered frankly.

"Not much, Professor. I'm against them."

There was a small eternity of silence, punctuated by ghastly sogging noises, like the cries of a wounded midget drowning in oatmeal, emanating from the Professor's pipe. He chuckled softly, leaned over to Doris, and addressed her in a stage whisper.

"I've been letting you keep this young man quiet too long, my dear. I think he could tell me some things I ought to hear." Then, to Ernie, he explained, "For years now, I've been teaching prospective teachers to teach, and soon I'll be in charge of the teachers who teach prospective teachers to teach. I seem to be moving farther away from the real thing as time goes by. Now, you're right up in the front lines, so to speak. You have a first-hand awareness of the problems we educators theorize about. Would you be willing to tell me what you think is wrong with the idea of observations?"

The Professor surprised him. This was the first time they had ever really talked to each other, and so far the Professor was handling it well. He sounded almost real; not, as in the past, like a man playing a favorite role. Ernie dove in.

"Well, for one thing, they're not honest. They can't be. For instance, if I were to teach the perfect lesson tomorrow, my chairman would still have to find flaws in it; and if I taught the worst lesson he'd ever seen, he'd still have to find something to praise. Now, I admit that there's not much chance of my doing either one, but I'd like to know that I can go to the top or the bottom, and not be committed to a kind of cozy middle ground before I even open the classroom door. You can't really lose, but you can't really win, either, so why knock yourself out? I think it just encourages mediocrity."

"Do you think that's true everywhere?"

"I really don't know, Professor. It's true in Glen Park High School, though. I've spoken to people in other departments, and they say it's the same when they're observed."

The Professor nodded. "Still, if that's the only dishonest thing about—"

"Oh, it's not," Ernie said cheerfully. "They just *can't* be honest. When a chairman or a principal walks into a classroom, the whole situation changes. The kids react differently, and the teacher teaches differently."

"Better or worse than usual?"

"Just differently. And that's scientifically true," Ernie said profoundly. "I don't know it exactly, but there's a law that says when you're observing something, some phenomenon, you should always bear in mine that the very fact that you're observing it changes the phenomenon. Do you know anything about that, Doris?"

Doris, wide-eyed, shook her head helplessly. "I'm awful in science, Ernie," she explained.

"So am I," he reassured her, squeezing her hand. "I just remember odd things like that." He grinned at the Professor. "They're great when you drop them in out of context."

"You don't think teaching is a science, then?"

"Not at all."

"An art?"

"Well, closer to an art. I don't think you can pin it down like that, Professor." Ernie paused. "That's another thing that's bad about observations," he said brightly, as if it had just occurred to him, which it had.

Mrs. Flecker turned to her husband and favored him with a sweet smile. "Aren't you glad you asked, dear?" Then, to Ernie, "Go on, Ernest. I think you've got him."

"I'll certainly think twice before I schedule any more observations," the Professor said, shifting in his chair. "Or ask any more loaded questions."

"Gee, I didn't mean—"

"Just pulling your leg, Ernest. Go ahead."

Ernie took a few minutes to fool with his cigarettes, snuffing one out and then lighting another, meanwhile getting his ideas straightened out, then he plunged ahead. "The whole thing is, what's the point?"

That drew three blank stares.

"What I mean is that nobody really knows what good teaching *is*. They can come into a classroom and watch a teacher perform, and then all they can honestly say is that they liked it or they didn't like it. But they can't really condemn anything."

"I can't buy that, Ernest. You're saying that there's no standard of judgment except personal preference. Surely there's such a thing as good teaching and bad teaching."

"Oh, certainly, but I don't think anyone can judge them on the spot. The only way anyone can judge, really, is in retrospect."

The Professor gave him a puzzled frown.

"Well, you can look at one man and say 'He's been taught well,' and you can look at another and say 'He's been taught badly.' But that's afterward. You can't tell in the classroom."

The Professor grunted.

"Look at some of the English schools you read about in Dickens," Ernie went on. "They must have been horrible places, compared to the schools we have today, but they produced a Dickens."

"And what else did they do to him? Dickens was a very troubled man, Ernest. I'm sure you know that."

"Everybody's troubled, but Dickens was a great writer. Maybe if he had been educated differently, he wouldn't have been troubled, and we wouldn't have his novels."

The Professor grunted again.

"Almost all great authors complain about their schooling, but the fact that they're great authors means that the schooling couldn't have been all that bad. It worked."

"Perhaps great authors thrive on adversity," the Professor suggested.

"Then maybe we need more bad teachers if we want more great authors," Ernie said triumphantly. It was his most consoling thought of the evening, and he hoped he'd remember it, just in case things got bad with Mikropoulous.

"Well . . ." the Professor said, frowning.

"Don't give up the ship, dear," Mrs. Flecker said.

"I won't give up the ship, but I think I'll change course. Tell me, Ernest, why aren't there more great teachers? What's stopping them?"

"Conformity. Everyone is supposed to teach the same way."

"Don't you think there should be standards?"

"Oh, sure. The higher, the better. But I don't see any value in forcing all teachers to work in the same pattern. I think administrators ought to play up individuality, not play it down the way they do."

"How do they play it down, Ernie?" Doris asked.

"Uniform lesson plans, for one thing. No matter what kind of a lesson you're teaching, you have to approach it the same way. In theory, anyway. I don't and most of the others don't, but we're expected to. When we're being observed, we darn well better, or we're in trouble."

"I can see you don't like the idea," the Professor said, "but is it as bad as you paint it? At least it assures a certain orderly minimum of instruction from anyone who follows it, and it gives a new teacher something to lean on until he develops a style of his own."

"Granted, but most administrators seem to me to see this uniform lesson approach as a great solution, when actually all it does is what you say—provide an orderly minimum."

"Surely there's some latitude allowed, Ernest," the Professor objected. "I can't believe that any principal or chairman wants a school full of human teaching machines."

"Well, flexibility certainly isn't encouraged. Whether you're teaching a lesson on punctuation, or poetry, or anything else, you're expected to use the same basic approach, and I just can't see it. You're supposed to motivate, and the kids are supposed to participate, and everything is supposed to be tied up in a neat little package lasting exactly forty minutes."

"Put that way, it certainly doesn't sound very exciting," the Professor said, smiling at Ernie. "What do you suggest as an alternative, though? Surely you don't propose anarchy."

"Not anarchy, exactly, but a lot more independence. I think a trained, experienced man—or woman," he added, tossing a quick apologetic nod to the ladies—"should be free to teach any way he likes, as long as it gets results. If he can't think of a better way, let him use the uniform lesson approach, but only until he finds the right way for *him*."

"And if he doesn't find the right way for himself?"

"Let him look for another job. He's not good enough to be a teacher."

"You're quite severe."

"Think of your own days as a student, Professor. Don't you remember the things you learned from the interesting teachers—even the ones who might have struck you as slightly mad—better than the things you learned from the nice normal mediocrities?"

"I hope you don't think everyone who's normal is necessarily mediocre," the Professor said with a dry little smile. "I must confess that as a chairman, I'd rather have a group of normal people working for me than a pack of wild-eyed eccentrics. Perhaps I'm just getting old."

"Don't be *stuffy*, dear," Mrs. Flecker admonished him. "I think there's a bit of the eccentric hidden under your dignified professorial façade and Mr. Quinn is giving rise to some doubts. He was going to grow a *beard* a few years ago, you know," she said to Ernie.

"Oh, really?" Doris said enthusiastically. "I think you'd look wonderful in a nice trim little beard, Professor, honestly I do! Why don't you grow one this summer, just to see how it looks?"

"Why stop there? I'll get a cloak and a silver-headed walking stick. Right now, I think I'll get a drink. Anyone else care for one?"

The ladies declined, but Ernie decided to go along. It was good cognac.

"I'm going to have some soda and ice in mine this time, Ernest. Care for the same?"

"Sounds all right. Okay."

"Darling, you're not going to get away," Mrs. Flecker called as the Professor began manipulating bottles and tongs. "You still haven't answered Ernest's question."

"Don't you have some people to call, dear?" the Professor asked, with an unconvincing smile.

"The calls can wait until tomorrow. I want to hear what you're going to say."

"What question do you mean?" the Professor said, with a sigh.

"About the interesting teachers—the eccentrics," Mrs. Flecker said. "Do you remember what they taught better than you remember what the ordinary teachers taught?"

"I'd have to think about that," the Professor said, not turning.

"I'm on Ernie's side," Doris announced, moving closer and squeezing Ernie's hand to emphasize her loyalty. "We have a man for history—I guess it wouldn't be ethical to mention a colleague's name, would it?"

"You don't have to," the Professor answered, returning with two fresh drinks. "I know Oxenreiter."

Doris laughed. "I guess everybody knows Oxenreiter. He's the most eccentric man alive, but you just can't forget what he tells you. He's so *vivid*. He draws funny cartoons on the board, and he brings in a box of toy soldiers and uses them to illustrate battles, and he even acts out whole incidents from history. When he did the assassination of Marat, I nearly fainted. It was as though I was seeing the real thing, honestly. And he reads Robespierre's speeches, and Burke's . . . he's really a great teacher. He makes you want to learn."

"That's just what I mean," Ernie said, squeezing her hand to emphasize his reciprocal loyalty. "How can you condemn a man as unorthodox if he makes his students want to learn?"

"There are degrees of unorthodoxy, Ernest. One man's eccentric is another man's raving looney, you know."

"Maybe that's a good thing, Professor. After all, education is supposed to prepare you for life, and life is full of looneys. It might actually be a disservice to kids to have them taught entirely by normal people, you know? Being taught by an occasional nut would act as a kind of immunization program." Ernie was grinning broadly as he said this, but actually, he didn't think it was such a bad idea.

"I must say you've got some novel views on education, Ernest. An eccentric in every school." The Professor was silent for a moment, then he grunted again.

"You're getting stuffy again, dear," Mrs. Flecker warned. "I think you've given him some ideas, Ernest, although he'll *never* admit it."

"Oh, I'll admit it. If I inaugurate a course in Introductory Eccentricity someday, I'll give full credit to Mr. Ernest Quinn, I may even try to prevail upon him to teach it. Tell me, Ernest, is there anything else that bothers you?"

"Oh, lots of things," Ernie said cheerfully. "Do you really want to hear them? I can go on for hours."

The Professor held up his hands in alarm. "Tomorrow *is* a working day. I'd like to get to bed by dawn, anyway. What's the worst thing, besides observations?"

"The idea that a lesson can't be a complete success unless every one of the students contributes something," Ernie shot back immediately. "I guess you'd call it 'The Rule of Universal Participation.' It's ruinous."

"That's hallowed ground you're treading on," the Professor warned. "What's wrong with having students participate?"

"If they have something to contribute, it's fine. But when they don't, I think it's idiotic to expect them to talk just for the sake of talking."

"You can't expect to give a straight lecture course in a high school."

"I don't. That would be going to the other extreme and it would be just as bad. All I'm saying is that there's a time to lecture and a time to discuss."

The Professor made a little noncommittal gesture with his pipe. Ernie pressed on.

"Besides, I think it's wrong to give a student the idea that every word he utters is a pearl of wisdom. I don't remember who said it, but there's a great saying that the beginning of wisdom is the realization of your own ignorance. Well, these kids are never going to realize how little they really know if they're given the impression that teachers hang on their every word."

"It's supposed to build confidence, isn't it?" the Professor pointed out.

"That's the last thing the kids at Glen Park need. They could do with a little insecurity. They just keep getting worse as they go along. I'm taking a graduate course now, out at the university, with Professor Seabold—do you know him?"

"I've met him a few times. He has quite a name in his field, I understand."

"Yes, he does. I don't really like him too much, but he knows his stuff. Now, I'm paying forty-five dollars a credit to listen to what he has to say, because I think it'll be worth hearing. But half the time I don't hear *him*, I hear some pretentious fool who's trying to make an impression by quoting something from *PMLA* and raising some stupid question about it, just because he's been told, all along the line, that he must speak up. I think this clown, and all the others like him, are just wasting my time and money. I don't want to hear *them*, I want to hear Seabold."

"Don't you ever ask questions?" the Professor asked. It was a clever thrust, almost a touch. Ernie parried quickly.

"Only when I want to know something. Not just to hear my own voice."

The Professor leaned forward, frowning, shook his head very slowly, and threw up his hands in a gesture of futility.

"You know, I disagree categorically with most of your positions, but you're a damned convincing talker! I'm sorry I ever started this. I certainly got more than I bargained for."

There was polite laughter—the Professor really wasn't so bad, Ernie thought—and then Mrs. Flecker mentioned coffee and she and Doris left to work out something along those lines. Ernie lit another cigarette and the Professor began an elaborate routine with his pipe. Watching him go through the blowing and filling and tapping and tamping, Ernie still found the theatricality a bit irksome, but he was beginning to like the Professor a little more—or dislike him a little less. He couldn't really say which. Mrs. Flecker's revelation about the beard threw all his previous calculations off. But he still had the impression that he was talking to a character, the Professor, played by John G. Flecker, and not John G. Flecker himself. Perhaps there was no John G. Flecker, only the "Professor." It was something to think about later; along with the "Chairman."

"You like teaching, don't you?" the Professor asked abruptly.

"Yes, I do. I wish I could really do it someday, instead of sandwiching it in between meetings and conferences and observations and form-filling-out and all the other nonsense." Ernie drained his glass and sat back. "I probably sound like an embittered failure, with all these complaints."

"If you didn't like teaching, you wouldn't complain. Want another?"

Ernie thought this offer over for a few seconds before replying. A few more drinks and he'd wake up tomorrow with a pinball machine going full blast inside his head and a taste in his mouth like the bottom of a janitor's pail. And he had to be reasonably alert when he got home, so he could check over those damned lesson plans. But it was good cognac. And tomorrow was going to be lousy anyway.

"All right, thanks. This is awfully good cognac."

"Isn't it? A fellow at the school brought it back from Europe."

Europe. The magic word. Ernie had a sudden feeling of crisis, as if a great opportunity to make it or break it in one fell swoop (Was it "fell swoop" or "swell foop"? Never mind that now) had been dumped in his lap. If he could get the Professor talking about Europe and how great it would be for a young man to be able to spend a year or two over there before settling down, the ice would be broken. He could make it sound as though the

Professor had gotten him all fired up with the idea, and then Doris couldn't really get angry when he told her he wanted to go. She'd be willing to wait for him, and he'd have it all, just the way he wanted it.

"Have you ever been to Europe?" Ernie asked casually.

"Not since the war. I was with Army Intelligence."

"Did you like it?"

"Well, I didn't like the *war*. Europe was pretty enough, but I can't say I saw it at its best."

"Do you ever think of going back?"

"Sometimes," the Professor said absently, handing Ernie a fresh drink and abandoning the topic.

Thanks a hell of a lot, Ernie thought. You're a great help. He was trying to work up a new approach when the Flecker ladies entered bearing coffee and cakes. Well, he thought dismally, scratch one bright idea. One *more* bright idea.

The talk turned to harmless social chatter. Mrs. Flecker mentioned a few new novels, none of which Ernie had read (but he had two of them in his voluntary bookcase); a Bergman movie which was fraught with meaning for the Fleckers, and which Ernie still hadn't deciphered; the college drama society's plans for the fall, which augured dismal failure; an outrageous pun Doris had heard in her Economics class (What did the Italian say when he parked his car in the lobby of his apartment house? "The Fiat's in the foyer") and an even worse one Ernie had dreamed up while watching a dreary documentary on India (How did the maharani explain the fact that she kept all her money locked up at home and never carried it on her person? "Better safe than sari"); and, finally, small domestic matters: arrangements for Friday's party, people to be notified about the Professor's promotion, how badly the change of duties might affect the summer vacation plans, and so forth.

A bit before twelve, the Professor suppressed a yawn. Ernie took the hint.

"I think I'd better be on my way. I have to be in top form tomorrow, you know."

"If you can handle your *chairman* the way you handled my *husband*, you haven't got a *thing* to worry about," Mrs. Flecker said cheerfully.

She wasn't so bad, really. Neither of them were. Why is it that

I can't stand thinking about them, but I don't really mind being with them? Ernie wondered. Am I really *that* much of a phony bastard? Maybe.

"Good luck tomorrow. Give 'em hell," the Professor said, flashing a reassuring I'm-with-you smile.

"Thanks. And congratulations again."

There had been enough conversation for the time being, and it was some time after Ernie and Doris had reached the front porch that they got around to talking. Doris put her hands around Ernie's shoulders and looked up at him in a way that made him ache, it was so sweet and perfect.

"Ernie, it was so nice of you to come tonight, with all that work you have, and that awful observation tomorrow."

"I missed you. I haven't seen you since Saturday."

"I felt so sorry for you, Ernie. I know you didn't feel like talking about school, and teaching, and all, but you were so nice to the Professor. He likes you, you know."

"Well, I wouldn't be too sure about that, Doris. I was a little blunt with him."

"He likes that, Ernie."

"Doris?"

"Yes?"

"Let's not talk so much."

And so there was no more talking until they heard the Professor remark, loudly enough to be heard at the front door, that it was getting late and he thought he'd start up to bed. A gentle hint, but a hint, nonetheless.

"Will I see you before Friday, Doris?" Ernie asked.

"Oh, Ernie, I have four horrible finals this week. I have to study like mad. Really, I *have* to."

"Every night?"

"Well . . . the really monstrous ones will all be over by Thursday."

"Thursday night, then."

"Thursday night," Doris said, smiling up at him.

"I'll be here around eight."

And soon, then, they said their final good night and Ernie headed off for the train. He hadn't really settled things with

Doris, but he had made a decision about something that had been nagging at his mind since the bus ride this afternoon: a way to beat them all. He would knock Mikropoulous cold tomorrow, and then, when he was sure of a job, he could ask Doris to marry him and go to Europe on their honeymoon. A whole summer in Europe, with Doris—he would eat his cake and everybody else's, and still have enough left to feed an army. Unless something went wrong.

But don't think about that.

PART TWO

Ernie awoke Tuesday morning feeling as though a cat—not a cool Siamese or a petulant Angora, but a low-bred, alley-prowling, lop-eared, tattered bum of a cat, a cat devoid of that typical cattish flair, a cat of nasty personal habits and a generally undesirable character—had kittened in his mouth repeatedly during the night. It wasn't the cognac, it was the damned cigarettes. He had gone through nearly a pack last night as he sat up, sipping coffee and smoking to keep awake while he went over his lesson plans like an auditor on the trail of a missing dime. Now, the sensation inside his mouth was something no human should have to endure. It felt as though his tongue had been tarred and feathered. With ostrich feathers.

He opened his eyes and shut them again, immediately. They felt like open wounds. Or little red-hot raisins. Or cinder holes in a dirty sheet. He lay still for a while, trying to think of other, more painful similes, and then the voices of spring swept through his bedroom door.

"Get up, you lazy good-for-nothing! It's seven o'clock!"

That was third call. He must have slept right through first call ("Time to get up, Ernie") and second call ("Ernie Quinn! Get up, lad! I won't call you again"). Fourth call would come in the form of a wet dishcloth flung down on his face, and the thought of it was enough to bring Ernie to a sitting position on the edge of his bed.

He trudged into the bathroom and did all the standard morning things to his face, hair, and mouth, but nothing helped. At 7:15 he was slouched in his place at the kitchen table, ready for abuse and breakfast. They came as a matched set, like Sodom and Gomorrah. Morning was unburdening time for Mrs. Quinn.

"Fine thing, a young lad like you, up until all hours of the morning," his mother greeted him, thrusting a glass of juice into his hand. "You don't care if you keep the whole house up all night."

"Everybody was asleep when I came in."

"And who wouldn't be, at two in the morning? Thank God, we're not all like you, gallivanting about all night with some professor's daughter."

Her logic was unimpeachable. From behind his newspaper, Ernie's father grunted his support.

"I didn't get home that late. It was around one."

"That's late enough. How do you want the eggs?"

"Boiled."

"And why couldn't you go to bed then? You were up in your room until four o'clock."

"Two-thirty. I had school work to do."

"Why couldn't you do it in the afternoon, when you had the house to yourself?"

"I did. I was working until nine o'clock."

"Well, it's a fine job you picked for yourself, working all day and all night and not getting enough sleep. It's a wonder you're not in the hospital, the way you ruin your health with the late hours and the cigarettes and coffee and the running around."

"I drink a lot. That's my health secret," Ernie said sullenly into his empty juice glass. His father lowered the paper enough to glare at him, then resumed his reading.

"Don't get fresh with me, lad. Maybe your friends all think it's very clever, but I'm still your mother."

"I'm sorry."

"Here," his mother said, handing him a towel containing two hot eggs. He broke them into his dish, stirred them into a soupy mess, and began to eat.

"I don't know, lad, I just don't know," his mother began. "I'll never know what got into you, leaving a fine job with a nice future so you could be a teacher, up all night and reading all the time, and still carrying on as if you didn't have to get up in the morning."

"I like it, Mom. I enjoy teaching." Ernie enjoyed the carrying on, too, but thought it better not to say so right now.

"I don't know why you can't take the civil service, like your father, and get something steady where you work regular hours and live like people should live," she went on, ignoring him.

It was a regular morning ceremony, but this morning was a little worse then usual. The relatives must have been rough on her last night, Ernie thought, needling her with success stories of Uncle Tim at the gas company and Cousin Bill at the bank, dwelling with loving relish on such details as fringe benefits, profit-sharing plans, and pensions, while she had to make excuses for a son who enjoyed reading books and teaching poetry. He wanted to explain the whole thing to her, had tried, unsuccessfully, a number of times—but there was a wall between them. Ernie felt that he understood pretty clearly what the problem was: his mother looked at him and saw the smoking ruin of a good upstanding file clerk, leveled under a bombardment of fancy words written by a lot of dead foreigners; Englishmen, at that. She would have understood—not liked, certainly, but understood—losing him to a brassy-haired little trollop, but losing him to books hurt her, and she had to fight back as best she could. The family had encouraged Ernie's going to college because they believed, in a simple, unquestioning way, that "you had to have an education." They were not sure just *why* you had to, but you had to. Now, seeing that Ernie was working hard and showed no signs of getting rich, they were beginning to feel doubts.

All Ernie's mother wanted for her son was a good gray job in a good gray company; and when her son had been given the opportunity and thrown it away, her world was shaken to its foundations. She was fighting a losing battle, and both she and Ernie knew it, but at least the fighting gave them a common topic. There seemed to be nothing else for them to share. Ernie didn't like it this way, but he could think of no solution.

". . . till three in the morning. You can't keep it up, lad," she concluded.

"I'll get to bed early tonight, Mom. I won't even go out after supper. I'll just stay in and go to bed early." It was a peace offering. He couldn't see Doris, anyway.

"Take some care of yourself, Ernie. You look so tired," his mother said, suddenly softening, laying her hand on his.

"I will, Mom. Honest, I will."

They looked at each other, for the first time that morning, and in many mornings, not as antagonists but as mother and son.

Ernie wanted to say something that would help to put things right, and he felt that she wanted to hear it; but she removed her hand and went back to the stove, seeming embarrassed by her display of concern.

"Finish your eggs, lad. You'll be late."

"Okay. Is the coffee ready?"

"There's no time."

"Half a cup?"

"You'll miss your bus, lad."

"I'll gulp it. Please, Mom, I need it. I'll get my bag and come back in for the coffee right away."

"All right! All right! Do what you like," his mother sighed, rattling a cup and saucer to show her irritated resignation. "Go in late, and maybe you'll be happy then. Maybe they'll fire you and bring you to your senses."

The mention of the word "fire" brought Ernie to his senses right then and there. He had never quite explained to his mother the precarious employment situation of a full-time substitute teacher. The thought of coming home someday soon—perhaps this afternoon—and trying to convince her that he really was a good teacher and teaching really was a good profession but there just wasn't any job for him at Glen Park High School any more suddenly loomed before him in its full horror. If that happened, he would have to leave for a while, and that would be the end of Europe, and Doris, and, in all likelihood, Ernie. Living at home wasn't much fun, but at least he could save a few dollars for an escape fund. It was a major worry, and as soon as he had undergone the Mikropoulous ordeal he was going to have to devote his energy to it on a full-time basis.

"I guess you're right about the coffee," Ernie said, rising hurriedly. "I'd better be running."

Start off each day with a song, he thought bitterly as he headed off to confront the world. Let's try "The Dead March" from *Saul.* Call it "Ernie's Theme."

The morning passed slowly and uneventfully, its only good feature the absence of any sign of Mikropoulous. When the fifth period arrived, with all the speed and none of the grandeur of a glacier, Ernie headed for the nasty little sty of a faculty room on the third floor. His stomach protested its betrayal with ominous subterranean rumbles, like a long-extinct volcano getting ready for a spectacular comeback, but Ernie remained adamant in his determination to spend his lunch period preparing for the observation. There would be time to eat afterward, during the seventh period.

But that would mean seeing Lynn, and she'd probably think he—no time for that now, he warned himself. Worry about it later. This period is reserved for worrying about the observation.

The observation . . .

Observations were horrible, hateful things, and Ernie knew from painful experience that Mikropoulous had a flair for making them more horrible and hateful than nature intended. There was a bad time ahead. It wasn't so much the idea of someone coming in to watch him work (He preferred any euphemism to the term "observation" with its connotation of trick mirrors, hidden tape recorders, and loaded questions; of complicated and painful analyses of his bodily fluids by bespectacled little men in white tunics who shook their heads sadly at their findings and mumbled unintelligible Latin polysyllables suggestive of advanced internal decay; of fat, jovial alienists conducting visitors to a massive door with a small peephole and saying "Here's an interesting one. Young fellow thinks he's Socrates. Keeps saying 'Is that not so?' and doesn't want to wear anything but a sheet' ") that bothered Ernie; it was the feeling he got whenever Mikropoulous came slithering through the back door of his room and started taking notes, the unnerving sensation that he had been suckered into a game in which everyone knew the rules except him, and he was the only one bound to follow them. The rules, as Ernie had deduced them, were twice as formalized and five times as absurd as a students' dueling code. Mikropoulous knew them by heart, believed in them with fervor, and applied them with rigid Old Testament justice.

It was a regular ritual. First of all, you had to write the next day's assignment on the blackboard, check attendance and readmittance slips, and collect homework—all this before you even started to think about the lesson for today. It was flatly impossible. Ernie managed to get all these things done—well, *most* of them—but never in an orderly fashion. He usually gave the next day's assignment when it occurred to him, most often right smack in the middle of something else ("This poem is an example of the Imagist school of poetry, which began—oh, yes, you'd better read these next six poems for tomorrow—which began in America early in—and write out the answers to the questions at the end of the poems, too—in the twentieth century. Everybody got that assignment?" This approach always caused confusion, shared equally by Ernie and the students. He told himself that it helped create a rapport), but he always managed to slip it in somewhere. He was pretty good about attendance, too, especially since that boy had turned up in Utah when Ernie had been happily and innocently marking him present for three weeks. Readmittance slips weren't really a problem. A student handed you a little card and you signed it and gave it back. If he forgot it, that was *his* problem, not the teacher's. Ernie was certain that the day was coming when some bright young assistant principal would figure out a way of *making* it the teacher's problem, so he enjoyed himself while he could. Homework he tried not to think about. He usually succeeded beyond his expectations.

So much for the preliminaries. Even if you managed to remember all of them and attend to them in the approved fashion, you weren't out of the woods. You had scarcely even reached the first tree, as a matter of fact, because now you had come to the point where you actually started to teach.

There were a number of ways to get into the business at hand, all of which were quite bad. Some of the books recommended opening things with a question, something on the order of "Well, Jimmy, what are we going to study today?" but Ernie could never convince himself that Jimmy wouldn't say "How the hell should I know?" or, even more likely, hurl his book to the floor and snarl his defiance. So that was out. Others prescribed a brisk statement of purpose, such as "Today we're going to learn about parliamentary procedure!" This was even worse; first of all, because it was a damned lie—no one was going to learn about *anything* if they could possibly help it, and the teacher knew it, and the students knew it, and they each knew that the other knew it—and second of all because it put the teacher in a vulnerable position. If a student ever raised a hand and asked "Why?" it would be the end of everything.

Ernie had adopted a kind of skulking method of approach which consisted in avoiding all visual contact with the class until it was too late for them to defend themselves. He would enter the class clutching a sheaf of mysterious papers, or he would immediately begin to rummage through a drawer, or write something confusing and incoherent on the blackboard, and while the class' attention was focused on the mystery he would mumble something like "Verbals today . . . parts of the verb . . . nouns and adjectives . . . not really so difficult . . . Exercise A. . . ." Then he would advance under cover of the confusion. This approach was particularly effective with his first two classes, whose intellectual resources were almost totally depleted by the task of finding their way to the classroom. They were easily duped, even by him.

Then there was the problem of motivation. For Ernie, it was more an insurmountable obstacle than a mere problem, but there was no avoiding it. On every one of the mimeographed English Department lesson plan forms that Glen Park High School thoughtfully furnished its teachers (then collected at intervals, on one day's notice—a practice introduced by Dr. Norman Shefin, the teachers' friend, and eagerly seconded by all department heads, who were exempt from the whole filthy business), there was a space headed "Motivation" which had to be filled in. There was no escape. In the other spaces, the ones headed "General Aim," "Specific Aim," "Pivotal Questions," "Medial Summary," "Terminal Summary," and so forth, you could say almost anything so long as it was cloaked in suitable pedagogical language ("Grammar," for example, became "Increased awareness of structural relationships"), but in the motivation space you had to say something clear enough for anyone, even Dr. Shefin, to grasp immediately. Even so, you had to be careful not to be truthful, or there would be trouble. Ernie, for instance, used intimidation ("This will be worth about thirty points on the final examination, so be sure . . ."), bribery ("If we can finish all of these questions in class, then we won't have to . . ."), and howling lies ("This book may seem dull to you at first, but once you start reading it carefully . . ."), but he knew perfectly well that he could not fill in the motivation space on his lesson plan with such terms as "intimidation, bribery, and howling lies." It simply would not do. Ernie's task was to compose a bit of touching fiction—a different one for each lesson—which left anyone who read it with the impression that this teacher was a sort of educational Pied Piper whose mere entrance into a classroom was sufficient to kindle a wild desire for knowledge on the part of some thirty-odd (*very* odd, in some cases) adolescents whose interests up to that moment had been restricted to stealing hubcaps, sniffing airplane glue, and standing zombie-like on street corners, with tiny radios embedded in their ears.

The whole business of motivation depressed Ernie as much as it pleased him, because it always aroused in him the feeling of the penniless waif standing outside the candy store with his nose pressed to the glass while he watched the rich kids inside squandering nickel after nickel with gay abandon. As far as he could remember, no one anywhere along the line from grammar school to graduate school had bothered to motivate *him*, and it just didn't seem fair, somehow. The sole motivating force behind his years of schooling had been fear, in one form or another. In grammar school, it had been mortal terror, aided and abetted by such old-school techniques as clouts alongside the head, Herculean punish lessons, vague threats of unspeakable horrors that awaited bad boys in some dusty attic room (He still wondered whether they really did have a spanking machine in his old grammar school), interminable hours sitting in a deserted classroom, motionless as death, while the happy voices of the playmates he would never see again drifted tauntingly through the windows, and worst of all, notes sent home to his father, which meant that he would have to go through the whole awful business again when he got home.

High school turned out to be an improvement over grammar school only in the sense of duration: four years of suffering were better than eight, any way you looked at it. Still, they didn't skimp on motivation. The clouts on the head were harder and more frequent, the vague threats were replaced by agonizing actualities, and the childish nonsense of staying after school was replaced by Saturday-morning "study groups" designed along the lines of a Gestapo interrogation. All in all, they had managed, thanks to careful planning, good organization, and brilliant utilization of the materials at hand, to make the four years of high school just as unpleasant as the eight years of grammar school. You really had to hand it to them, Ernie admitted grudgingly. No one had ever told him precisely *what* you had to hand to them, but he had a number of ideas on the subject, any one of which would have evened things up nicely if it could be arranged.

Then came college. Unfortunately for Ernie and most other men his age, along with college came the draft. This helped to make his college career about as carefree as an old-fashioned Russian sleigh ride, complete with wolves. Just as the Russians used to toss a baby or a grandmother (played by Madame Maria Ouspenskaya, of course) to the wolves at intervals, the dear old alma mater used to cast out a handful of unfortunates to the draft board twice each year; by the time Ernie was a senior, the pressure within the ivied halls was slightly higher than that at the deepest point of the Mariana Trench. After graduation, being drafted was almost a relief. Almost, but not quite. It turned out to be grammar school all over again. Ernie could still remember the sergeant who loomed huge and terrible—he was only 5′5″, but he managed to loom just the same—in the pre-dawn blackness of Fort Dix and growled, "Any of you clowns who don't shape up damn quick, you'll go see the man." No one ever told him who the man was, or what he did. No one had to. Ernie knew. The man had a gigantic khaki-colored spanking machine (or, as they would have put it in the Army, a machine, spanking, M-1). But the Army had the one saving grace that it included a free trip to Europe, something they hadn't thought of in grammar school. The accommodations left something to be desired, resembling, as they did, the lower decks of a seventeenth-century Portuguese slaver, but if you survived you were in Europe and it was worth all the Purgatory involved. Of course, if you got ptomaine poisoning on the second day of your big leave in Paris, it sort of took the edge off things; but that, Ernie told himself philosophically, was life. *His* life, anyway.

Even now, in graduate school, the same old motivation applied. To be sure, no one came around walloping the M.A. or Ph.D. candidates alongside the head if they didn't do their homework, and there were no letters sent home to Daddy (or the VA, in the case of veterans), but there was still that old demon fear working for them, more subtly this time but just as strong, and Ernie had yet to see a professor come bounding into a graduate classroom with a bag of tricks to make students clap their hands, and shriek, and beg to be taught.

Remembering all this, Ernie found it difficult to get very pious on the question of motivation. He tried to rationalize, telling himself that although nobody had ever motivated him, he still had managed to come pretty far, educationally speaking; but he was honest enough with himself to admit that even if someone could prove to him that positive non-violent motivation was absolutely indispensable to good teaching, he would still resent the whole business merely because it irked him to see other people being pampered and having it good when he had had it so very bad. He realized that this made him an old dog-in-the-manger, a mean, spiteful, petty-minded prig, and a general all-around bastard. But he didn't let it bother him. In this respect, at least, Ernie was a normal human being: fully aware of his faults, he cheerfully persisted in them because he *liked* them.

Probably the most annoying feature of the motivation convention from a practical point of view was its disruptive effect when introduced into one of Ernie's traditionally non-motivated classes. Being a new teacher, Ernie was not entrusted with one of Glen Park High School's star-studded honors classes. His typical class contained approximately thirty-five sleepy, surly, tenaciously unintellectual students who, over the months, had come to adopt an attitude of fatalistic resignation to the fact that for forty minutes a day, five days a week, they must subject themselves to boredom and occasional harassment at the hands of a deranged young man suffering from the delusion that the intricacy of English grammar and the glory of English literature are of some value, and, what is even more ludicrous, some interest to them. They have never accepted this insane premise, but for the sake of convenience they have assumed a virtue where they have it not. A wise philosopher once said that the first requirement of civilization is an ability to adapt to the absurd (If no wise philosopher has said it, it's about time one of them did), and these youths, wise beyond their years, have adapted.

With the passage of time, they have settled into an almost comfortable routine of ennui. At a given moment, the teacher enters in a flurry of disorganization, mumbles a few disjointed phrases, then proceeds to babble on about a host of trivialities that will forever remain a mystery to his listeners. An occasional question, now and then a restrained rustle of polite laughter at what the teacher, from his expression, appears to consider a witticism, and at last the merciful benediction of the bell, and another day's suffering has ended. Then, one day, into this idyllic scene, this tranquil oasis of Zen calm, comes the serpent of motivation.

The scene resembles the opening act of an Edwardian melodrama; it is apparent from the moment that the teacher enters the room that something is amiss. Today there is no covert shuffling of papers, no mumbled phrases tossed over the shoulder as he walks over to open and close the door, no curious non-objective scrawl hurriedly traced on the blackboard; instead, there is an orderly disposal of business, a fond avuncular smile reminiscent of a television pitchman, and more surprisingly, there is a coherent and obviously carefully prepared speech.

"We all think we know a lot about words, but it's good to stop and check up on ourselves every once in a while. Words are tricky, and if you're not careful they can fool you," the teacher begins.

A tense silence pervades the room. Nothing really bad has happened yet, but everyone can feel it coming.

"Let me show you what I mean," the teacher continues, turning and writing RUN in big, clear block letters on the blackboard.

Three of the more impulsive students twitch nervously in their seats, ready to take the word at face value and bolt from the classroom. But curiosity conquers impulse, and they decide to stay. They have never seen a man's mind disintegrate before their eyes, and the spectacle promises to be more diverting than the usual uneventful class period.

"Now, that's an easy enough word. We all use it a dozen times a day, I'm sure. But how much do we really know about it? For one thing, what part of speech is it?" The teacher looks about him, an expression of genuine concern and anxiety in the face of this deep mystery charging his features. Then, like a thunderbolt, he falls.

"Will you tell us what part of speech it is, Philip?"

Philip looks up like an animal at bay. Mixed feelings of shock, terror, anguish, and hostility pluck at his heart. For months he has looked upon his English class as a backwater of calm and restful obscurity, a sort of gentlemen's club provided by a gracious Board of Education, where he can unwind after the rigors of trigonometry and refresh his spirits preparatory to the challenge of Earth Science II, and now, in an instant, his illusion has been cruelly demolished. Not only does this sly, unscrupulous Judas in the front of the room know his name, he is asking him a direct question. The surge of violent passions precipitates a sudden seizure of aphasiac amnesia, and he gives vent to horrid choking grunts, meanwhile shaking his head spasmodically from side to side.

"Well, that's all right, Philip," the teacher says smoothly, unmoved by the appalling spectacle. "Can you tell us, Sharon?"

"It's a . . . it's a . . ." Sharon bawls, her voice rising with each word, "I don't know!"

"Well, Jimmy, you had your hand up," the teacher says, a slight tension noticeable in his voice. "Maybe you can tell us."

"Yeah, I know. It's a preposition."

"A preposition. How do you know it's a preposition, Jimmy?"

"'Cause it's little, and you told us all them little words are prepositions. And it's little, so it's got to be a preposition."

At this point it is obvious to even the least perceptive of men that the lesson is a shambles and is rapidly becoming something worse, perhaps even a full-scale debacle (*Debacle, Son of Shambles,* starring the former Mr. America and the entire population of Frascati, and badly dubbed). The teacher is on the road to disaster, and if he does not act quickly he will be there in a few minutes. He has already reached the outskirts.

There are several courses open to him. The simplest, most obvious, and certainly most appealing is to seize the bull by the horns and give the class the correct answer, but this is frowned upon by many educators as being a destructive influence upon the students' initiative. Ernie was forced to admit the soundness of their judgment; from observing the initiative displayed by his own pupils, he had come to the conclusion that student initiative was a delicate, fragile quality, and shattered easily, leaving sharp fragments. He treated it with the utmost caution, making no excessive demands on it. The method Ernie usually used in a situation such as this was a variation in which he did not actually *give* the class the answer, but suggested it pretty plainly, working along the same general lines one uses in playing peek-a-boo with an infant. The results, while not spectacular, were at least not disastrous. That was good enough for Ernie.

Motivation loomed as such a ghastly bête noire for Ernie that he often found himself in danger of forgetting the infinite number of other points covered by Mikropoulous during an observation.

The first time he was visited, he had put so much effort into a truly foolproof motivating gimmick that he had actually hit upon one. The class, inspired by the novelty of his approach, displayed unmistakable signs of life and the lesson went off smoothly—so smoothly, in fact, that they went through forty minutes' material in less than twenty-five, and Ernie was forced to resort to everything but juggling and bird imitations to fill up the remaining time. Shaken by this experience, he had drawn up a plan for his second observation containing enough material to last him for two normal weeks of teaching, only to find the class in a trance. That was even worse than the first time, but the end result of both fiascos (fiasci?) was the same. Ernie had attempted to create a diversion by outdoing himself in motivation and blinding Mikropoulous to the other faults in his technique, but the diversion failed to divert and Ernie went down in flames.

For one thing, there was the matter of voice. Ernie had never been aware of any glaring vocal flaws, and had, in fact, prided himself on having a reasonably pleasing voice. True, people did not come for miles merely to listen with closed eyes and rapt expressions as he recited the rules governing the comma, but neither did they clap their hands over their ears and make faces when he opened his mouth. He tried not to be smug about it, and seldom boasted, but he always cherished the secret belief that he could, with a minimum of effort, become a giant of the theater.

Mikropoulous fixed all that. In his report on the first observation, he remarked of Ernie's voice, "I found it difficult to hear you toward the end of the lesson. Your voice lost volume and your enunciation became less distinct," giving the impression that Ernie conducted a lesson by standing in the front of the room with a mouthful of mud, grunting softly to himself. Hurt and embittered, Ernie took special pains to speak in a fine, ringing voice all through his next observation, enunciating his words with the exaggerated care of Sheridan addressing Parliament. Mikropoulous helpfully informed him that his voice was too loud and he had a tendency to overcorrectness.

Gestures were treated in the same way; no matter what Ernie did, he was doing the wrong thing. If he stood sedately behind the desk, one hand resting lightly on the pages of the book while the other remained demurely behind him (A posture Ernie favored

—it reminded him of old Robert Donat movies), that was wrong. If, on the other hand, he moved about the room as he spoke, emphasizing the major points of the lesson with easy, natural gestures that would have been immediately intelligible to any normal child of five, that was wrong, too. Mikropoulous' report gave the impression that he had, in the first instance, been privileged to observe a curiously interesting specimen of the catatonic phase of dementia praecox, or, in the second instance, had been an onlooker to some outrageous scene precipitated by a half-crazed drunken Neapolitan street vendor. In either case, Ernie felt like a silly ass, or worse.

And Mikropoulous' talent for deflation did not stop there. He had an endless store of depreciating phrases to apply to a teacher's manner of dress, diction, and handwriting; initiative and classroom attitude; method of approaching, eliciting, asking, and answering questions; choice and employment of instructional material, including use or non-use of blackboard, over- or under-reliance on textbook, use of charts, filmstrips, or recordings, and even the teacher's choice of illustrative metaphors and anecdotes. Ernie knew he had them, because he had used every damned one of them in writing up his observation reports on Ernie. Being observed by Mikropoulous was, as far as Ernie was concerned, like playing Russian roulette with a fully loaded pistol.

Ernie managed to spend his entire free period brooding over these varied thoughts and all their known subdivisions, and when the bell rang to announce the end of the fifth period he reacted like a frightened spastic at the realization that his ordeal was three minutes away. He snatched at a cigarette, lit it, and began puffing away furiously as he rummaged through his bag with increasing panic, seeking his lesson plan. He could not find it. He was on the verge of believing that Mikropoulous, or one of his devoted followers (Members of a secret band of fanatics known as FINK—Federation of International Killers—distinguishable only by a tattoo inside the left earlobe, they were sworn to destroy all new English teachers, particularly males named Ernest), had slipped into the faculty room and rifled his papers while he was deep in thought, but then he noticed his lesson plan lying on the table, just where he had placed it at the beginning of the period. He peeled it off the sticky, coffee-smeared surface, started to stuff it into his bag, then, thinking better of it, decided to carry it to class by hand. The fresh air might do it good.

He started for the door, the dampened lesson plan curling carnivorously about his hand as he moved, helping to make life a little bit worse. As he reached the door, it opened and Aaron walked in, looking furtive.

"Who died?" Aaron asked cheerfully. "You look terrible."

"I'm going to be observed. Got to run."

"Mikropoulous?"

"Of course, Mikropoulous. I couldn't be lucky, and have someone like Hitler, or Attila the Hun. It has to be Mikropoulous. Look, the bell is going to ring in about two seconds, and I don't want to be—"

"Okay, okay. Want some advice?" Aaron said sweetly.

"Sure. What?"

"Zip up your fly."

Ernie dropped his bag and made a quick check, found everything in order, and looked up furiously at Aaron's kindly smile.

"You're a scream, Aaron. A real scream," he said venomously.

"Just building up your confidence. Good luck."

Ernie was framing a suitable reply, a philippic rich with scathing references to Aaron's family history, morals, physical appearance, intellect, and sense of humor, when the class bell intruded itself. With a weak, unconvincing "Go to hell," he flung out of the room. There was no longer time to fritter away on petty grievances. The crisis was here.

Mikropoulous—thank God for small favors—had not arrived early. There was one black mark, at least, that could not be scored against Ernie. He entered the room, ready to dodge a flying eraser, but apparently the students had seen him coming. They were all seated.

He became suspicious immediately. What were they up to? A whoopee cushion planted under Shelli, the fat girl? A stink bomb in his desk? A mangy dog concealed in the book locker? There must be something. What?

He walked to his desk, trying hard to look calm and confident, like the eager young executives-on-the-make who people underwear ads, but inwardly he was terrified that he would fall on his face, belch loudly, or lose his trousers before he got there.

He made it. Swallowing hard, he forced a cheerful smile as he arranged his papers. The lesson plan, still tacky, adhered to the desk like a decalcomania. There was something eerily symbolic about that, but he decided to brood about it later, during the seventh period. He was going to have a great deal to brood about during the seventh period today; one more item wouldn't make much difference.

"Well, good afternoon," he said cheerfully, fooling no one. "Today, you remember, we're going to look at a few of Shakespeare's sonnets. If you'll open your books to page—" The lesson plan was blurred in this spot. He should have known. "—to the right page, we'll get started in a moment. Would you mind checking the attendance, Sharon?"

"Okay," Sharon said listlessly. "You got the seating chart?"

"Oh, yes. Here it is," Ernie said, handing her a square of cardboard covered with confused scrawls and crossings-out. "While Sharon is checking the attendance, I'll put the assignment for tomorrow on the board," he announced to the rest of the class—who really didn't give a damn, and showed it.

He turned and began to write tomorrow's assignment in the corner of the blackboard. Halfway through it, he heard the back door open and close softly, and a large body settle into a seat. He stole a quick glance, just to see if his worst fears had been realized. They had. Enter Mikropoulous, dressed in a blue suit and a little brief authority. Ernie returned to the task at hand, concluding the message with what he considered a good, sound, teacherly admonition: "Answer all questions in complete, correct sentences." Maybe someone would, if he made a point of it.

He returned to his desk, picked up the seating chart where Sharon had abandoned it, and decided to let the matter of attendance drop. It was time to start motivating.

The motivational approach he had selected was sure to be a success in any high school classroom in America. It deserved to be, if only on the basis of the sheer physical suffering involved. In search of modern echoes of the Renaissance love lyric, Ernie had spent nearly an hour the previous evening listening to the unearthly hash of howls, whoops, shrieks, gurgles, and moans that comprised the lyrics of what one gibbering Fagin had labeled "The

Teen Top Ten." Such echoes as he sought were few and far between. Whatever the reason, a modern youth, at the age when Chatterton had whipped up his forgeries, Pope had written four books of an epic poem, and Romeo, after having cut quite a swath for himself among the Capulets, had done himself in, could express his tenderest emotions in no more imaginative words than "Yah! Yah! Yah! Yah! Yah! Yah! Baby!" What disturbed Ernie even more was the universal assumption that a young lady to whom such terms of endearment were addressed was expected to be pleased and flattered. If Romeo had gone into the Capulet garden with all that caterwauling and howling, he would have had a flowerpot flung at him from Juliet's balcony (Considering the fashion in sanitary facilities at the time, he could have counted himself lucky if nothing nastier than a flowerpot greeted him). But a young man of the present day, emitting these sounds while writhing and gesticulating in a most unseemly manner, was greeted with squeals of erotic delight by his fair listeners. Faced with things like this, Ernie despaired of ever really understanding what people meant when they spoke of "progress."

Out of his evening's torment, Ernie had managed to glean a few lines that would serve to support his approach. These included such touching expressions of passion as "Baby, Baby, I Love You Big, When I Think of You I Flip My Wig," "I Saw Them Holdin' Hands in the Assembly," and "Jeannie, Jeannie, Jeannie, Jeannie, Jeannie." At least they were in English. Sort of.

Thus armed, Ernie began.

"No one has come out and said it, but I'm sure a lot of you wonder why you're asked to read poems written by an English poet who died about three hundred and fifty years ago. Do you have any idea why?"

There was a sudden silence, then Arlene's hand shot up and a smug expression suffused her features. Ernie knew that he was going to get a nice, pat, shallow answer that she remembered from some other teacher in past years. Arlene had all the words, but she couldn't get the music. But even Arlene's bromides were better than silence.

"Yes, Arlene. Can you tell us why?"

"Because William Shakespeare is the giant of English letters. He was born in 1564 and he died in 1616."

"Well, that's certainly true, Arlene. But what do you think people mean by calling him a 'giant of English letters'?"

"Everything he wrote was great," Arlene said defensively.

"Let's see how the others feel," Ernie said, glancing about desperately. Harvey, a tall, serious boy who sat in the back of the room by himself and gave a false impression of knowing everything, seemed to have an idea. "Harvey, what do you think?"

"I think Shakespeare is great because he wrote about almost everything, and most of what he said is still true, even now. That's why everybody likes to quote from Shakespeare when they want to sound very profound, because people know *he's* smart, so if you know a lot about him then *you* must be smart, too."

"That's good, Harvey. Can you think of any one specific thing he said that's still true today?"

"Well, all that stuff about politics . . . I can't remember the exact . . ."

"I think Jack can help you out," Ernie said pleasantly, glad to get Harvey off the hook. "How about it, Jack?"

"When they got Brutus to be a front man for them. All those guys who wanted to get Caesar, you know? They figured everybody knew Brutus was honest, so if they could get him on their side everybody would say they must be right because Brutus wouldn't do anything dishonest, so they'd get away with it."

Jack's statement left something to be desired in the way of grace and lucidity, but his idea seemed reasonably clear to the class. Flushed with triumph, he continued.

"They still do that today, so it proves Shakespeare was right. As a matter of fact, my father said that's why this guy Levine was nominated for mayor last fall. He's honest, but all the men behind him are a bunch of Reds and grafters. My father—"

"That's fine, Jack. I don't think we want to be quite that specific," Ernie broke in, snatching away Jack's soapbox before he could get into full swing on the seamy side of local politics. He looked around around the room fast, and did a badly concealed double-take when he saw Arnold's hand waving vigorously. Ernie had long ago categorized Arnold as a functional mute and given up his case as hopeless. Now—unless he merely wanted to leave the room—Arnold actually wanted to contribute something. "Yes . . . Arnold?" Ernie said gently, not wanting to frighten him.

"That speech Mark Antony made. Right after they killed Caesar," Arnold began warily.

"Yes, I'm sure we all remember that speech. Go on, Arnold."

"It was great!" Arnold blurted.

A brief pause.

"It certainly was," Ernie agreed, blessing Arnold with a smile. Somewhere, the shades of Demosthenes, Cicero, Patrick Henry, and Edmund Burke heaved a sigh of relief and settled back into repose. Arnold was not yet ready to arouse the masses, but at least he had broken his silence. Ernie was so pleased that he momentarily forgot himself. Seeing Judy's hand go up, he called on her.

Calling on Judy was always dangerous and with Mikropoulous in the room it could spell disaster (that's d-i-s-a-s-t-e-r). Judy, Ernie had learned, was dating a college sophomore. Their dates must have been the model of decorum, because judging from her classroom performance, Judy employed them in picking her suitor's brains for outrageous and impossible questions to fire at her teachers. She always prefaced these questions with a curious glance around the room, a slow half smile of amused tolerance at the quaint antics of the backward children among whom she had been marooned, and a steady, stiff-armed wave of the hand which was at once languid and imperious. Her general attitude was one that Ernie found annoying—doubly annoying because she was one of the top students in the class. It reminded him of the intolerably smug girls in the television commercials, the ones who always use the right deodorant. Their poor benighted friends go about surrounded by a miasma suggestive of the Chicago stockyards, repelling males three miles away, while these fragrant snips trail crowds of hypnotized, sniffing, admirers. It bothered him. Judy's question, on this particular occasion, bothered him even more.

"Mr. Quinn," she said sweetly, "isn't it true that Shakespeare was a homosexual?"

"Ah . . . well, there *are* one or two critics who think so, but actually . . . I don't know, I really don't think it's that important to an understanding of—"

"Oh, but it *is!*" Judy burst in. "I mean, if a man is writing erotic poetry, and it can be shown that he's writing from the viewpoint of a sexual deviate, that changes the whole thing!"

She was probably the only kid in the class who knew the meanings of "erotic" and "deviate" and could use them both in a single sentence. And she had to do it today, of all days. Ernie looked back at Mikropoulous to see what effect all this was having on him. What he saw was not reassuring: Mikropoulous was writing away at top speed, and Ernie got the impression that he was having the time of his life. He returned quickly to Judy.

"You may have a point, Judy, but as far as the case of Shakespeare goes, this is all conjectural. Besides, it's a problem for the biographers, not for us. Our job is to get to know the poems."

"But that's exactly what I'm trying to say, Mr. Quinn," Judy persisted. "How can you know the poem if you don't know all about the author? That seems obvious."

Ernie felt a wild urge to grab her by her long, ugly, ponytail and fling her out of the window; or, better still, fling her at Mikropoulous and get rid of two birds with one stone.

"Well, it may seem obvious, but it's really not a part of our study. I'd like to get back to something Harvey suggested, if no one has anything else to add." He paused about three-tenths of a second for a reply, then went on, "Harvey mentioned that most of what Shakespeare said three hundred and fifty years ago seems to be valid today, and I was wondering if you found that to be true for the sonnets you read last night. I was thinking particularly of the one that begins 'When in disgrace with fortune and men's eyes . . .' Would one of you young men care to read it aloud for us?"

Absolute silence.

Then, out of a clear sky, came divine inspiration. Not divine, actually; more a compound of hypocrisy with repulsively base fawning, and not out of a clear sky, either; it came from something Fred Millard had said at lunch the day before. But in it, Ernie saw a way of snatching survival, if not actual triumph, from the jaws of defeat. Trying to conceal the glee in his voice, he said silkily, "You know, I just realized something."

The class was glad to hear it. Whatever it might be, it gave them a momentary reprieve.

"There's someone with us who can read Shakespeare the way he deserves to be read," Ernie went on, already feeling a slight twinge of disgust with himself, but doing his best to let his practicality override his self-respect. "Mr. Mikropoulous, would you be willing to read that sonnet to us?"

Mikropoulous looked up, and for a moment Ernie had doubts about his cleverness, but then the chairman's carefully barbered jowls broke into a quiet smile of complacent smugness and Mikropoulous rose grandly. Ernie would not have been surprised if he had ordered everyone to kneel and begun to intone a blessing in Latin, but nothing quite so dramatic was forthcoming.

"I'm flattered . . . Mr. Quinn," Mikropoulous said in a soft, unctuous voice, "and what's more, I'm going to . . . accept . . . your offer." He looked about, and it was clear from his "Oh, you lucky boys and girls!" expression that he would not have thought a tumultuous ovation out of order; not getting one, he continued. "Mr. Quinn knows how much I . . . value the spoken word. I'm going to ask you to . . . close your books while I . . . recite this poem. And I'm going to ask you to . . . try to . . . listen . . . in a very . . . special way. Imagine . . . that these words are being spoken to you . . . today . . . for the very first time. They've never . . . appeared in print, and they've never been . . . spoken before. Will you do that?" There were a few nods. "Very well. Close your books."

And Mikropoulous began. Ernie had to give the man his due. As a human being, Mikropoulous was one of the few truly colossal bastards Ernie had ever encountered, but as an interpreter of poetry he was a spellbinder. He was a pro, and he could carry off something like this with a flair and a polish Ernie had seldom encountered. Every touch was perfect, right down to the business of having the kids close their books. It served the sound, solid educational purpose of focusing their entire attention on the reader; it also—and Mikropoulous knew it—made it difficult for them to check up on him if he missed a word here and there. A real pro.

He closed the book gently after the first two lines, and held it cradled before him as he continued, looking from face to face, then toward the end, gazing off into the distance, rapt. The man could get more out of fourteen lines than Ernie had seen some people get out of a five act play. By the time he was scorning to change his state with kings, the class—Ernie included—was hypnotized. Mikropoulous ended the sonnet, paused dramatically for just the right amount of time, then gave a slight, gracious nod and whispered, "Thank you." It was a magnificent performance.

Mikropoulous resumed his seat in the rear of the room, and

Ernie took command once more. He felt like a personified anticlimax, but there wasn't much he could do about it. So it's chin up, lad, and let's get to it, he told himself.

"It's we who should thank you, Mr. Mikropoulous," he said, then turned his attention to the class. "Now that you've heard the sonnet, would you care to try putting it in your own words? Miriam?"

If anyone could do it, it was Miriam. She was one of the few students Ernie could rely on in cases like this. He saved her up carefully, like D'Artagnan's wound-salve, for use only in emergencies.

"Well, first Shakespeare says that sometimes he gets very disillusioned, and he feels as though he's in disgrace with everybody."

"Fine, so far, Miriam. By the way, if you want to look at the poem, you may. You don't have to keep your books closed any longer. Yes, Harvey?"

"It's okay, Mr. Quinn. That's what I was going to ask."

"All right. Are you ready to go ahead, Miriam?"

"Yes. When he feels like this, Shakespeare says, he envies everybody and wishes he could be like them. But then he thinks about this girl—"

Judy's hand went up like a railroad semaphore.

"—and just thinking about her and how she loves him makes him feel wonderful, and then he wouldn't change places with *any*body, not even a king!" Miriam concluded triumphantly.

"That's very good, Miriam. Judy?"

"But Mr. Quinn, we don't know he's talking about a *girl*. I mean, if he was *really* a homosexual—"

"You've got a point there, Judy, but let's just assume that he's talking about a girl, all right?"

Judy withdrew into a sullen silence. Ernie sensed that it was a tactical withdrawal. Once she had taken care of the wounded, she was going to regroup her forces for a slashing counterattack at his weakest point. His defense was brilliant in its simplicity: don't call on Judy again, no matter what. If she raises her hand because she's dying to leave the room, she'll just have to die. We can't please everybody.

"Getting back to this sonnet, is there anything that anyone would care to add to Miriam's interpretation?"

There wasn't.

"All right, now, let me ask you this: Is this poem still true today? What do you think, Harvey?"

"Yeah, I think so."

"All right, then, can you give me an example? Can you think of anyplace where you might read or hear something like this today?"

The bait was offered. It hung suspended, waiting for the strike. Harvey eyed it warily, circled, hung back—then snatched at it.

"In songs. You hear a lot of songs about how a guy feels low and then he thinks about his girl friend and then he thinks everything is really okay."

"Something like 'Baby, Baby, I Love You Big'?"

"Yeah, that's right, Mr. Quinn! That's a good example," Harvey said, sounding happily surprised.

Ernie noticed expressions of mild interest, curiosity, shock, and amazement dawning on the hitherto passive faces of his students at the idea that a teacher knew anything at all about their world. Apparently they thought that no teacher ever listened to a radio; if one ever did, it was to an obscure FM station at midnight in a darkened room, where he sat, a pale hand clasped to his forehead, listening to Albert Schweitzer play Bach. He decided to give them another jolt.

"There's also 'I Want to Be Your Eternal Teenage Love'," he suggested. "Can you think of any more?"

They could, and they did. Hands began going up all around the room (not Judy's, though—mercifully, she was still pouting), and as Ernie called on them, he found himself growing more confident about the progress of the lesson. So far, things were going well. Not perfectly, to be sure, but better than he had expected. He tempered his feelings somewhat by reminding himself that half the period was left; more than enough time for someone to shout an obscenity, punch Mikropoulous, or throw a fit. That made him feel a lot better.

"It seems to me that most of you would agree that Shakespeare isn't quite the square some students think he is. In this sonnet, at least, he seems to be pretty up-to-date," Ernie said, after the students had unburdened themselves. "Let's try another sonnet. Look at the one that begins, 'Let me not, to the marriage of true minds . . .'"

They began looking it over, Ernie meanwhile looking *them*

over for a suitable victim. It would have been fun to ask Mikropoulous to read again—and it probably wouldn't have taken much coaxing—but Ernie didn't see any sense in crowding his luck (and thank you, Lord Chesterfield, wherever you are). So far, it was moving along nicely; one push and it might tip over.

"Will anyone volunteer to read the sonnet to us?" he asked hopefully.

Once again, silence. Ernie was ready to call on a boy when he noticed a hand making a hesitant trembling movement almost under his nose. He glanced down and met Martin's pleading eyes.

"I'll do it, Mr. Quinn," Martin said. His tone, expression, and general attitude conveyed the impression that he was volunteering to hurl himself into a volcano to save his people from the wrath of the angry fire god. Martin was a shy boy; at least, he had always seemed shy to Ernie; but one never knew. It was, after all, still spring. Martin might be pledging for one of the fraternities that defiled Glen Park High School, or perhaps trying to impress a girl.

"Good, Martin. Go right ahead."

Martin went ahead, doing his best to sound as though he meant every word. He still had the jarring habit, common to every student, of stopping dead at the end of each line, regardless of sense or punctuation, and accenting the unnecessary pause by a fall in his voice; but he was not outrageously bad. Not in Mikropoulous' league when it came to reading poetry, perhaps, but not all that bad. Ernie had long ago come to the conclusion that trying to get good poetic interpretation from a student was like trying to play Chopin's "Fantasie Impromptu" on a hollow log. Martin offered a ray of hope.

"That's good, Martin. Thank you. Now let's try to do the same—yes, Shelli?"

"He says 'writ'!" Shelli cried, shocked.

"He does?" Ernie mumbled, taken aback by Shelli's dazzling talent for the *non sequitur*. "Oh, you mean in the last line . . . yes, he does. You're right, Shelli," he went on, recovering slightly but still wondering what he was expected to do about it. He decided to try an old diversion, and posed a general question.

"In the last line of this sonnet—as Shelli has pointed out—Shakespeare says, 'I never writ, nor no man ever lov'd.' Does anyone know why he says this, instead of 'I never wrote'?"

Harvey's hand went up, tentatively, as if he had tested the upper atmosphere and found it too hot for a prolonged stay. It did not look as though the hand was going to remain up very long, so Ernie acted fast.

"Yes, Harvey?" he said quickly.

"Maybe he didn't know any better. I guess he was smart and all, but maybe he just made a mistake in grammar and nobody ever changed it."

"That's an interesting suggestion, and I think you'll find a lot of people willing to go along with you on the idea that Shakespeare's formal education was small. It's one of the basic arguments of the people who say Shakespeare didn't really write the plays. But in this case, there's another—yes, Miriam?"

"Wasn't it all right to say 'writ' in Shakespeare's time, Mr. Quinn?" Miriam asked rhetorically. She knew perfectly well that it was, but she preferred not to rub it in.

"Yes, it was, Miriam. Shakespeare didn't really make a mistake, it's just that the rules of English grammar were a lot looser in his day. Do you remember the famous example from *Julius Caesar*, Miriam?"

"Oh, yes, where he says 'the most unkindest cut of all.' Today, that would be incorrect because it's a double comparative, but it was correct for Shakespeare."

It was a double superlative, but since no one objected, Ernie kept his peace. He would have felt like a swine if he corrected Miriam. He owed her too much. Of course, he was being chivalrous at his own expense, and he knew it. Mikropoulous could be depended upon in his writeup of the observation to make a great thing out of an uncorrected grammatical error, an imprecise definition, or any other such oversight on Ernie's part. It would be done in his famous "You were great, but—" style, in which the first paragraph recorded Mikropoulous' awe, reverence, and gratitude at having been privileged to view a reincarnation of Socrates, then each succeeding paragraph (except the last) proceeded to introduce, with preliminary apologies, remarks on a series of shortcomings, blunders, and outrages, while the last paragraph suggested that perhaps after years of study, prayer, fasting, and self-denial, all under the guiding hand of a benevolent chairman, there might be some chance of the observee's becoming an adequate teacher. Ernie felt certain that Mikropoulous' report would read something like this anyway, and now, at least, he had an idea of just what shortcomings Mikropoulous was going to pounce upon. It did not make him any happier, but it provided a certain sense of security.

With Shakespeare's grammatical difficulties disposed of, Ernie returned his attention to the sonnet, aware that Shelli's interruption was going to have a disruptive effect on his progress. The attention span of some of his students was only a notch above that of a three-month-old kitten's, and Ernie knew that at this moment, if they were thinking about Shakespeare at all—and that was a risky assumption to make—they were feeling a slight peevishness at his ability to get away with sloppy grammar, and not any concern about his intentions in the sonnet Martin had read. Some of them, in fact, had probably forgotten that Martin ever read it to them.

"Well, now that we're clear on that problem of Shakespeare's grammar, let's see what he was saying in the sonnet Martin read," Ernie said relentlessly. He could see the unspoken question, "What sonnet?" flicker across the lips of some of his scholars, but he refused to be put off. It took a bit of coaxing, but he finally got Linda Sue, Marvin, and Matty to piece together a reasonable answer between them. Their classmates watched, relieved.

Ernie made a quick time-check: about twelve minutes to go; enough time for another poem, and then maybe a general summary, if he needed to fill up a few minutes at the end. Not bad, he thought, not bad at all. All may be well.

"They're really not so bad or difficult after all, are they?" Ernie asked the class, smiling wisely and a bit condescendingly. "Let's try another one. Number forty this time, 'Not marble, not the gilded monuments . . .' Anyone?"

Again, the class exercised Spartan self-restraint. As Ernie's eyes swept over the group he saw one student after another with eyes fixed on the page before him, intent on Shakespeare's lines and grimly determined not to look up until a victim had been named. Then he looked full into a pair of soft, wide, soulful brown eyes that held mingled hope and timidity, like a cocker spaniel's at feeding time. They belonged to Patty, a small, sweet-looking girl who reminded Ernie of Little Annie Rooney in the comic strip. Patty looked like the sort of person who would read inspirational verse and actually feel inspired.

"Patty, would you read this for us?" Ernie asked gently, afraid she might burst into tears at any but the kindest of tones.

"I'll try, Mr. Quinn," she said aspiringly.

She began to read, and she was doing well. Halfway through her recitation, Ernie noticed a bit of agitation and quivering in the back row, on the far side of Mikropoulous. Roy and Robert, two big, happy-go-lucky congenital grinners, were exchanging leers. He looked around the room quickly and noticed two or three other faces fixed in furtive, dirty grins.

Ernie was puzzled for a moment, not by the phenomenon but by its cause. He was aware of the ability of most adolescents to inject an obscene significance into anything they heard or read, and merely wondered what had triggered the reaction. He realized almost immediately that it had been the phrase "sluttish time" in line four. He could picture the ideas scampering around in their nasty little minds like rats in tenement cellars, and decided to exterminate them posthaste.

"'. . . and dwell in lovers' eyes'," Patty concluded.

"Very well done, Patty. Thank you."

Patty lowered her eyes and smiled demurely. She glanced at Martin, and when their eyes met Martin turned a deep red and began to fuss with his book. Aha! Ernie thought. But there was work to do; no time to muse on the tender beauties of awakening love.

"Will someone try to put this sonnet into his own words? Roy, how about trying it?"

Roy looked up in sudden panic, his eyes wide and a "Who, me?" expression on his round face.

"I can't. I don't understand it," he said, shaking his head.

"That's odd. It looked to me as though you were enjoying it immensely."

Robert, sensing Ernie's next move, was trying to make himself invisible. He was resting his forehead on his hand, shading his eyes, while he buried his nose in the book. It was a good try, but fruitless.

"Robert, can you help Roy out?"

"I didn't do nothing, Mr. Quinn!" Robert said, wounded.

"No one says you did, Robert. I'm just asking you to put the poem in your own words."

"I didn't understand it," Robert sulked.

"I thought you did. You looked so enthusiastic while the poem was being read."

"I was thinking about something else. I wasn't laughing at the poem."

"Oh. My mistake," Ernie said innocently. "As long as you were thinking about something else, it wasn't really rude and inconsiderate, was it?"

Robert shrank into his seat.

"Well," Ernie asked, "can anyone paraphrase the sonnet?"

Harvey came to the rescue. He stated, a bit too succinctly, that a good poem will last longer than a statue. Miriam took over from there, expanding, explaining, specifying, until even Mikropoulous was satisfied, judging from his expression.

With about two minutes left, Ernie began a final summary. He watched Mikropoulous rise, ease his way to the door, and slip out silently. As the door clicked shut, Ernie paused in mid-sentence and gave a great deep sigh of relief. Most of the class were too absorbed in the prospect of their approaching freedom to notice it, but he caught a comradely grin on the faces of Miriam and Harvey. Judy, he noticed, was still sulking. Good.

And then the bell rang and it was over.

On his way to the faculty lunchroom—the orthodox route this time, since there was no seventh-period lunch for students—Ernie busied himself with a post-mortem on the observation. He had taken a little too much time building up his motivation; Mikropoulous would catch that. But the idea of having Mikropoulous read a sonnet to the class was a stroke of genius; and the way he brought it off, making it sound as though Mikropoulous had come in at Ernie's own request, not to observe but to be put to use, was delectable. Aaron would love it. He should have made more of Shelli's question about "writ," maybe worked it into the homework assignment or made up a project around it; but at least he hadn't passed over it. She raised a question and she got an answer. That ought to satisfy anyone. He had an uneasy feeling that it wouldn't satisfy Mikropoulous, but then, nothing did. He decided not to think over Mikropoulous' probable reaction to Judy's question. What's done is done, he told himself; don't think about it.

Ernie had not been in the faculty lunchroom during the seventh period before. Upon entering, he experienced the strange, paramnesiac sensation one gets from seeing a new place and finding it somehow familiar. The room itself *was* familiar. That was not what struck him. It seemed to him that he was reliving his daily fifth-period lunch. At the old-timers' table was a group of veterans, similar in appearance to the group he saw every day some two hours earlier. Their gestures were the same as those of their fifth-period counterparts, their voices had the same familiar keening quality, and the indistinct snatches of their conversation that came to him sounded like a subtly modified version of the hagiology recited each day by his fellow diners. When they fell silent, he half suspected that they were meditating piously on the golden days of Harry Podnak and the iron discipline at Thomas A. Edison Vocational High School during the Mulvehill regime. At a farther table, as if to reinforce the illusion, fate had seated two faded blossoms from the Social Studies Department who were chatting wistfully about the sweet children of the past. They could have been stand-ins for the Misses Rose and Payseley.

But the resemblance broke down when he checked the other tables. Next to the Old Soldiers' Home were seated two of the younger teachers, Mr. Di Maestro and Miss Gern, and they were, as always, looking intense and concerned. Ernie nodded and kept moving. He didn't particularly like them. They were always worrying, noisily, about the myriad forms that bloomed in their letter boxes, whining, complaining, and denouncing; but they always filled them out correctly and handed them in early. They reminded Ernie of those phonies at college who used to come in to the final examinations in a simulated frenzy of desperation, and then wound up getting the highest mark on the test. You may not be able to change them, Ernie thought, but there's no need to associate with them. It just encourages them. Phonies are phonies.

At the table where he usually lunched with Aaron and Fred, Ernie saw Lynn reading a book and drinking a cup of coffee. She looked up and smiled a greeting.

"Hi!" she said cheerfully.

"Hi," Ernie said, walking over.

"Was today the big day?"

"The big, bad day," Ernie said. "Mind if I join you?"

"Sit right down," Lynn said, shutting the book and pushing it aside.

"I'm going to get some lunch. Would you like another coffee?"

"All right, thanks. I hope you're not too hungry, Ernie. The kitchen's closed after the sixth period. All you can get is pie."

It figured. Life was going on as usual.

"That'll do. Mikropoulous did something to my appetite, anyway."

Ernie trudged off, ordered two cups of coffee, and looked over the offerings. He finally selected a small, dismal wedge of something that might once have been apple pie but now resembled a smear of yellowed library paste between two soiled blotters. He paid, grudgingly, and returned to Lynn's table.

"Here, Ernie," Lynn said, digging into an enormous shoulder bag, "let me pay you for the coffee."

"Oh, come on, Lynn."

"No, I insist. It's not as if we were on a date. On a date it's different," she said, smiling.

Oh, oh, he thought. She's getting pushy.

"Please, Lynn," he insisted. "I never take money from women. It makes me feel as if I should be dancing tangos with widows at a seaside resort."

She laughed. "All right. I don't want to make you feel bad. And I can't tango, anyway."

Ernie steeled himself and went to work on the pie. It was pretty bad; like eating a piece of wet newspaper. He hoped he would have a chance to use that.

"How was it?" Lynn asked when he had finished.

"Awful. Like eating a piece of wet newspaper."

"Not the pie," she said, "the observation."

"Oh, that. Well, that was like eating a piece of wet newspaper, too." He paused thoughtfully. "No, I'm exaggerating. Actually, it came off pretty smoothly."

"Good. And how did you make out with Miss Grimm yesterday?"

Somehow, the phrase "make out" didn't seem to apply to Ernie's dealings with Miss Grimm. But he let it pass.

"Stalemate. She couldn't get me for missing the faculty meeting, but I think I'm on her list now. Something she said got me angry. I tried to be cool, but I think she noticed."

"What did she say to get you angry?"

"Well, it was really what she implied: that I'm a lazy bum who'll never come up to her exalted standards, and I'm lucky she tolerates me in her school. You know."

"She doesn't really mean that, Ernie," Lynn said, as if she were talking to a peevish child.

"I don't care whether she means it or not," Ernie said, taking his cue from Lynn and adopting the tones of a peevish child, "she has no right to say it or even to suggest it. This isn't *her* school. I don't work for *her*. She's just another employee, Lynn. Who the hell is she to sit in judgment on me or anyone?"

"She *is* the assistant principal, Ernie. She has to keep things running smoothly."

"By making the teachers feel as though they're in a penal colony? That's nonsense."

"You have to understand her problems."

"No, I don't," Ernie said, shaking his head emphatically. "I'm fed up to the teeth with understanding people's problems. I have to understand the kids, the parents, Miss Grimm. . . . Maybe I ought to try to understand Mikropoulous, too."

"You're in a great mood, Ernie."

Ernie made a wry face and nodded slowly.

"The observation must have been pretty bad," Lynn said. "Come on, tell me about it."

"It wasn't so bad, honest. That's not what's bothering me. I'm just getting fed up."

"With what?"

"Everything. I'm sick of having to make excuses for not doing things I know are stupid, and having to worry about whether or not people approve of the way I teach. This isn't the way it should be."

"How should it be, then?"

"Hell, I don't know. Different. Better." He jiggled his coffee cup around and dug a cigarette out of his crumpled pack, then looked at Lynn and grinned sheepishly. "I'm great company, right? You're trying to be sociable, and I'm snapping at you and complaining away a mile a minute. I'm sorry, Lynn."

"That's all right, Ernie. I understand. You've been under pressure. It's natural."

So Lynn was an understander. Ernie would have accepted a

sarcastic remark, a stinging rebuke, even a ringing denunciation, but right now he didn't want to be understood—not by Lynn, anyway—and he was disappointed with Lynn, who had impressed him, at first, as a co-conspirator. She wasn't like Doris. He knew, right then and there, that there was no one like Doris, and he would be a fool to keep trying to avoid accepting this wonderful fact any longer. And realizing this, he began immediately to wonder how Doris really felt about him. Oh sure, she *liked* him, but did she really . . . ? He didn't want to talk to Lynn any more; he wanted to talk to Doris, or at least think about her—those damned final exams of hers, he thought, in wild frustration. I won't see her until Thursday night! What if she thinks things over and decides . . . no, stop it! he demanded.

"I'd better be going, Lynn. I have to work out something for the eighth period," he said, rising.

"You're conscientious. Do you spend all your time preparing lessons?"

"Most of it. It seems that way, anyhow."

"You ought to relax."

Pushy, he thought. Much too pushy.

"I guess I should. Well, it's not for much longer. Summer's almost here."

"What are you going to do this summer, Ernie?"

"I really don't know. Look for a job, maybe."

"Don't get so discouraged," she said. "The last few weeks are the hardest."

"Yes."

There was an awkward silence.

"Well, I don't want to keep you from anything important, Ernie. Come down tomorrow, if you can spare the time," Lynn said, a trace of petulance in her voice.

"Yes, I will. So long, Lynn."

"So long, Ernie," she said, reaching for her book.

Bitchy, he thought, as he left Lynn at the table. Awfully pretty girl, but pushy and bitchy. Not like Doris.

Ernie arrived home on Tuesday afternoon seething with pious resolutions. He would mark the compositions from yesterday. He would begin working out some of his final class grades. He would read a hundred pages of the new Golding novel. He would trim his fingernails. And he would go to bed by ten, not a minute later.

He announced his good intentions to his mother and his grandfather, who were unimpressed. After a snack of pie and coffee, Ernie changed to a pair of chinos and went to his room to immerse himself in his labors.

As he finished deciphering the second composition, he realized that his eyes were a bit heavy and his attention was wandering.

He put down his red pencil and leaned back thoughtfully, to appraise the situation. It was not quite four o'clock. Surely there was time for a nice refreshing nap. Just a half-hour or so, no more. It would make a new man of him. He would breeze through his work with time to spare. It was the only sensible thing to do, really. Just a half-hour; and not even a nap, not actual sleep, just a restful shutting of the eyes, a gathering of thoughts, a retreat from the confused alarms and sudden flights of the day.

The next thing Ernie knew, he was imprisoned in a burning wagon, rumbling clumsily over a bumpy road at top speed while a hostile crowd of onlookers shouted jeers and threats. He sat up, making awful surprised grunts, and saw his mother violently shaking the foot of his bed.

". . . good-for-nothing loafer! Supper's been ready for fifteen minutes and your poor father's just in the door after a day's work and you're sound asleep like a millionaire without a care in the world! We won't have that kind of thing in this house, it's not right, a healthy young lad sleeping away his days like an invalid!"

"I'm awake. I'm really awake," Ernie mumbled.

"Get up and go in to supper! Oh, you ought to be ashamed to face your father, Ernie Quinn."

"Well, you *told* me I ought to take better care of myself," Ernie said plaintively. "That's all I was doing."

"I didn't mean for you to sleep away the afternoon like a dirty bum, and you know I didn't. How do you think your father feels, him coming home all worn out and hungry for a hot meal, the poor man, and his lazy lump of a son asleep in his bed when everybody else is working?"

Ernie couldn't think of a very good answer, and he knew that even if he came up with something Oscar Wilde would have envied, it wouldn't make an impression. He arose and went in to dinner. He was received into the bosom of his family with a warm and touching display of hostility.

"Look at him! Look at the sleepin' beauty!" Grandfather gummed jubilantly. "Ah, he's no Quinn, not that one. The Quinns never slept their days away like a lot of English dukes."

"When did *you* get up?" Ernie asked him sweetly.

"Listen to the disrespect!" Grandfather howled with all the righteous indignation of one who had bounced up at the crack of noon. "Listen to the way your son talks to his own grandfather!"

"None of that, now, lad!" Ernie's mother snapped, and his father glowered his support. "Your grandfather's worked hard all his life, so he tells us," Mrs. Quinn went on, "and he has a right to lie around in his bed until the afternoon, and it's not for us to call him a lazy good-for-nothing if he does."

Grandfather frowned, uncertain as to the implications of this speech; but the arrival of the food ended his interest in rhetoric. The meal passed without further incident, and Ernie made a discreet tactical withdrawal after dessert.

He managed to finish marking his compositions that night, and even figured out final class marks for half his first-period class. But there was no time for Golding or fingernails. Even so, he was not in bed until twelve-thirty. Thus passed Tuesday.

Wednesday was a day spent on pins and needles. Ernie checked his letter box in the morning, but there was no note from Mikropoulous to arrange a conference on the observation. He checked before lunch, and again when he was leaving, but there was still no word. This gave rise to a number of deep thoughts, very few of them reassuring:

1. There was not going to be any conference at all. Mikropoulous was just going to dump Ernie unceremoniously, perhaps without a word. On the last day of school he would shake Ernie's hand and say "Good luck in your new job, Quinn," and walk away.

But that was impossible.

2. All right, then, there *was* going to be a conference, and it was going to be a horror. Mikropoulous was holding it off in order to give himself time to go over the lesson with a fine-toothed comb

and find inconsistencies, errors, and absurdities unheard of for generations. He was going to flatten Ernie with a barrage of petty criticisms, pounding away until Ernie himself, collapsing in tears, offered his resignation and his apologies.

That was a distinct possibility.

3. Or, there was going to be a conference, and it was going to be a quickie, one of Mikropoulous' three-minute specials, and Ernie would emerge from it knowing no more than when he had entered. That way, Mikropoulous didn't really commit himself to anything.

That was an even more distinct possibility.

4. Or, Mikropoulous had been assassinated, or eloped with Miss Payseley, or been cut down in a running gun battle with the FBI, or sought political asylum in Turkey, or been kidnaped by disgruntled seniors, or run away and joined the circus, or fallen on his head and been stricken with amnesia.

These were pretty remote possibilities.

5. Or, Mikropoulous had something up his sleeve, and was working out a plan that would catch Ernie by surprise.

That, or something very close to it, was highly probable.

These speculations kept Ernie occupied on his homeward ride, and supplied enough motivating fear to enable him to make up the final class marks for three whole classes. Then, after a brief suppertime skirmish with his grandfather and a hurried but highly emotional telephone conversation with Doris, he was off to his room, where he actually read an entire issue of *Saturday Review* without interruption, and dipped into *Time*. For a few hours, Mikropoulous and the network of unpleasant associations surrounding him were almost forgotten, as Ernie brushed up on the nastiness running rampant in the world outside Glen Park High School. Thus passed Wednesday.

Ernie arrived at school Thursday morning in an unusually cheerful mood. Tonight he would see Doris; his mother had had no extraordinary grievances to present at breakfast; life seemed to be worth living, if you were careful about it. Then he checked his letter box and felt the first qualms of the day. There was a note from Mikropoulous fixing the seventh period today for the post-observation conference.

That would be scanned, and Ernie spent the better part of the day scanning it from every possible angle.

The two previous conferences had been held after school, and had lasted about an hour each. A seventh-period conference could only last thirty-five or forty minutes, and would probably be even shorter than that. Ernie couldn't decide whether that was good or bad. He was positive that this last observation had been the best of the three; maybe Mikropoulous, like most critics, was at his best when dealing with someone else's worst, and now that Ernie had finally done a good job, Mikropoulous had lost interest in long conferences and just wanted to dispose of the damned thing so he could get his records straight. That would be fine, if that were the case.

But a shorter conference could also mean that Mikropoulous didn't feel that Ernie had shown enough improvement to warrant spending a lot of time in discussion, and just wanted to get the unpleasantness over with quickly. That wasn't so good. Or perhaps Mikropoulous would have preferred holding the conference after school, but was too busy with end-term clerical details, or had a meeting to attend. That wasn't so bad. But if Mikropoulous was that busy, why would he bother squeezing Ernie's conference in at all, unless he considered it important? And did he consider it important because he was going to tell Ernie there was no opening for him next year, or because he was going to tell him he was being kept on? And if Ernie wasn't kept on, what would he tell his family? And what about Doris? And the trip to Europe? And if he *was* being kept on, would he really be happy sweating out the whole thing for another year, with Grimm getting wise to him, and Mikropoulous hounding him, and Mrs. Ramsay tracking him, and Lynn being pushy-bitchy all over the lunchroom?

I'll never make it, he thought. I should have been one of the Geste boys. They had the right idea. Why the hell did the French go and disband the Foreign Legion?

By the time the sixth period ended, Ernie had reasoned away all favorable aspects of the approaching meeting with Mikropoulous. Nothing good, he knew, was going to come out of the seventh period.

He paced slowly down the empty corridors toward the chairman's office, keeping close to the wall, trying not to look into the secure hermetic sanctuaries of the classrooms, where life was going on in innocent and happy ignorance of his approaching crisis. He felt like a desperate man on his way to a rendezvous with some indefinable danger. Agent C21 sprang into action.

. . . disguised as Mravintz, the informer, had penetrated to the deepest stronghold of MINUTCON, the dreaded chambers of the Supreme Chairman of MERDE, the Ministry of Execution, Revenge, and Death. It was a desperate plan, but C21 was a desperate man on his way to a rendezvous with danger.

His fingers closed on the smooth, cold cylinder in his jacket pocket. To all appearances it was an ordinary fountain pen; but at point-blank range, this innocent-looking cylinder could project a tiny cyanide pellet with deadly accuracy.

Agent C21 paused at the Supreme Chairman's door, and a cold smile twisted the grim line of his lips. He tapped gently, then entered . . .

"Sit down, Mr. Quinn. I'll be with you in a minute," Mikropoulous said, looking up from the papers on his desk.

Ernie settled himself in the victim's chair. At this hour, the sun was not yet at a point where it could hit him full in the eyes. He took that as a good omen.

"Do you mind if I smoke?" he asked.

"Certainly not. Here you are," Mikropoulous said cordially, pushing an ashtray over to Ernie's side of the desk.

Ernie wasn't sure whether this was good or bad. He thought of the traditional cigarette given to a man facing a firing squad, and then he had to rein in hard on Agent C21. Mikropoulous ended his speculations.

"Well, Mr. Quinn. We can make this . . . conference . . . short and sweet, if you'll forgive the . . . cliché. The lesson you taught yesterday was . . . the best I've seen you give all year. A great . . . improvement."

"Thank you. Thank you very much."

"Quite all right. Glad I can say it." Mikropoulous paused, looking down at Ernie's hand, which was clenched in his jacket pocket. "Is there anything wrong with your . . . hand?"

"My . . . Oh, no, no, it's just . . . my fountain pen," Ernie babbled, removing the smooth, cold cylinder from his pocket and displaying it awkwardly, getting his fingers well inked in the process.

"I see. No need to be uneasy, Mr. Quinn, none at all," Mikropoulous said, smiling benignly. "Actually, I have very few comments to make on yesterday's . . . lesson, and since you'll be . . . receiving a copy of my report, I see no need for . . . duplicating our labors, as it were. There's something else I'd like to . . . discuss with you."

Ernie felt like letting out a wild yell of relief and slapping Mikropoulous' broad back. They were finally getting down to some specifics about next year, and he was going to be kept on. It *had* to be that. It couldn't possibly be . . .

". . . final grades," Mikropoulous droned. "You see, since this is the end of your . . . first year with us, I thought you might have some . . . questions about procedure, or perhaps some . . . doubts about . . . particular students. I'll be asking for your final class marks next week, and I wanted to . . . offer my help in clearing up any problems you might have today, instead of . . . waiting until the last minute."

Ernie was unacquainted with Vergil, but he knew that *someone* had said "I fear the Greeks, even when they come bearing gifts," and he agreed. What was Mikropoulous up to now?

"That's very nice of you."

"It's part of my job, Quinn," Mikropoulous said nobly. "Tell me, do you foresee many . . . failures?"

"Well, I haven't figured out all my grades, but I think I'll have about ten. Maybe twelve, but no more."

"That's about six or seven percent," Mikropoulous said after a short pause for mental calculation. "I'm glad to see you avoid the two great . . . pitfalls of beginning teachers."

"What are they, sir?"

"Many new teachers lack . . . confidence in themselves, and feel that they haven't the . . . right to fail anyone, while others are . . . a bit too assertive, and try to prove their . . . high standards by failing half their students. You've avoided both extremes."

Ernie nodded, grateful for the compliment, but still wondering what was coming.

"How about the . . . other end of the spectrum?"

"Do you mean the top grades?"

"Yes, of course," Mikropoulous said pettishly.

"Oh. I've been a little more generous with them than with the failures. I have about twenty-five or thirty students who seem fairly certain to finish the term with an eighty or better."

"That's not excessive. I notice you have some very good . . . students in your classes. I saw several . . . promising youngsters yesterday."

"That's a good class," Ernie said, glad to give them a plug now that they had helped pull him through his darkest hour of the week—his darkest hour of the week so far, that is. "There are five kids who are almost positive nineties, and two more who are close enough to make it if they do well on the final exam."

"A very good class," Mikropoulous said, nodding in agreement. "Any failures?"

"Not in that class, no."

"Which of your classes has the largest number of failures?"

"The first period juniors. I see four definite failures."

"Mmm . . . let's see, now . . ." Mikropoulous mumbled, hunting through the papers on his desk until he found a folder, then extracting a page and studying it closely. "English 611, isn't it? Nola Benson, Sidney Brinckman, John Carlin . . . is that the class?"

"That's it," Ernie said, a bit uneasily. Any time someone dug out a paper, he was sure it was going to contain damning evidence against him.

"Who are the failures?"

"Steve Hirsch and Donald McLoughlin . . . Joe Fisher . . . and . . . oh, yes, Shirley Trindle."

"That's quite an assortment," Mikropoulous said sympathetically. "I had one or two of them last year. I believe I . . . failed McLoughlin."

"I hate to do it, to tell you the truth," Ernie confessed. "He's such a good-natured, happy-go-lucky clown I keep hoping he'll come to his senses. But he just doesn't do a thing. He hasn't passed a test this semester."

"That really doesn't leave you . . . much of a choice, does it? No need to feel bad, Quinn."

"I guess not. I didn't feel too bad about the others, anyway.

Shirley and Joseph are two of the most hostile kids I've ever met. I knew I wasn't reaching them at all, but when I checked their records I found that no one else had ever reached them, either. I spoke to their parents, but that didn't help much. They just threw up their hands and said 'Go ahead, fail them.' And Steve Hirsch's parents didn't even bother answering my letters. I wrote to them three times, and didn't get a single reply."

"You didn't? Now that's a surprise," Mikropoulous said, a look of perplexity crossing his great face.

"Yes, it is sort of unusual."

"More than just unusual in . . . Steve Hirsch's case. Why, he's never failed a subject before, to my knowledge."

"Oh? Well he's failing one now. He's going into the last week of the term with a class mark of thirty."

"Very disappointing performance for a boy with . . . his ability," Mikropoulous said gravely, shaking his head in disapproval. "But of course, you're the judge of that."

"I tried to be as fair as I could," Ernie said, suddenly feeling that he had been put on the defensive and was expected to explain himself. "I gave him a chance to make up the work he owed me, but he didn't seem to care at all. And then, when his parents didn't reply to my letters about him . . . well, there wasn't much more I could do."

"No, of course not," Mikropoulous reassured him. "Still, I'm puzzled about his parents' not contacting you. It's not like them at all."

"Well, they didn't. I haven't heard a word from them."

Mikropoulous gave a little sniff of bewilderment and gazed down at the class sheet pensively.

"I make it a point never to question a teacher's . . . grades, Quinn, but I wonder . . ." he trailed off mysteriously.

"Yes?"

"Well, I wonder if you're doing the right thing here . . . for yourself."

"I don't think I follow you, Mr. Mikropoulous," Ernie said. He could feel the sudden tightening of his guts. Mikropoulous was leading him along smoothly and skillfully, as if he had had considerable practice at this sort of thing. But where were they heading? Ernie wondered.

"We've been looking at things from the . . . teacher's viewpoint, Quinn. Now let's look at them another way. Just suppose that you were a . . . disinterested third party who knew nothing of Mr. Quinn, or Steven Hirsch, or Glen Park High School, except what the . . . records told you. What *would* those records tell you?"

"The facts," Ernie said carefully. He was not going to stick his neck out any further than it already was.

"Exactly! And just what facts would they show?" Mikropoulous exclaimed, like a man on the point of revealing some obscure and astonishing truth.

"The facts. The plain facts, that's all," Ernie said. He was getting impatient now, and a bit jumpy. He was beginning to feel like an appetizing trout that had been securely hooked. He could fight gamely and try to throw the hook, but he didn't have a chance. The deep fat was already sputtering in the pan, and whenever Mikropoulous got tired of the sport, all he had to do was reel Ernie in. Mikropoulous began to reel.

"The facts: a bright student from a good home has been doing well for two years. He comes in contact with a . . . certain new teacher. At this point, the boy stops working and fails the course; his first failure, and a very drastic one. Now, Mr. Quinn, mightn't a . . . detached observed, a . . . disinterested third party . . . interpret this as a failure on the part of the *teacher?*"

"He might, but he'd be wrong if he did."

"I'm not saying he'd be right, Quinn. I'm merely . . . pointing out a possibility."

"It's a pretty remote possibility, isn't it? What 'disinterested third party' is going to be looking at these records?"

"Dr. Shefin might, for one. Or someone from the Board of Education. Perhaps even the boy's father," Mikropoulous said offhandedly. "He's connected with the Board, you know."

And there it was.

"I didn't know that, but I don't see that it makes any difference." Ernie paused. "Does it?"

"Of course not. This is a democratic school system, Quinn," Mikropoulous said grandly, "and no child is given special treatment or consideration because of parental influence."

"Then why are we bothering so much about Steve Hirsch? He deserves to fail. He'll fail. That's that."

"Don't be so suspicious, Quinn. I'm your chairman, and part

of my job is helping you to become a good teacher. Right now, you're . . . inexperienced and you're liable to make mistakes in judgment that can hurt you in your career. My . . . interest in this boy has nothing to do with his father. I'm concerned for you. The fact is, I recall some . . . difficulty you had with Steven earlier in the term. Something like that might well affect your . . . ability to judge his performance objectively."

"I didn't have any 'difficulty' with Steve Hirsch, Mr. Mikropoulous. He made a wisecrack and disrupted the class one day, and I put him on detention. That was the end of it."

"Still, you don't like him, do you?"

"No, I don't," Ernie said flatly. "But I think I'm enough of a man not to fail a kid just because I don't like him."

"Of course," Mikropoulous said, nodding. "Then . . . his grade is a closed issue."

"Yes. I appreciate your concern, but there's really no good reason to change it."

"I understand. Well, that's all, Quinn. You may go now," Mikropoulous said, turning away and looking out the window.

This tactic threw Ernie for a loss. He had managed, during the past few minutes, to build up a small supply of righteous anger, and now he had no outlet for it and it was showing signs of going bad and turning into confusion. What the hell was Mikropoulous up to? Obviously, Steve Hirsch was supposed to pass—why was Mikropoulous dropping the question so abruptly? Ernie began to waver a little.

"I don't . . . I'm not trying to cause any trouble, or anything like that. I hope you understand."

"Of course I understand, Quinn," Mikropoulous said pontifically, turning to face Ernie. "You're acting on . . . principle. That's the right thing to do, and I'm sure that no matter how things turn out, you'll have no . . . regrets." He paused, beaming, then added, "Then, too, you might think things over and perhaps . . . change your mind. That's always a possibility, isn't it?"

"Oh, it's . . ." Ernie began, lamely; then, with a sudden resolute firmness that surprised him, he said, "No, I'm afraid it isn't. There's no reason for me to change any of my grades."

"Perhaps not," Mikropoulous said, unruffled, "but one never can be sure. Tomorrow morning you may look upon this whole affair with . . . different eyes. I'd like you to . . . think things over and give me your final answer then."

"All right, Mr. Mikropoulous. Is that all?"

Ernie wanted to get out. More than that, he wanted to vault over the desk and pummel Mikropoulous mercilessly, but he knew that that wouldn't solve things. And besides, Mikropoulous was pretty big. It might not turn out well at all. The best thing to do was to go.

"There *was* something . . . oh, yes. About next term, Quinn."

It was absolutely incredible. Ernie thought he was ready for Mikropoulous, but this interview had turned into a painful revelation. Mikropoulous could swindle a roomful of Balkan diplomats right out of their drawers, and they wouldn't even suspect him until they felt the cold air on their behinds. He was a sly, slippery, conniving son of a bitch, but what a pro! He had turned away as he spoke, and was facing the window again, gazing into the distance with an air of innocent unconcern. Ernie admitted, reluctantly, that he was being shafted by a master of the game.

"I've heard some talk about appointments by the Board," Mikropoulous began languidly. "Nothing concrete, but if they're any indication of . . . what's to come, some of the . . . substitutes will be out of work next year, I'm afraid."

"It's a little late to start looking around."

"The whole matter is still very uncertain, Quinn. I'm going to . . . check into it. I may be able to let you know . . . oh, say, tomorrow. You'll be dropping by anyway to . . . let me know about your . . . decision on the grades. Will that be all right?"

"Fine."

"I'll expect you, then," Mikropoulous said, turning and looking Ernie squarely in the eye, a faint smile on his broad face. "You can let me know about your grades, and I'll be able to tell you about your position for next year."

"That's very convenient. May I leave now?"

"Certainly. Think over what we said, Quinn, and don't judge things too hastily. You don't want to hurt a promising career because of a few rash decisions, I'm sure."

Ernie nodded impatiently, turned, and walked out fast. That old Kafka feeling was coming back, stronger than ever. He could almost see himself lying flat on his back in the hall outside the chairman's office, his little legs waving in a high degree of unpleasant agitation while Mikropoulous, dressed for the occasion in a smart blue uniform with gold buttons, such as bank messengers wear, pelted him with small red apples. It was a rotten feeling. But that was natural; no doubt about it, he was in a rotten spot.

But what the hell can I do about it? he thought despairingly, and began to hunt for an answer.

There were a few standard courses of action. First of all, bitch to someone. Aaron would probably be in the faculty room. But even Aaron wouldn't know a way out of this mess. Fred wouldn't be much help. Ernie was fairly certain what Fred's advice would be, and he didn't want to hear it. Bob Ferriss would be no help at all, even if he were in school. Before Ernie could finish his story, Bob would be writing letters to congressmen and editors and organizing a "Save Ernie Quinn" campaign complete with torchlight parades, hunger strikes, and a march on City Hall, all led by Bob Ferriss in person. No, thanks. Lynn claimed to be good at consoling; but after the way he had put her off the other day, Ernie couldn't picture her wanting to console *him;* more likely she would bounce up, clap her hands gleefully, and cry "Good! Good! I hope he fires you!" No, Lynn was out, too. And the thought of breathing a word of this to anyone at home was too horrible to entertain for more than a split second.

There was no one to turn to but Doris. And how could he explain the situation to her? He turned this over in his mind for a while, and it seemed worse each time he turned it over. It might not have been so bad if only her father were anything but a professor of Education—chairman of the department, in fact. Ye gods!

But suppose, in spite of everything, she was willing to listen. What could he tell her? What *was* the situation, anyway? Mikropoulous had implied quite clearly that Ernie had to pass Steve Hirsch in order to have a chance of staying on at Glen Park next year; but it was only implied, never stated, never put in writing, never made into any kind of clear-cut ultimatum Ernie could throw back at Mikropoulous. There had been no offers, no promises, no deals. Mikropoulous was as pure as a lamb. Ernie could go in tomorrow and tell Mikropoulous that Steve Hirsch was getting a final grade of ninety-five, and Mikropoulous could smile and say that Ernie Quinn was getting his unconditional release, and what could Ernie say? Of course, that wasn't going to happen. Steve Hirsch deserved to fail, had earned a failure, struggled for it against all odds, and was going to get it, and no sly son of a bitch of a fat sneaky chairman was going to change that. And once Ernie had told Mikropoulous of his decision, there would be no opening for next year. Funny coincidence.

Doris would believe him. Ernie knew that. But it would be smart to have some kind of factual evidence of what was going on, just so Ernie would be able to prove that he wasn't losing his job for any reason connected with his teaching; was, instead, being fired—or, rather, let go with deep regrets and best wishes—for, as Mikropoulous put it, "acting on . . . principle."

On second thought, Doris might not believe him. She might think she was getting mixed up with some wild paranoid who was convinced that "They" were out to get him. He remembered a few hints he had dropped early on in his acquaintance with Doris, precautions against an unwarranted entanglement, just in case she didn't turn out to be as nice as she seemed to be, vague references to strange uncles and odd cousins. Would she remember these things now, when he wanted her to love him and believe in him? Would she think he was a nut?

Probably.

If only he could make Mikropoulous come out and say what he was up to, admit that he was pressuring Ernie to do something that no teacher, no man worth a damn would ever do, then he could leave Glen Park High School with honor and dignity and —to be practical, for a change—some kind of a recommendation. Right now, the job at Glen Park didn't mean a damned thing to Ernie any more, but he could never ask Doris to marry him if he had no job and no hope of getting one. And marrying Doris was the one thing he wanted to do now. Naturally. At this late date, and without a dazzling letter of recommendation, he would never get a teaching job in any kind of decent school. That was probably why Mikropoulous had put off the question of next term for so long.

Maybe I could beat it out of him, Ernie thought. He's got about sixty pounds on me, and the reach, but it could be done. Keep moving, use the left, tire him out, then get to work on the gut. Just like Billy Conn fighting Joe Louis, the way Grandfather always described it. But Conn lost.

No, there must be a better way, he told himself, searching his memory. How about writing a scathing satire and publishing it anonymously, slipping copies into all the letter boxes and shaming Mikropoulous into a public confession? It would mean work, but at least it wouldn't involve violence. He began digging through his memory for a suitable model. Dryden . . .

> All human things are subject to dismay;
> When chairmen summon, teachers must obey.
> This Ernie found, who to the office late
> Was summoned to hear judgment on his fate . . .

Yes, Dryden would have been able to handle a situation like this, no doubt about it. And he would have done a beautiful job on Mikropoulous, too, pinning him down in a few lines:

> A man so devious that he seemed to be
> Made not of flesh and blood, but mercury:
> Vague in his speech and always on the sly,
> There was no artifice he would not try;
> But, in the space of one revolving sun,
> Was jury, judge, and hangman, all in one.

Very good. But now Ernie's memory was working. Dryden wasn't the only model. Pope could do a hell of a job on someone he wanted to get; like that poor fag Lord Hervey that he made into Sporus:

> Yet let me squash this bug with bulging sides,
> This Attic s.o.b. that cheers and chides;
> Whose tricks . . .
> Whose tricks . . .

Well, work on that one. But Pope and Dryden were a little bit too similar in style; how about getting away from the heroic couplet and trying something else? Ernie thought for a few seconds, then it came to him: Lord Byron. There was a man who could wring a thing like this dry:

> Mikropoulous! You bastard, you're a chairman,
> Chairman of English here at Glen Park High;
> I've learned—to my dismay—you're not a fair man
> In dealings with poor fellows such as I,

And now I'm on my guard. You'd best beware, man,
Your day of reckoning is drawing nigh.
You build us up, and then you try to topple us;
Perhaps I'll do the same to you, Mikropoulous.

Yes, Byron would be good for something like that. But the rhymes would be a problem. "Mikropoulous" wasn't the easiest word to find a rhyme for. Blank verse would be a lot easier, but blank verse was too damned serious and philosophical. Nobody wrote satires in blank verse. Ernie thought of Wordsworth, and that, naturally, made him think of Coleridge. Now, *he* had possibilities:

Like one, who down a corridor
Doth walk in fear and dread;
His shoulders sag, his footsteps drag,
He dares not turn his head,
Because he failed a boy whose Dad
Is on the Board of Ed.

Still, Coleridge was a pretty serious type. Anybody who can read German philosophers and get excited about them is bound to be serious. Maybe free verse would be best. You could really fool around with free verse, and work in all kinds of effects. But there was free verse, and free verse. Whitman would never do, and Eliot was too smart. And even if Ernie could write like Eliot, Mikropoulous would never understand it. There had to be someone, preferably someone contemporary, with a good ear and a wild sense of humor; someone who could say something serious without taking himself too seriously and make you laugh without ever losing the awareness that you were laughing at your own risk.

Yonder f a t chairman contemplates
dr
op(lo)p
ing
a certain—you(ng fellow named Quinn)
know the type—
troublemakinglish
teechur.

If you're going to go that far, Ernie thought critically, why stick to poetry at all? This was an absurd affair; why not try drama, treating the situation with all the resources of the stage?

You could start with two tramps, caved-in, defeated little men with odd names—say, Cuspidor and Labyrinth—standing on an almost-bare stage. Props could be kept to a minimum: a desk; a chair. They could be waiting for someone, or something, that would never arrive; something out of the golden past; maybe Harry Podnak. Call it "Waiting for Podnak." And while they waited, weird things would happen. A big, mean guy named Mikropoulous would come on stage dragging a teacher, Ernie, on a leash. . . .

Absorbed in his plans of literary vengeance, Ernie had wandered down the hall to the main stairway without any definite objective in mind. At the head of the stairs, he checked his watch and found that he had nine minutes before his next class—enough time for a fast cup of coffee and a cigarette. He would have preferred a stiff belt of the Professor's cognac, but the cafeteria was no place to get it; coffee would have to do. The nice part was that he could slip in the back door and get the coffee directly from Mrs. Lummis, and thus avoid an embarrassing confrontation with Lynn. Things were bad enough already. Maybe in a day or so.

He clattered down the stairs, reached the last landing, just before the main floor, and stopped dead in his tracks. From the landing he could see the hall on both sides of the staircase, and what he saw froze his blood, it was so damned symbolic. Approaching the staircase from the left was Lynn Rogers. Coming up fast on the right, like the twin moons of Mars—which they resembled in outline, and, appropriately enough, in color, since they were both wearing yellow—were Mrs. Ramsay and an unfamiliar Valkyrie who could only be Rowena. Straight ahead, through the open door, lay Miss Grimm's office. They were really closing in now, and Ernie half expected to hear a soft footfall behind him as Mikropoulous crept up brandishing a kidney dagger. He looked back quickly, and was relieved to find the stairs empty. Ramsays to the right of him, Lynn to the left of him, Grimm before him; he could imagine the volleying and thundering: "Oh, Ernest, you must meet my daughter Rowena!" "Too busy to come down for a cup of coffee, Ernie?" "Well, Mr. Quinn, have you reconsidered that flimsy excuse you tried to palm off on me?" He turned and raced up the stairs. To hell with the coffee. It was a time to worry about survival.

When the eighth period finally ended, Ernie stayed behind in the empty classroom to try to think things out clearly. He had been reconsidering the situation during the period, and he felt a bit less dogmatic than he had in Mikropoulous' office. He dug out his mark book to see if he might possibly—just possibly—be able to find some honorable way of passing Steve Hirsch. After all, he *had* been tired when he figured out the grades, and he wasn't that good at math anyway, so there could have been a mistake. And if this really was Steve's first failure, maybe Ernie ought to give him the benefit of any existing doubt.

With the mark book open before him, there was no room for doubt at all. Steve's average, figuring in all the failures, the tests he had missed and never made up, the assignments he had never handed in, and the blasé manner in which he had contributed his mite to class discussion, came to a pitiful 29.7. Even if he pulled a perfect grade on the final, an extremely unlikely eventuality, Steve could not make a passing grade. There it was, in black and white, cold and impartial. Steve Hirsch had to fail.

Of course, if the tests he missed, and the assignments he didn't hand in, were given a straight failing grade of fifty, he'd have a better average. He would still have to do well on the final, but he'd have a chance.

Ernie sat back and thought about this for a few minutes. It could be done. But damn it, he hadn't done it for anyone else, and he had never marked on that system before. Why start now?

To keep the job, stupid, he told himself coldly.

He felt the need for a cigarette. Shutting the mark book and burying it in his bag, he moved out of the room, slamming the door behind him, and started down the hall toward the faculty room.

Someone called his name. He turned and saw Steve Hirsch, as neatly dressed and snotty-looking as ever, hurrying to catch up to him.

"Mr. Quinn, I'd like to talk to you."

"Sure. What about?"

"My grades," Steve said, breathing heavily. He had moved a fraction faster than normal walking speed for a distance of about ten yards, and he was heaving away like a pearl diver. The little punk probably smokes two packs a day and drinks like a Dublin charwoman, Ernie thought.

"It's a little late in the term, isn't it?" Ernie said, using the grand old cliché.

"Well, I heard this rumor about failing."

"Where did you hear it?"

"Oh . . . around the school."

"Where around the school?" Ernie pressed.

"Just around. You know, people talking."

"Let's not waste time discussing rumors, Steve." Ernie started to move on.

"I was talking to Mr. Mikropoulous. He said you told him I was failing."

Professional ethics. Right between the shoulder blades, and then sharply twisted. Thank you, Mr. Chairman. Ernie made his decision on the spot.

"He's right. Is that what you wanted to hear?"

"I never failed anything before!" Steve cried.

"You've been lucky. Or else you worked a lot harder than you did in my class."

"You never said I was failing!"

"Oh, knock it off, will you, Steve?"

"Yeah, just like that, 'Knock it off, Steve.' This means I have to go to summer school, and I have a failure on my record. But you don't care."

"I care. Look, I don't get any awards for failing people."

"Then why can't you pass me?"

"Because there's no basis for it. You just didn't do the work."

Ernie noticed then that two of Steve's classmates, Shaggy McLoughlin and a Polish boy named Eddie whose last name trailed off into a thicket of unpronounceable consonants, both of them on the beefy side, were standing just down the hall. They were out of earshot, but they appeared to be interested in the proceedings. The little fink! Ernie thought. He's going to call in his boys and jump me! He hadn't thought Shaggy was that kind of a kid, but this was no time for character analysis. They were pretty big, and there were three of them. They could give him a bad time before anyone . . .

. . . a quick karate chop, and the first of the would-be assassins crumpled. C21 whirled, catlike, and came face to face with Colonel Kakamimi of the Inner Guard of MERDE. A cruel smile flickered across . . .

No time for that, he warned himself. Just edge toward the stairs and make a run for it.

"I think your friends are waiting for you, Steve."

"Yeah, my friends. I wanted them to see what kind of a teacher I got stuck with."

"Watch your step, boy," Ernie said. Maybe there'd be time for one quick punch before he took off.

"My English teacher," Steve said, moving toward Ernie, "a dumb little shit who thinks he can walk in off the streets and make—"

Ernie caught him squarely on the cheek with his best backhand. "I told you to watch your step."

"You dirty son of a bitch, you hit me!"

"That's right, I hit you. Twice," Ernie said, letting him have one more. "Now crawl away."

Steve backed off, rubbing his reddened cheek. "Thanks, English teacher, that's just what I wanted."

"I'm glad I could oblige."

"I came here to ask about my grade, and you hit me, twice. In front of two witnesses," Steve said, smiling a triumphant smile of surpassing nastiness. "You're through, teacher. If I don't pass, you're through."

"That's pretty clever, Steve. Who taught you that one, your father? Mikropoulous?"

"They haven't got anything to teach me, and neither have you. You just go in and tell your fat slob of a chairman that I'm going to pass. Then maybe I'll let you keep your job."

"What makes you think I want it, now?"

"You want it. You're just like all the rest. You've got a good thing and you want to keep it."

Ernie laughed contemptuously. "You call *this* a good thing?"

"You know what I mean. And I can fix it so you stay or you go. My old man can do it."

"We'll see what your father does. Maybe he'll do just what I did."

"Are you serious? I'm his son. He'll never take your word against mine. You're through."

"All right, then, I'm through. Beat it."

"You better start cleaning out your desk, English teacher," Steve said, edging away. "And start looking in the want ads."

"And you better start running before I give you one for the road, punk," Ernie said, moving toward him. "I have nothing to lose, remember?"

Steve moved. Ernie felt glad for a brief moment, full of the warm satisfaction of a good and much-needed job well done. But even in the midst of his good feeling, he knew that very soon he wasn't going to feel glad at all. He had been done in, and not by an old pro but by a scheming kid. He wanted to work up a high indignation, a fine sense of outrage; but the best he could manage was a fuming, impotent feeling of humiliation. All questions of injustice aside, being made a patsy twice within the space of two hours was too much for him to bear. At the rate things were going, he would be sucked into a game of three-card monte run by a team of kindergarten hustlers before the day was out. And he would probably lose his shirt.

"You sneaky bastard!" Ernie snarled, shaking his fist at the empty corridor down which Steve had gone. "You rotten little weasel!" Then he thought of Hamlet's "unpack my heart with words" line, which he had recited to his seniors with such great fervor only a week ago, and had to laugh at himself. Poor Hamlet, he reflected. He thought *he* had problems. Steve Hirsch and Mikropoulous could give cards and spades to the whole Danish court and still leave a stage full of corpses at the end of Act V. And they'd probably get Fortinbras, too, and Horatio. Or at least have them fired. What the hell, he thought, trying to be philosophical and rise above the whole nasty business, it's always been this way. Tarquin and Caesar each had his Brutus, Charles I his Cromwell . . . and I have Steve Hirsch.

Ernie spent most of the trip home brooding profoundly over this most recent turn of events. He had figured Steve for a spoiled, snotty little bastard before the term was a month old, but he had never suspected that under Steve's nasty exterior beat the heart of a Jacobean avenger. All the other spoiled, snotty little bastards he had met had turned out to be towers of Jell-O. Steve was a surprise; not at all like Lloyd, whom Ernie had, up to this moment, considered the archetype of the spoiled kid. But then, there was probably no one in the world quite like Lloyd.

Lloyd's father was a successful lawyer. His mother worked as a nurse three evenings a week, not because her financial assistance was needed, but because she wanted to make things easier for Lloyd. Lloyd was going to go to Yale, then to Harvard Law School, and then join his father as partner in a family law firm. Naturally, he would not be able to work and still do justice to his studies—God forbid that Lloyd should have to work his way through school, or life, or anything else—so his mother was building up a nice little account to defray his personal expenses during the grueling years of study that lay ahead.

The only fly in this otherwise fragrant ointment of parental solicitude was Lloyd. At the rate he was progressing, it would be an impressive achievement for Lloyd to graduate from high school before the age of twenty-four, and even then, his record would be such as would cause an outburst of belly laughs across the city of New Haven if it happened to be presented seriously to the Director of Admissions of Yale University. Somehow, these facts had never dawned on Lloyd's parents. They had seen his report cards, on which at least half the grades were entered in red ink; they had seen his themes, every one of which came back to Lloyd so heavily festooned with red insertions, corrections, and plaintive comments that they resembled less an English composition than an enlarged color photograph of a bloodshot eye; they had spoken to his teachers, each of whom treated the subject of Lloyd's academic future in the same manner as a doctor informing the next of kin that the patient will not last out the night; they had been warned and warned again, and the warnings fell on deaf ears. Their Lloyd was going to graduate with honors, go to Yale and Harvard, and then begin a legal career that would end only in the office of Chief Justice of the United States Supreme Court. That's the way it was going to be, and nothing was going to convince them otherwise.

Lloyd, meanwhile, treated the whole business with patrician disdain. Let his elders fret; he knew what he wanted to be, and it had nothing to do with Glen Park High School, Yale, Harvard, or the Bar Association. Lloyd wanted to be a disk jockey. He prepared himself assiduously for his chosen profession, spending, according to his mother, some six hours a day listening to his favorite disk jockeys, taping their best moments for review and study. It was his mother's description of this practice, with the stock observation, "We just don't know what to do with Lloyd," that elicited Ernie's suggestion of what seemed to him to be the obvious first step: take away the tape recorder. But that was out of the question, as he learned. "Oh, we couldn't do that," Lloyd's mother said, shocked at this display of pedagogical fascism. "We've *never* been firm with Lloyd."

Thinking about this afterward, Ernie was able to re-create in his imagination a series of tableaux depicting the early life of Lloyd in the gelatinous disciplinary atmosphere cultivated by his parents: Lloyd drop-kicking the Limoges dinnerware as Mother looked on and timidly whispered, "Darling is going to make Mama unhappy"; Lloyd carving his initials in the sofa while his mother cooed, "Darling shouldn't do—he might hurt his little hands"; Lloyd snatching off his grandmother's glasses and doing a brisk flamenco on the lenses as Father said gently, "Lloyd, dear, maybe Grandma doesn't want to play that game"; Lloyd at the age of ten cheerfully relieving himself on the living room rug while Mama pouted, "Now, Lloyd, you *know* that isn't nice"; Lloyd at the age of twelve stocking his room with the largest collection of pornography outside the British Museum while Father, loitering sheepishly about the doorway, asked, "Are you *sure* you wouldn't like me to read you some Winnie-the-Pooh?" There were many touching episodes in the pageant of Lloyd, but the one Ernie dwelt on longest was the climactic scene, a projection into the future, in which Lloyd, age thirty-two, was carried off, securely restrained, to a place where he would reside within soft walls for the rest of his life; his mother and father were looking on, saying to each other tearfully, "But how could it happen? We did everything for him, and we were never, never *firm* with him."

It was kind of sad. Lloyd really wasn't such a bad kid, and Ernie hated to see him ruined. There was no guarantee that he *was* ruined, to be sure, but there were pretty strong indications. Any way you looked at it, Lloyd had a lot to overcome. Ernie even felt a little sorry for Lloyd's parents. They were trying like hell to be good parents, but they just couldn't make themselves do the one thing they had to do. They were probably afraid that Lloyd would stop loving them if they ever got "firm." The poor bastards, Ernie thought, realizing that at this point they were probably right. You had to start early, or it was no good. If you let a kid commit every crime known to man for the first sixteen years of his life, and then, one day, out of a clear sky, you gripped his lapels and snarled, "Okay, punk—one move and I'll break every bone in your body," and it was obvious that you meant it, there was going to be a certain strain in the parent-child relationship from then on.

Ernie's own ideas on child rearing were clear-cut, as they usually are in unmarried men: fixed rules, consistently enforced, with no nonsense and no arguments. It seemed so obvious, and yet no one—to judge from the few small children Ernie came in contact with—was trying it. He remembered dreadful afternoons when the neighborhood mothers, with their full complement of children, dropped in to visit his mother, with much the same effect as a playful contingent of drunken Vandals dropping in on Rome. The sofa was turned into a makeshift trampoline, the drapes became jungle vines, and the entire house was transformed into the Hampton Court maze, where happy boys and girls ran, leaped, and squealed, to the accompaniment of jarring offstage thumps and crashes. Ernie's mother, who had made his head ring if he so much as squirmed in his chair on the rare occasions in his childhood when she took him visiting, was mysteriously transformed into a paragon of benevolence in such a setting. As her home was slowly and methodically reduced to a shambles, she would murmur, "Oh, that's all right," or, "Don't worry about the lamp, it's not working anyway," or, "We were going to be getting a new television set soon, so it doesn't really matter." The visitor was, if possible, even more casual. She might whisper a periodical "Don't do that to the wall, darling," but that was all. Darling, in the meantime, would go right ahead and do that to the wall and anything else within reach. About the only beneficial effect Ernie could see in these social calls was the fact that they furnished his mother with something to keep herself occupied, and made his life a bit more peaceful. It took three full weeks for her to get the house looking like the residence of civilized human beings again. By then, life being what it is, it was time for another young mother to descend upon them.

Ernie was determined that there would be none of this nonsense in *his* house. He had worked out an eminently satisfactory scheme. All it required was a dog, a huge black dog with wild yellow eyes and a short brutal name suggestive of a blood-stained muzzle and dark deeds on the moor. Something like Fang, Tor, or Wolf was what Ernie had in mind, but he hadn't really decided on that yet.

He wasn't sure of the breed, but something along the lines of the Arctic timber wolf, perhaps with a touch of wolverine in his ancestry, would do nicely. This dog would be allowed to roam free whenever small children visited. At their first exuberant cry he would enter the room, belly low, tongue lolling, salivating freely, and stalk menacingly toward them.

"He'll be fine as long as they stay perfectly still," Ernie would say reassuringly. "It's only when he's startled . . . the children have had tetanus shots, haven't they? My, he's really taken a fancy to Debbie! Don't scream, Debbie, he won't break the skin. Yes, he does like the little ones, as long as they don't make any sudden moves. There was a little boy down the street he was just wild about. It was so nice to see them play together! Then one day . . . I think the boy tried to pet him . . . poor little fellow! We'll never know just how it happened, I guess." Here Ernie would pause, shake his head, and sigh. "He'd be just about your Jimmie's age now. Don't tell me you have to leave so soon! That's a shame. I think Tor was just getting ready for a romp with Jimmie . . ."

This was one of Ernie's favorites—even better than the C21 series, which tended to become strenuous—and he spent a good deal of time on it, polishing the lines and adding little embellishments—a gesture here, an intonation there—with the painstaking craftsmanship of a Flaubert. He had even developed some fine defensive play. His favorite was the one he would use to counter the objections of the mother who, having allowed her offspring to grow up as free from civilization's restraining hand as Rousseau's Emile, expected Teutonic discipline from everything and everyone else. Such a woman, Ernie knew, would, immediately upon his dog's entrance, turn the conversation to such topics as muzzles, choke leashes, and "putting him to sleep." Ernie had a comeback that was beautiful in its simplicity.

"Yes, I guess I have been a little indulgent with old Fang," he would say as the dog walked in, dropped a terrified child at his feet, and sat eagerly awaiting a pat on the head for his skill at retrieving. "I can't bring myself to be firm with him. Truth is, I love the little rascal. I guess you really can't understand it unless you have a dog of your own." There were a number of other lines Ernie was proud of ("I just can't seem to control him," and "It's only a phase—the dog of two-and-a-half always goes for the jugular," for instance), but this was his favorite.

Ernie enjoyed this particular fantasy, but he had few illusions about the chances of its ever being realized. It was not so much the thought of a posse of irate neighbors marching on his house, like something from the last reel of a Frankenstein movie, that gave him pause; it was the near-impossibility of getting any woman to go along with it. They were all soft on kids. But Doris seemed sensible enough. Perhaps, with coaxing, she could be induced to give it a whirl.

Ernie arrived at Doris' house a few minutes before eight that night. He had decided to tell her the whole grisly story of Mikropoulous, the grades, and Steve Hirsch, and maybe even about Europe, and then see how she reacted. He was sure she would understand. If she didn't, he could always throw himself in front of the train on the way home. That ought to make *someone* happy.

Doris answered the door. She looked like an advertisement for girls, with the lamp in the hall throwing a soft backlight on her hair and leaving her face partly in shadow, but still light enough for Ernie to see the sudden smile when she looked up at him.

"Oh, boy, you look good to me, Doris," Ernie said, pulling her close to him and kissing her hard. She felt great. He squeezed her close, kissed her again, then just stood still, being happy, as she nestled against his shoulder. She even smelled good. Ernie would have been content to stay in the doorway all evening, but like all good things, his idyl was interrupted.

"Who's at the door, dear?" Mrs. Flecker called from inside.

"It's Ernie, Mother," Doris answered, hardly moving. Ernie kissed her once more, fast, before everyone inside could come trooping out on the porch. "I guess we ought to go inside," she said, not moving.

"I guess so. But to tell you the truth, I'd rather stay out here and neck than go in and talk to the Professor. He just can't compete with you."

"The Professor's out tonight. He had to see Dean Adams about something."

"Gee, that's too bad," Ernie said, grinning.

"Yes. The Dean called and—oh, you big phony! You're glad!" She tried to look severe.

"Not really *glad*. Not glad he had to go see the Dean, anyway. I feel sorry for anybody who has to go to meetings. But I'd still rather neck than talk, so—"

"You're hopeless. Come on inside," Doris said, taking his hand and leading him in. He followed, obediently.

As they entered the living room, Mrs. Flecker looked up from her desk. She peered over her glasses, looking like Margaret Leighton about to deliver a clever line, something very Noel Coward or Terence Rattigan, but all she managed was, "Hello, Ernest."

"Hello, Mrs. Flecker," Ernie replied. "Did I interrupt you? You look busy."

"Oh, it's just details. I've got *thousands* of letters to write, and things to straighten out so the party goes smoothly tomorrow night. You *are* coming, aren't you?"

"Yes, I'll be here."

"Good. You can protect Doris. There are two or three dirty old men from the English Department that I *have* to invite, but I wouldn't trust—"

"Oh, *Mother*," Doris said indignantly.

"You didn't see Professor Northrup at the Christmas party, dear. Honestly, Ernest, I think the man has little cloven hoofs instead of feet."

"Fear not," Ernie said, with a hammy flourish. "I shall wear my magic armor. And carry a hatpin."

"The hatpin is a *marvelous* idea," Mrs. Flecker drawled with an arch smile. "What are you two doing tonight?"

"I don't know," Ernie said. He looked at Doris, who shrugged. "Do you need any help getting things ready for tomorrow?"

"I've thrown up my hands, Ernest. We'll mix our own drinks, but I'm going to have everything else catered. It's sweet of you to ask, though."

"Is there a good movie playing anywhere, Ernie?"

"I don't know. Have you got a paper?"

"Where's the paper, Mother?"

"Inside, dear, in the family room. I think there's a new Bergman playing somewhere nearby."

"Come on, Ernie, let's check it," Doris said, leading the way.

The lights were off in the family room; that suited Ernie just fine. Doris finally broke loose and switched them on, chastising him furiously in a whisper, but looking rather pleased. She picked up the paper and began thumbing through it while Ernie slumped on the sofa.

"Come on over. There's plenty of room."

"Now, you behave. I want to look at the paper."

"'I know a game worth two of that.'"

"That's not original," Doris said without looking up. "I've heard that line before."

"*Aria da Capo*," Ernie admitted. "We saw it at the college. Remember this line? 'Is it Tuesday, Columbine? I'll kiss you if it's Tuesday.'"

"It's Thursday, and you behave yourself. Here it is, Ernie. The show starts at eight-fifty. Can we make it?"

"I really don't feel like seeing a Bergman movie. He's all spiders and rape and gloom. I'd rather see a good, dopey, Technicolor musical."

"Philistine."

"And so would you, so don't 'Philistine' me."

"I would *not*," Doris said, coming over and sitting at the other end of the sofa, keeping a firm grip on the newspaper. "I enjoy foreign movies."

"They're just like American movies, only dirtier. And they have subtitles."

"They're not dirty, they're realistic. You're an *awful* Philistine."

"Here, let me look at that," Ernie said, taking the paper and pretending to study it intently. He had worked something out along these lines, and this was his first opportunity to use it. "Now, here's a good one. A lusty, bawdy, earthy tale of young love among the Neapolitan olive pickers, produced by Lecherino Lecherini, directed by Vittorio da Flower, starring Voluptua di Gennerata. It's called *La Donn' E Nubile*. And there's a French movie playing with it—"

"Oh, stop it, Ernie. You're terrible!"

"I know. It's called *Neuf Ouefs*, and it stars Monique Risqué and Jean-Pierre De Bauche. It's so realistic no one under forty-five is admitted."

"You really *are* terrible," Doris said, but she was laughing. Good. He would use this one again. At the party, maybe.

"I'm not terrible, I'm a Philistine. It's not bad, really, as long as you keep away from shepherd boys with slingshots," he confided.

"All right, Nut, I guess you don't want to go to the movies. What shall we do, then?"

"Want to wrestle?"

"You stop it, now. Mother's in the next room."

"I couldn't care less," Ernie said, sliding over toward Doris. "I don't want to wrestle with *her*."

Doris jumped up nimbly just as Ernie got within striking distance.

"Do you want to watch television?"

"Now who's the Philistine?" Ernie said smugly.

"I think there's a Bogart movie on at nine," she said, ignoring him. "You can check it in the paper."

"You'd better come over and help me. Us English teachers can't read good."

"You'll just have to struggle with it."

"Killjoy," Ernie mumbled. He pawed through the paper until he reached the television listings, checked them, and announced, "You're right, Miss Flecker. That was a very impressive performance. You deserve a reward."

"Behave, Ernie," Doris said. "Honestly, you'd think you were home on leave from a polar expedition or something."

"I can't help it, Doris," Ernie said, rising and closing in on her. "I'm very demonstrative. It's my way."

"Let's go for a walk," Doris said hurriedly, making for the living room. "We can get back by nine and watch Bogart."

"Okay."

Ernie caught her before she got to the doorway. She talked a good fight, but at heart, Doris was a collaborator. When they entered the living room, Mrs. Flecker looked up.

"Are you going to the movies?"

"We're just going to take a walk, Mother. There's a Bogart movie on at nine, and we'll be back to watch it."

"Is it a good one, dear?"

"It's one of his early ones, Mrs. Flecker," Ernie volunteered, hoping to frighten her off. "A gangster thing."

"Oh, dear. I was hoping it might be *Casablanca*. That hasn't been on for ages."

"They'll run it soon," Ernie consoled her. "At three-thirty on a Tuesday morning, right after a Mr. Moto."

"Come on, Ernie." Doris tugged at his hand. They said their goodbyes to her mother, who sighed a martyred sigh and returned to her letters.

It was a pleasant early summer evening, and with Doris by his side Ernie was able to appreciate just how pleasant an early summer evening can be. A few of the neighbors were out on their porches, and Ernie showered them with imaginary mortar fire. He wanted privacy.

Doris was great. She had a way of letting him know she was there and wanted to assure herself that he was there too, and Ernie loved it. She took his hand in the simple matter-of-fact way a child consigns herself to an adult at a street crossing. She slipped her arm through his as if it belonged there. It was wonderful being with her. Naturally, something had to spoil it.

"Ernie," she said suddenly, "what are you going to do? I mean in the future; what are your plans?"

He winced. He had tried to convince himself that tonight was going to be a night of great truths and deep revelations. Now he was sick at the thought of telling Doris what was happening to him. He took a deep breath and started evasive action.

"Well, I don't know, really. I don't think about it too much."

"Don't you ever wonder what you're going to be? What your life will be like?" she pressed.

"You make it sound as though I should be like Pippa. Maybe that's not a bad idea. 'Ernie's in trouble, all's right with the world.' "

"Now, there you go again. Ernie, you always get off the subject. You have to face up to reality, not avoid it."

"Have you taken a good look at reality lately? Nobody in his right mind would want to face up to it."

"Ernie, you *have* to!"

"Why? Reality is Mikropoulous, and Glen Park High School, and my grandfather, and all of the rest of them."

"What's so terrible about them?"

All right, honey, he thought, if you want it, here it is, straight from the shoulder.

"What's really terrible about reality, Doris, is that I know what I'm going to be. I'm going to be unemployed. In a few days I'll be out of a job, and—"

"What happened?"

"A lot of things." He stopped, took both her hands, and looked down at her. "Look, honey. I can probably keep my job at Glen Park if I just agree to play the game and do something I know is wrong. But I don't want to play the game. It's their game, all the way, and I hate it. If I don't play along, I may not be able to teach any more, but that's—"

"Ernie, what did you do?" She sounded quite anxious.

"I hit one of the kids. In front of witnesses. He set the whole thing up to pressure me into passing him, and I fell for it."

"But he can't get away with that, Ernie!"

"I think he can, Doris. His father is a big shot on the Board of Education."

"What about your chairman? Can't he do anything?"

"Mikropoulous? He practically came right out and told me to pass this kid, no matter what his grades were, or I'd be out of a job. That was *before* I got conned into hitting him. Now, with that to hold over me, I expect he'll fire me on the spot tomorrow unless I go into his office on my knees and swear fealty."

"Oh, Ernie, poor Ernie," Doris said, reaching up to touch his cheek softly. Her eyes were shining, and she looked beautiful. "You were trying so hard to be a good teacher."

"Not *that* hard," Ernie said, placing his hand over hers.

"It isn't fair."

"Life isn't fair. Don't get upset, Doris."

"How can I help getting upset? This is so wrong! They need people like you, Ernie."

"You're prejudiced," Ernie said, kissing her gently. She threw her arms around his neck and clung to him tightly. She was just so great, Ernie thought, so really perfect. She really cared, and she wanted him to know she cared. This was the kind of girl a man hopes, all his life, to meet someday, the kind of girl he hopes will love him. And Ernie had met her, and it looked as though she loved him, or came so close that it hardly made a difference. And Ernie had no job—not for long, anyway—and no future, and only a few dollars to his name. His Europe money; that was a laugh, now. But that's the way it usually works, he reflected; he was the kid who got the brand-new sled on the Fourth of July.

"What are you going to do, Ernie?" Doris asked as they walked back home.

"Well, I suppose the sensible, practical thing to do is to pass this punk, and hope Mikropoulous will bury the whole incident."

"Are you going to do that?"

"I was never very sensible. Or practical. But if you want me to, I will."

"Ernie, I couldn't ask that!" She sounded genuinely shocked. "I think that would destroy you. A person has to do what he thinks is right, not what's practical."

"Good girl. I'll be poor, but honest."

"Ernie . . ." she said thoughtfully.

"Yes?"

"Ernie, do you think the Professor might be able to do something? He knows a lot of—"

"No! Absolutely not, Doris. I don't want him to get mixed up in this."

"But what's being done to you is so *unjust!*"

"Yes, but I just don't like to fight it that way. It would boil down to a case of who has the best connections. 'My contacts can outpressure your contacts,' or something like that. This way, no matter what happens, I'll at least know I did the right thing; at least I did what I thought was right." He felt a vague, ironic echo of Mikropoulous' words, but ignored it. "That's really important to me."

"Don't you want any help at all?"

"None at all. Why should your father get involved in my problems? He might get hurt, you know. How do you think I'd feel if *he* lost his job, too?" He paused, then, with a soft, self-depreciative laugh, he went on. "Do you know who's always been one of my heroes? Cyrano de Bergerac. I must have read the play five times, and God only knows how many times I've seen the movie, but the speech in Ragueneau's pastry shop still makes me want to stand up and cheer every time I hear it. 'Here comes —thank God!—another enemy!' I guess I'm trying to play Cyrano. You know—'I stand, not high it may be—but alone!' "

"Not all alone," Doris said, squeezing his hand hard.

"Thanks, Doris."

They walked on in silence, and Ernie began to come out of his mood and act more cheerfully. By the time they were within sight of the Flecker house he was talking almost confidently of the future. But he thought it best, right now, not to mention his ideas on being a book bum.

"There's always the bank, Doris. They'll take me back. Or I might try newspaper work. That's an awfully interesting job. I might even try to write."

"What would you write about?"

"I don't know," Ernie said thoughtfully. "I'm sort of handicapped. I never went to a prep school."

"Do you have to go to a prep school to be a writer?"

"It looks that way. Either that, or grow up in the deep South. I'm completely out of it."

"Why don't you write a shocking exposé of our schools? You could certainly do *that,*" Doris suggested.

"No one would believe it," Ernie said flatly. "I'd have to turn it into a comedy, and right now I don't see anything amusing about our schools."

"No, I guess not. I'm sorry, Ernie."

"There's nothing for you to be sorry about, Doris. I'm not really that sorry myself. The only thing that I kind of regret is that this probably means the end of my teaching career for good. I was getting to like it."

"I think it's a shame. You could be a great teacher, Ernie," she said emphatically.

"Well, yes," Ernie said, after a short, judicious pause. "Yes, I guess I could. But what I'll really miss is the vacations. I was hoping to get to Europe once in a while, over the summer, but you can't do it on a two-week vacation. Oh, well."

"At least you've been to Europe once. Sometimes I think I'll never get there."

"You'll get there," Ernie said reassuringly. He hoped she wouldn't press him for details. Fortunately, there was no time. They were at the house.

"Ernie, it's quarter after nine!" Doris exclaimed. "We missed the beginning of the movie."

"Before we go in—not a word to anyone about my problems, Doris. Promise."

"I wish you'd let me talk to the Professor. He could do something, I'm sure."

"No, please. Remember Cyrano."

"All right, Ernie. If that's the way you want it."

Waiting for the train that night, Ernie soothed himself with the memory of Doris' parting words: "Whatever happens, Ernie, I'm on your side." She was so great, so absolutely perfect, and she was on his side. She didn't think he was a nut, or an anarchist, or anything like that. And she hadn't gotten nervous at the very mention of Europe. She was with him, all the way. That was all that mattered, really.

He took a deep breath, squared his shoulders, and leaned back against the brick wall of the station. All right, he thought. All right, you bastards, come and get me. Now I'm ready for you. I can't lose now.

Well, not too badly, anyway.

PART THREE

On Friday morning, Ernie was ready to act with firmness and resolution. And speed. It had occurred to him, in a last disturbing night thought at the very edge of sleep, that Steve Hirsch would probably run to Mikropoulous at his earliest opportunity with a wild tale of teacher brutality, and that Ernie's best course was to get there first and take the offensive.

Mikropoulous still had not arrived when the first period began, so Ernie did the next best thing. He took his second period study group, or "Animal Farm," as he had fondly christened it, to the library, and abandoned them there. After a hurried explanation to the librarian, who kept up a steady, desperate incantation of "But they're only supposed to come here on Mondays and Thursdays!" he went directly to the chairman's office.

"Ah, Mr. Quinn, you're . . . early," Mikropoulous greeted him. He did not appear surprised by Ernie's early arrival, though.

"Yes. I want to talk to you about Steve Hirsch."

"I thought you might."

"Not about the marks; about something else."

"I know, Mr. Quinn. Stephen was in to see me during the first period. He was very upset."

That's one point for the little bastard, Ernie thought. He's certainly efficient. Well, it won't do him any good.

"He ought to be upset. I want to have him suspended. And if I can have him expelled, I want him expelled."

"You surprise me, Mr. Quinn," Mikropoulous said mildly.

"I'll probably surprise you even more when I tell you what really happened yesterday. I suppose you've heard Steve's version of it already."

"Yes. He told me that you struck him several times. Is that true?"

"Not exactly. 'Several times' is a slight exaggeration. I hit him twice."

"Well, you did strike him, though. Is that correct?"

"It is. Did he tell you why I struck him?"

"He didn't seem to know, Quinn," Mikropoulous said, looking sincere and perplexed. "He said that he approached you to . . . inquire about his final grade, and you grew angry and struck him."

"Then he didn't tell you that he called me a dirty son of a bitch?"

"Please, Mr. Quinn! There's no call to use such . . . language."

"I agree. That's why I hit him. He called me other things, too, you know."

"You needn't repeat them now, Quinn," Mikropoulous said primly. He paused for a moment, then asked, "Tell me, did anyone else hear the boy say these . . . things to you?"

"No. There were two boys—friends of Steve's—down the hall a way, but they couldn't have heard anything we said."

"But they did see everything that happened."

"Probably. They certainly could have."

"Yes. Yes, they certainly could," Mikropoulous said, nodding weightily. "As a matter of fact, Quinn, they did. They saw you . . . conversing with Stephen, and then striking him. But they have no idea of what was said."

"They were out of earshot," Ernie agreed.

"An unfortunate circumstance, that."

"Why?"

"Well, I'm sure you can see how it . . . complicates matters. There are witnesses to your action, but there are no witnesses to the . . . cause of your striking the boy. No one but yourself heard him call—"

"Wait, now. What have witnesses got to do with this?"

"Nothing, I hope, Quinn. I'm sure you'll agree that it would be in your best interests, and the boy's, and the school's, if this were . . . settled quietly, before it . . . grows to proportions beyond our means to control."

"I'm not so sure what you mean by 'settled,' Mr. Mikropoulous," Ernie said cautiously.

"Simply this: both you and Stephen did something you . . . regretted almost immediately. Perhaps if you think it over—"

"Are you trying to make a comparison of what I did and what Steve did?"

"Well, in a sense, Quinn, there is a similarity. You know—" Mikropoulous began.

"That little weasel is an extortionist!" Ernie exploded. "He tried to set this up so that I have to pass him or be in trouble up to my ears! He said he'd have his father get me fired!"

"Oh, come now, Quinn. He's a sixteen-year-old boy," Mikropoulous said impatiently.

"Hitler was a sixteen-year-old boy once, too. So was Genghis Khan."

"Don't be ridiculous."

"I'm being serious. You can't just overlook what Steve did yesterday."

"What I'm trying to say, Quinn," the chairman said with a placating gesture, "is that it might be wiser to overlook . . . everything that happened yesterday."

"Wiser for whom?"

"For all concerned, Quinn. Perhaps you don't realize it, but this is a bad spot for you. You certainly stand to gain the most from a . . . quiet resolution of this whole affair."

"Why?"

"Consider the facts, Quinn."

Those damned facts again, Ernie thought. No one cares about the truth as long as they get the facts straight.

"I think the facts are on my side. He deliberately sought me out and provoked me—"

"You can't prove that, Quinn."

"He gloated about it! After I hit him, he said that that was just what he wanted!"

"And who heard him say that?" Mikropoulous asked, leaning back in his chair and folding his arms.

"I did. Isn't that enough?"

"Perhaps."

"Perhaps? You mean, if it's my word against his, my word isn't good enough?" Ernie asked, unbelieving.

"Your word, Quinn, makes this adolescent boy sound like a . . .

Machiavelli. There's nothing in his background to support this . . . characterization. I can see where your story would leave doubts in a listener's mind."

"Don't you believe me?"

"Now, I didn't say that, Quinn."

"All right, then, you believe me. Would you support me?"

Mikropoulous looked at him warily. "Support you?"

"Well, you're my chairman. You said you wanted to help me. If this thing can't be solved quietly, can I count on your support?"

"Just a minute, now, Quinn," Mikropoulous said, shifting in his chair and looking around the office uncomfortably, like a drunken bit player looking for the prompter, "You don't seem to . . . understand the situation at all. You're heading for trouble. I'm giving you all the support I can."

"You are?" Ernie said, innocent as a lamb. "I couldn't tell."

"I certainly am, Quinn. I'm showing you a way out of this, and if you're sensible, you'll . . . take advantage of it."

"What's the way out?"

Mikropoulous relaxed at these words from Ernie. He leaned forward over the desk, clasped his hands, frowned off into space for a moment, then revealed his solution.

"I'd like to have you and Stephen come to my office this afternoon. We'll talk this whole affair over. If he's willing to apologize—and I'm speaking of a sincere and genuine apology—for anything he may have . . . said to you, will you abandon the notion of suspending or expelling him?"

Ernie thought it over. It sounded good. He didn't like Steve, but if the kid was willing to apologize, he could be big about it. Hell, he thought, anyone can lose his temper.

"That sounds all right to me, Mr. Mikropoulous."

"Good, good," the chairman said, beaming.

"Of course, he still fails English," Ernie added.

All beaming stopped. Dark clouds lowered on the chairman's brow and he looked at Ernie much the same way as Charlemagne must have looked at Ganelon when they heard the first faint notes of Roland's horn.

"Now, Quinn . . ."

"I'm willing to forgive and forget, but I'm not going to give the kid a present, besides."

"I believe we had agreed to discuss Stephen's grade today.

I thought we might go over the matter this afternoon, after . . . clearing the air."

"I must have misunderstood you. I thought you wanted to know my final decision on Steve's grade this morning."

"I'm perfectly willing to give you more time to . . . think things over."

"Thanks. Oh, about next year."

"What about next year?"

"You were going to let me know whether or not I'll be kept on for next year."

"I should be able to tell you this afternoon," Mikropoulous said blandly.

That was enough for Ernie. He had thought, for a few minutes, that he was doing well; had even gotten a bit cocky; but somehow, the advantage had been lost. Things were back to normal. It was Mikropoulous' game, played on his field, by his rules, and Ernie didn't have a chance. He decided to go down fighting.

"Will you let me know before or after I tell you Steve's final grade?" he said.

"I really don't know, Quinn."

"Try to guess."

"I simply haven't made my mind up yet, Quinn."

"Well, I'll help you make up your mind. Steve flunks. He fails. I almost backed down yesterday, but now I know better. If the only way to keep my job here is to grovel—"

"Climb down off your charger, Quinn," Mikropoulous said scornfully.

"Into the dirt with you and the rest of them? No, thank you!" Ernie snapped back, flaunting his white plume proudly. He rose to his feet, ready to deliver a grand and long-suppressed denunciation of Glen Park High School, and all its works, and all its pomps, and all its chairmen. "This is supposed to be such a great school, and one punk kid with a father who can pull a few strings can make you fold up without a peep. You make me want to vomit, you and—"

"Shut up, Quinn! Shut up and get out of my office!" Mikropoulous blurted. He sat fuming for a moment, then started up, waving an excommunicating finger at Ernie. "Who the hell do you think you are, coming into my office and accusing me of . . . of . . ."

"Nepotism," Ernie said helpfully.

"Get out! You're through, Quinn, through at Glen Park and at every other school in this state, if I have anything to say about it. You're nothing but a nasty little troublemaker. You think you can walk in off the streets and—"

"What was that?" The words rang a bell, but Ernie couldn't place them.

"Get out of my office, Quinn. I'll attend to you later."

"Don't bother. I'm resigning. I'll hand Miss Grimm my resignation today."

"Wait a minute, Quinn. You submit your resignation to me."

Ernie could almost hear the sudden grinding of gears as Mikropoulous shifted back to his normal, carefully calculated operating speed. Ernie decided to stay in high.

"Fat chance. I wouldn't trust you with anything that's got my signature on it."

"Listen, Quinn—"

"Don't panic. I won't make waves. You're not worth it," Ernie said, turning and stalking out of the office.

Ernie stopped off in the faculty room for a cigarette and a few moments of emotional flagellation, but when he sprawled in one of the dilapidated chairs, feet straight out, head back, arms dangling, letting all the built-up tension drain out, he found it impossible to think of any way of making himself feel guilty. His family, he knew, would find several, but that wasn't going to come for a while. The job was gone, and there was very little hope of getting another teaching position; but it was all worth while. He felt clean. It had cost him dearly—in a sense—but for the first time in months, he felt that he could look himself in the eye.

At the thought, he decided to try it. He sprang up and walked lightly to the cracked mirror hanging by the window. He grinned at himself and began to laugh. He struck a grandiose pose and said aloud, "I stand, not high it may be—but alone!"

Alone. And unemployed. And unemployable in the profession he was beginning to enjoy. And practically broke. But what a moment!

Europe was out, but there was Doris. He wasn't alone, really. There was Doris, and now she'd have a reason to be proud of him.

He could picture their next meeting as it would be handled by Hollywood: a clear, starry evening with a gentle early-summer breeze stroking the treetops; he would pause with his hand on the gate, and as he stood, hesitating to take the last steps that would bring him to a confrontation with his beloved Doris' disapproving parents (played by Margaret Leighton and, perhaps, Michael Rennie), the front door of the Professor's house would open and Doris, eyes sparkling, hair shining, lips half parted expectantly, breathlessly, would emerge. Their eyes would meet. They would raise their arms slowly. Then, as the background music (Something schmaltzy—"Tara's Theme," or maybe the finale of "Slaughter on Tenth Avenue") swelled, they would run to each other, lock in a long, passionate embrace, and then, all possible complications forgotten, walk arm in arm into a golden future of loving happiness. That's the way it would be done in Hollywood, Ernie knew. Of course, in Hollywood, it could end right there, whereas life had to keep going, and it might not be to a future as golden as Hollywood could suggest. It might very well be to a future of peevish drudgery, replete with smelly diapers, overdue bills, and a general background of sweaty tenement squalor.

That wasn't very pleasant to think about, and as he went ahead and thought about it Ernie felt his exultation draining away, too, leaving plenty of room for the old doubts. He made a few feeble attempts to cajole himself into believing that all would be well, but they failed dismally. They might have had some effect if the surroundings were different, but optimism seemed somehow out of place in the faculty room. It was like seeing a production of *A Midsummer Night's Dream* at a Siberian labor camp. Ernie began to sink into depression.

The calendar hanging slightly askew on the wall caught his eye, and a line from some recent assignment flickered across his consciousness: "What is so rare as a day in June?" If I could get my hands on Lowell, he thought bitterly, *I'd* show him. It was all very well for the calendar to say June, and a Friday, at that; but Ernie's soul was settling into a dreary Monday morning in February, a day of gray skies and dirty snow, stinging hail and slush, and the promise of a long, bitter winter before the first crocus dared to show itself. He started digging in his memory for other lines that might offer a bit of encouragement, but they were not easy to find. They kept getting worse, as a matter of fact. "If winter comes, can spring be far behind?" You bet it can. "April is the cruellest month. . . ." Like hell it is. Then he thought back to Shakespeare, and there it was. The old pro came through with a sonnet Ernie recalled from the other day: "When in disgrace with fortune and men's eyes . . . haply I think of thee." His heart lightened a bit, and things seemed less miserable. He was not exactly singing hymns at Heaven's gate, but at least he no longer felt like young Werther. There was Doris; and there would always be Doris—he would see to that, somehow. The thought sustained him for the next few hours.

"Where's Fred?" Ernie asked as he planted himself, tray and all, beside Aaron in the lunchroom.

"Millard? I don't know. Probably up in Shefin's office being decorated."

"What did he do, write another article?"

"Who knows?" Aaron said with a blasé shrug. "Hey, how are you making out with Mikropoulous about next year? Don't talk with your mouth full."

Ernie hesitated, chewing thoughtfully on a leathery piece of rye bread. He decided to tell Aaron the whole story. Aaron, he felt, would appreciate it.

"I'm not going to be here next year."

"That lousy fat bastard," Aaron said, injecting venom into every syllable. "He kept you waiting until school was nearly over and then he told—"

"He didn't tell me anything. *I* told *him*. I quit."

"You did?" Aaron looked happily surprised. "Good. I'm glad to see you leave this place."

"Thanks, Aaron," Ernie said drily. "You have a way of making a guy feel right at home."

"You know what I mean, Ernie. You didn't like this place from the beginning. I could see it. I was hoping you'd wise up and get out of here before you got stuck."

"Why the hell didn't you say something?"

"I mind my own business. You never asked for my opinion, and I never offer advice."

"Yes. Well, it all worked out, anyway."

"So, come on, tell me about it," Aaron said, reaching for his coffee cup.

"What really happened was that I just got teed off and quit cold. Mikropoulous kept fooling around and putting me off. He never came out and said so, but he was just waiting for me to agree to pass one kid before he'd commit himself. That's really what did it."

Aaron, in mid-sip, raised an eyebrow in curiosity.

"Steve Hirsch. He's in my—"

Aaron exploded into spluttering, coughing, choking barks that finally turned to laughter. He mopped the spilled coffee off his suit and turned to Ernie, still flushed and watery-eyed.

"Never mention that kid's name to me when I'm drinking coffee! Steve Hirsch in one of your classes!" He shook his head in helpless amazement. "You should have told me. *Then* I would have given you advice even if you didn't ask for it."

"You mean this kid is known around here?"

"Steve Hirsch is the boy who never fails. His old man is on the Board of Education, so he's sacred. They always give him to one of the new teachers or the sweet old ladies. That way, he passes."

"I'm failing him this term."

Aaron shrugged. "Good luck. I bet the mark is changed before September."

"They can't do that, can they?"

"They can do anything, Ernie."

"I'll go to Shefin and tell him the whole story," Ernie said boldly.

"Where do you think Mikropoulous gets his orders? Shefin isn't going to stand up against Hirsch's old man, Ernie. Shefin wants to be a supervisor someday, and he's not taking any chances with his future."

"But this is just so damned *wrong!*" Ernie said, his frustration growing. "Doesn't anybody care?"

"Why should any of these people care?" Aaron asked, gesturing toward the occupants of the lunchroom. "It's not happening to them, it's happening to you. It's your problem. It never *could* happen to them."

"You think that everybody else in this school would just pass the kid and let it go at that."

"Sure. So would I, I guess, if it ever came to that."

"But why? What's everyone so scared of?" Ernie demanded.

"Hunger. You can go out and start in a new line, Ernie. You're young, and you're single. The rest of us here have to think about our profession. The people here can fix us good if we cross them."

"All right, look—suppose I wrote a letter to the Board, or did something like that. What could they do then?"

"They'd think of something. They might get Mikropoulous or a few others around here to say you were discriminating against the kid, or you're incompetent, or even crazy. It's been done."

"I sure as hell wouldn't sit still while *that* went on. I'd fight back. If they got people to lie about me, I'd get people to tell how they were pressured to pass Steve."

"Nobody else *had* to be pressured, Ernie. They all played along. Besides, who do you think would stick his neck out for you? They won't even join a union. It's too unprofessional."

"But they wouldn't be doing it for me, Aaron. It's a question of principle."

"Oh, come on, Ernie, this isn't an Episcopal prep school, it's Glen Park High. The greatest school in America. Ask Shefin, or Grimm, or Mikropoulous; ask anyone. Everybody here is on the make. They don't care about anybody but themselves."

"You don't think anyone would back me up, then, even though they know I'm getting the shaft?"

"Nobody who can do anything," Aaron said, shaking his head. "You could probably get that nut from the Social Studies Department, the one who's always making speeches in the faculty room —what's his name?"

"Do you mean Bob Ferriss?"

"Ferriss, that's the one. Where is he, anyway? It's been quiet around here."

"He's been out with laryngitis. It's pretty bad."

"Couldn't happen to a nicer guy. Well, when he comes back, you could probably get him to help you out, but that would only get him fired, too."

"That's a hell of a thing you're saying, Aaron," Ernie said, maneuvering his fork around in the rapidly cooling mashed potatoes. "If this is all it comes to, why did I bother to go to college? I should have gone to obedience school, like a puppy.

Then all Mikropoulous would have to do would be shout 'Heel!' and snap his fingers."

"Don't be bitter," Aaron said. Then, after a thoughtful pause, he corrected himself. "No, go ahead, be bitter. There's not much else you can do."

"I can quit. But it's a hell of a thing."

"It's true. Maybe they never mentioned it at teachers' college, but it's true," Aaron said, rising slowly from his chair. "You go ahead and eat that stuff before it gets cold. I'm going in for more coffee."

"Okay."

"Want anything?"

Ernie shook his head, and Aaron trudged off. As he disappeared into the doorway leading to the food counter, Fred Millard walked into the room, looked around, and headed for Ernie's table.

"Well, what have *you* been up to?" he asked as he laid his book down. "I was just talking to Mikropoulous, and he's livid."

"Difference of opinion," Ernie explained, after a heroic swallow. "Mikropoulous wants me to pass a kid and I don't think the kid should pass."

"Who is this kid?"

"Steve Hirsch. Do you know him?"

Fred nodded. "He's the boy who always passes. Like urine."

"Everybody around here knows that but me," Ernie said, peevishly.

"Cheer up. Mikropoulous will cool off by this afternoon. Go in and tell him you've reconsidered and everything will be forgotten."

Fred set off for the food counters, leaving Ernie alone once again, and thoughtful—as thoughtful as he could be in a noisy, crowded lunchroom where half-intelligible fragments of reminiscence and complaint floated on every smoky gust of air. Fred had an answer, and it seemed to be the right answer; for Fred, anyway. He had his trips to Europe, his new car, his nice apartment, and no apparent problems except an occasional twinge, which quickly passed. Maybe it *was* the right answer, but it was a hard one to accept. It's their game all the way, Fred seemed to think, so play it their way. You may never win, but you'll never lose, and that's something. Ernie weighed this, and found it wanting. He had gotten around to thinking about Don Quixote and the windmills when Fred and Aaron returned together.

"Aaron tells me you're resigning," Millard said.

"That's right. I didn't get a chance—"

"Don't be a damned fool, Ernie."

"Leave him alone, will you?" Aaron broke in wearily. "Let him do what he wants. You might have done the same thing fifteen years ago, Millard."

"I doubt it," Millard said coolly.

"Why am I such a damned fool to refuse to do something I know is wrong, Fred?"

"Martyrdom is out of fashion. You've got a job in a good school. Why not keep it?"

"There are other good schools, plenty of them."

"Do you think they're any different? For that matter, do you think anyplace will be different? This isn't a problem in education, Ernie, it's a problem in life. You have to learn when to give a little. You have to get along in the world."

"That may be true, but this is a matter of principle."

"Don't be dreary. Talk to him, will you, Aaron?"

"I don't know," Aaron said thoughtfully. "I think he's right. Crazy, maybe, but right."

"You would," Millard murmured. "You're as bad as he is."

"I've got a wife and kids, Millard. I can't afford to be as bad as he is. I have to be as good as you are."

"There's no need to be sarcastic. There are some things you can't fight. We know that, and Ernie doesn't. Don't try to make me the heavy just because I face up to the facts."

"Has anybody ever tried to fight this kind of thing?" Ernie asked.

"There have been a few. They didn't last long, either."

"No, they all quit," Aaron said, "and now they're making more in a year than we'll make in our whole lives."

"Maybe they are, Aaron, but I really don't give a damn," Fred said airily. "I'm comfortable enough right here. This is still a free country, you know. If anyone doesn't like what's going on at Glen Park High School, he's free to leave. I've found a home."

"Doesn't this bother you at all, Fred?" Ernie asked.

"Of course it *bothers* me. The hydrogen bomb *bothers* me, too, and Red China, and the Ku Klux Klan. They all *bother* me, but what the hell do you expect me to do, start a crusade? I can't change the world, and I know it. You can't change the world, either, but you don't know it yet. You'll learn."

"But a man has to do something," Ernie insisted. "We're all involved, just by being here."

"Not me, friend," Fred said, shaking his head. "I am totally uninvolved. Disengaged. Like a clutch. I coast along in neutral. I'll never overheat my engine."

"Yeah, but you can only coast downhill," Aaron pointed out helpfully.

Fred smiled. "So be it. You can call me a bastard, if you like—"

"Can I?" Aaron said. "Okay, you're a bastard."

"—but I really don't care. I thought you had more sense, Ernie. And Aaron, I *know* you have more sense, but you're not using it. You shouldn't encourage Ernie, you should try to straighten him out."

"Watch out, Millard. You sound as though you're getting involved," Aaron warned.

"No fear of that. I just hate to see a nice guy beat his brains out for no reason at all."

"Look, do you mind not talking about me as if I had two weeks to live?" Ernie asked irritably. "It's my life. I made my mind up."

"Fine," Fred said. "Now let's finish our lunch, shall we?"

When the bell rang to end the eighth period, Ernie headed straight for Miss Grimm's office. In his pocket was a rough penciled draft of his letter of resignation, carefully trimmed down to three cold, impersonal sentences, the product of his labors during the seventh period. In the faculty room, where Ernie had spent his free period drafting the letter, the wastebasket was filled almost to overflowing with discarded remnants of his earlier attempts, most of which resembled fiery nineteenth-century student manifestoes, seasoned with a generous sprinkling of Swift and a dash of Leon Bloy, and all of which gave promise of building up, through four pages of closely printed single-spaced type, to a conclusion worthy of Thomas Paine. After some deep thought and too many cigarettes, Ernie had settled for something less inflammatory and more traditional: "*Dear Miss Grimm: Please accept my resigna-*

tion from the faculty of Glen Park High School effective as of the end of the current semester. Circumstances have arisen which make it impossible for me to continue as a teacher in this school." He was particularly pleased with the concluding sentence, a construction which he considered a masterpiece of ingenious ambiguity: "*I shall always remember my year at Glen Park High School and the constant attention and interest you showed in my difficult first year of teaching.*" He could picture Miss Grimm reading it and looking around with her eyes narrowed and her tiny, suspicious mind churning, as she muttered to herself, "Now, what exactly does he mean by *that?*" The odds were that she would file it away and forget it immediately, but Ernie found it pleasant to imagine that he might cause her a few uneasy moments. It was small enough payment for the uneasy moments she had caused him since last September.

He entered her office, passed by the benches now packed with surly students awaiting their turn on the carpet, and stopped at Lynn's desk.

"Hello, Ernie," she said, unexpectedly bright and friendly. "What can I do for you?"

"I'd like to borrow some letterhead stationery and a typewriter. I have to write a letter to Miss Grimm."

"Complaining about the help?" she asked, smiling.

"Resigning."

"Resigning? Oh, Ernie," she said, looking up suddenly. She rose from her desk and opened the gate. "Come on in here. We don't want the students to hear everything."

They walked to an empty desk at the far corner of the room, by a window. There was a typewriter table near the desk, and Lynn pointed to it as she sat down. Ernie pushed it to the desk.

"That should satisfy the onlookers," Lynn said. "Now, what's this about resigning?"

"That's it, I'm just resigning. That's all, Lynn."

"Come on, Ernie. Is it Mikropoulous?"

"Partly. It's a lot of things, Lynn."

"I could tell you were upset the other day in the lunchroom, but I didn't think it was this serious. You really mean it, don't you?"

"I really mean it, Lynn," Ernie said, nodding. "I've had it

up to here," he added, tracing an emotional Plimsoll line across his Adam's apple.

"Well, you know what you're doing," Lynn said. "I'll type it for you, if you like."

"Would you? I'm a pretty sloppy typist. It's only a short letter, really," he assured her, digging out the rough copy and handing it to her.

She read it over slowly, speaking the words under her breath and nodding approval until she came to the last sentence. Her nose crinkled slightly in disapproval. It looked cute, but Doris could do the same thing, and cuter. Lynn was an awfully pretty girl, but she just wasn't Doris.

"That last sentence . . ." she began dubiously.

"What's wrong with it?"

"I don't know. It's just . . . well, you can take it two ways."

"Good! Fine! That's what I wanted," Ernie said, grinning happily.

"It is? All right," Lynn said, shrugging her shoulders, "that's how I'll type it."

She began to patter away at the typewriter, and in less than a minute handed Ernie a neatly typed letter that would have cost him an hour's work and indescribable frustration to have done by himself. He read it over, signed it, and tucked it into the envelope she provided.

"What now?" he asked.

"Well, she's pretty busy. If you like, I can ask—"

"If it's all right, I'd just as soon leave it here. If she wants to talk to me about it, she can let me know."

"I guess you can do that. I really don't know what the procedure is. Nobody else ever resigned."

Ernie gave a little unhappy laugh. "Another first for Ernie Quinn."

"Why don't you let me take it, Ernie? I'm leaving soon, and I always bring in the last-minute papers before I go. I can put this with them, and leave it on her desk."

"That's good. She won't get to it until we're both gone."

"Right. Ernie?"

"Yes?"

"I have to catch a train at four; that gives me about an hour. Why don't you ask me out for a drink and unburden yourself?"

"Well, actually, Lynn . . ." Ernie said uncomfortably.

"Just a friendly drink."

"You know, that's the first time anyone in this place ever used the word 'friendly' to me. Okay, Lynn, I'll wait for you by the time clock."

"I'll be there in five minutes."

Ernie made his exit, strolling with as much unconcern as he could simulate between twelve pairs of scandal-seeking teen-age eyes. He could imagine the gaudy tales about Miss Rogers and Mister Quinn that would be circulating through the Glen Park High School underground on Monday morning. There was a bright side to it, though: maybe some of the rumors would get to Mrs. Ramsay and scare her off. It would make his last few days a bit more peaceful, anyway.

Habit is habit; and although there was no longer much point to it, Ernie went through his letter box while he waited for Lynn to arrive. Among the debris was one pleasant surprise, the long-promised Spring-Summer edition of *Windswept*.

At first glance, there was nothing to distinguish *Windswept* from a thousand other high school literary magazines. It had the traditional abstract linoleum-block print on the cover; the same slick paper that left the reader's fingers feeling gluey, and smudged at the slightest touch; the same humorous articles, recondite, elephantine, and derivative; and the same intense, breathless, fragmentary poetry of personal revelation. But this issue was, Ernie hoped, different.

He opened *Windswept* to the table of contents, scanned it quickly, and gave a little triumphant snort of laughter at the sight of " 'Nepenthe,' by Lydia Lark Flingstock . . . page 14." He shut the magazine hurriedly and thrust it into his bag. He had struck a blow, and it had landed. It was not a very hard blow, true, but it was something. He was one up on *Windswept*, Mikropoulous, and the English Department, at least for the time being.

Lydia Lark Flingstock, along with a whole gallery of literary ladies whose work would never appear in *Windswept* or anywhere else, was Ernie's own creation. The back pages of one of his notebooks contained a series of brief biographies of these imaginary women authors, composed during a semester of numbing lectures on adolescent psychology at the university. The course had been totally unrewarding in any instructional sense, but Ernie's little covey of Galateas had afforded him endless diversion. There was Edna St. Vincent Molloy, the washerwoman poetess, to whom the muse had come one day when Edna was elbow-deep in dirty underwear and soap suds. There were Leda Swann and Deirdre Linnen, guiding spirits of the Irish literary revival, whose chanting, hypnotic fabric of myth and mysticism had given rise to a whole new school of native poetry, or "Erse Verse" (The foppish London critic who, in a slashing review, had named it "Arsy-versy," had been caned in Leicester Square by the young William Butler Yeats). There was the brilliant Keats scholar, Eva St. Agnes, the first woman to be honored as PMLA's "PMLA-mate of the month." There was chic, waspish Sibyl Lear, whose weekly column on the world of letters, "Assent with Sibyl Lear," was as fearsome to the pretentious as were the finely honed characterizations in her novels. There were Flatulanta Calydon, whose ethereal beauty belied the rich eroticism of her voluptuous rhythms; Sepulchra Cartouche, whose novels *Abyss*, *Void*, *Futility*, and *Zero* had become Bibles of existential thought; Rhoda Montade, authoress of a score of lurid swashbucklers; Morgan LeVey, loved by millions for her heartwarming book, *The Magic of Jewish Cooking*; and there was Caprolalia Pornhawker, who had given the literary world three fat novels delineating the sexual underground of a small Midwestern college town. These were Ernie's girls, and he loved them all.

Lydia Lark Flingstock was the most wistful of Ernie's creations, a spinsterish, petite creature who lived in seclusion in Nantucket, where she had retired after a tragic love affair with a handsome, callous young broker from North Adams. "Nepenthe," Ernie had decided, was one of Lydia's early efforts. Ernie had written it in its entirety during a lecture on role-playing, and then forgotten it until he began receiving notices from the desperate editorial staff of *Windswept*, beseeching him to extort submissions from his more literate students. He had managed to drum up a poem, two short stories, and a pen-and-ink portrait of Shakespeare that resembled the picture of Dorian Gray in its terminal phase; as he tucked them into an envelope, he thought of "Nepenthe." Lydia would have written it, he guessed, when she was about fifteen or sixteen, the age of most of his students. Why not give the kid a chance? The furtive joy of literary hoaxing was too much to resist. It was awfully small-scale literary hoaxing, to be sure, but the thought of Mikropoulous' seeing the poem in *Windswept* and demanding peevishly "Who is this girl? Why isn't she in my Young Writers' Club? Who's her teacher, anyway?" made it worth the effort. The sight of Lydia's name in the pages of *Windswept*, coming as it did on this particular day, was suggestive to him. He was through, but he had left someone behind him to torment and harass his persecutors. He knew perfectly well that "Nepenthe" might go unnoticed and Lydia Lark Flingstock might be a stillborn brainchild, but the thought of her as a kind of delayed-action Fury circling around Mikropoulous' enormous head was a comfort to him, and he needed comfort badly.

"Ernie, that's awful," Lynn said when he had finished his account of the Hirsch–Quinn–Mikropoulous affair.

"I'm glad somebody thinks so. Everybody else I've mentioned it to in this school just shrugs his shoulders and says 'That's life, kid. Too bad.' I never realized what a naïve character I really am."

"You don't want to be like *them*, though, do you?"

"Not at all. Would you like another drink?"

"No thanks. I have a four-hour train ride ahead of me, and I don't want to pass out halfway through it. You go ahead, if you feel like another."

"Okay. You're sure, now, Lynn? You really don't want another?"

"I'm sure."

Ernie returned a few minutes later with a double martini, brimful and ice-cold, clutched fondly in his hand. "This bartender makes a great martini," he said, after an approving sip.

"You've got guts. That's a double."

"What the hell. It's not every day I quit a job. Although, to hear my family talk, you'd think it was." He took a generous drink and said ruefully, "They'll really have a great time with this."

"If you want to change your mind, I can still go back—"

"No. It's done, Lynn. Let it be."

"What will you do now?"

"I don't know. Be a book bum, maybe. Pack up a satchel full of books, stow away on a tramp steamer. You know."

"What about your girl?"

"How did you find out about Doris?" Ernie said in amazement, putting down his glass.

"I didn't know her name, but I could tell you had a girl," Lynn said, smiling wisely. "You looked so guilty when I asked you to take me for a drink."

"Well, I did feel sort of . . . a little unfaithful. I was going to ask Doris to marry me this summer."

"You can still do that."

"There's a strange tribal custom among the American middle classes, Lynn. They believe that a man should be able to support a woman if he marries her. Personally, I'm against it, but the elders of the tribe enforce it pretty strictly."

"You still love her, don't you?"

"Very much."

"And does she know how you feel? Have you told her?"

"Well, you see, Lynn, I've been waiting until—"

"Oh, Ernie, you're hopeless!" Lynn said chidingly.

"What am I supposed to do? I was never sure of this job, you know, and I couldn't—"

"Is the job all that's stopping you?"

"I guess so," Ernie said carefully. Lynn was certainly pushy, and in totally unexpected directions. "Yes, it's the job."

"Well, stop worrying and ask her to marry you. A good teacher can always get a job."

"What about a teacher who can't give references? I certainly can't give Mikropoulous for a reference, not now, and who else—"

"Miss Grimm," Lynn said casually.

"Oh, come on, Lynn. That's not even funny."

"I'm serious, Ernie. She said something yesterday about your being a very promising young man."

"That was yesterday. Wait until she talks to Mikropoulous."

"Ernie, she can't *stand* Mikropoulous. I really think she'd give you a glowing recommendation just to spite him. And she doesn't like Steve Hirsch or his father very much, either. They tried to give her a lot of trouble last year."

"I never knew that."

"She doesn't go around telling people. She never told me—

not about the Hirsch business. I came across the correspondence one day. He wrote her some pretty nasty letters."

"How come she's still here? I thought Hirsch had everybody in the school system under his thumb."

"Not Miss Grimm. She's got friends in high places, too."

"Oh?" Ernie took a long swallow of his drink and reached for a cigarette. He extended the pack to Lynn, but she shook her head and began to rummage through her bag.

"Thanks, but I'll smoke one of mine. Filters. I'm a coward."

"But you don't inhale, do you?"

"I'm just playing it safe."

"Okay, now," Ernie said as he lit their cigarettes. "What about Grimm's friends?"

"She's got a younger sister. Fiftyish, very chic—a real Westchester matron type. She used to be an opera singer."

"Grimm's sister? !"

"Right. Well, anyway, she married this lawyer, and he went into politics, and now he's a state senator, or something like that. Whatever he is, he can introduce laws. No, *bills*. Before they're laws, they're bills, aren't they?"

Ernie shrugged. "I guess so."

"It doesn't really matter. Anyway, he's introduced a few bills on education, and Grimm helped him to get his information together. So if she wants a favor . . ."

"I get it. Ye gods, what a tangled web! And I used to think teaching was an ivory tower type job."

"You're learning fast."

"Not so fast, really. It took a whole year." Ernie paused, trying to think of something clever, or at least not insipid. "But I learned it's not ivory."

Lynn looked puzzled. "What's not ivory?"

"The tower. It looks like ivory, but it's actually a highly inflammable plastic that can go up in flames in a second. And I've been running around waving a blowtorch since last September."

"Now you know."

"Now I know," Ernie agreed. He liked the idea of the plastic tower. It would make a good setting for a C21 bit. Maybe the headquarters of MERDE could be moved. . . .

"Ernie, it's almost quarter to four!" Lynn cried suddenly.

"If I miss this train I'll have to catch a 5:10 full of leering commuters!"

"We can grab a taxi outside," Ernie said, rising and groping through his pockets.

"That's all right. You don't have to take me to the station."

"It's practically on my way home, Lynn. Come on, let's run."

On his way home from the station, Ernie had time to think. Luckily, he always thought better in taxicabs. There was no back-talk.

He wanted to think about Lynn. He had been wrong about her. And he had been wrong about Grimm, too, in a way. But they would have to wait their turn. The big problem right now was how to tell the family about his resignation. It was going to be unpleasant, no matter how he handled it; that was definite. A year ago, when he had left the bank, it had been bad, and then he at least had another job waiting. This time was going to be a lot worse, unless he figured out a good approach.

He could try indignation, sweeping into the house, flinging his bookbag into a corner, and shouting angrily and incoherently about dirty deals, treachery, and a man's honor. His father had done that a few times—not lately, though—and gotten a lot of sympathy and understanding. But his father hadn't quit his job. His father had put in thirty-seven years with the Civil Service, all of them in the same office. Ye gods, Ernie thought, no wonder he never says a word. If he opened his mouth, he'd scream.

Maybe a different kind of indignation, a slightly modified version, a kind of "call of Destiny" approach, would be better. Ernie thought about that for a while, and it seemed sound. He could walk into the kitchen, very solemn and serious, and say some profound things about how he wasn't getting any younger, and how a man has to find his place in life, and there's a right job for every man if he only has the determination to seek it out. But that was a little too close to what he had said when he quit the bank.

Of course, he could lie. But they'd find out. Somehow, they always found out, and then it was worse. Just *how* they found out was a secret that eluded him, but they always did. Even when he was a kid. He remembered the business of the dimes and the collection. His mother had always given him two dimes for the collection on Sunday, and when he hit the fourth grade he started taking a cut. He would get change, and put nickels in the collection basket, clearing a dime for himself every Sunday. Then one day his mother gave him marked dimes and searched his pockets after Mass. His head rang for a week. No, lying wouldn't do.

Perhaps, for a change, he could be gay and devil-may-care. He tried to picture himself strolling into the kitchen, coat slung carelessly over one shoulder in the Sinatra manner, whistling something catchy and smiling a distant, knowing smile. In the midst of a lively debate about the tactics of the new district leader, he would say casually, "By the way, I thought you might like to know that your boy is no longer a member of the teaching profession. Don't worry, I've got a few irons in the fire," he would assure them, covering a yawn. "I thought I'd take a few weeks off to consider some of the offers I've been getting."

The more he thought of that, the less he liked it. It always worked in the movies, but his family didn't react to things the way movie families did. It would never work for him.

He had reached the point where he was seriously considering a frank, honest statement of the facts when the taxi turned down his block. He looked out and saw a sight he dreaded. His grandfather was seated on the front steps, belligerently scanning the street for foreigners, known Republicans, and other undesirables, and one look at the set of the old man's jaw told Ernie that all his resentments were primed and ready to go at the least provocation, such as the sight of his grandson riding in a taxi. Grandfather had a fixation about young men who thought themselves too good to use the public transportation facilities so readily available to all and instead squandered their money by endless joyriding in taxicabs. Grandfather was incapable of believing that a man could choose to ride in a taxicab for sober, legitimate reasons; he gave Ernie the distinct impression that if some grisly accident should befall him, he would prefer to stand on a street corner, his life's blood gushing out in a torrent of gore, for forty-five minutes, rather than fling his savings away on a taxicab ride to the hospital.

The taxi stopped in front of the steps. Ernie saw his grandfather tense, suddenly alert, like a dozing cat who has heard a strange noise.

"Here you are, buddy," the driver said.

"Okay. Here," Ernie said, thrusting the fare and an absurdly inflated tip into the driver's hand. Grandfather, after a single glance at the occupant of the taxi, was up and moving, heading into the house like an unhorsed Paul Revere.

"Thanks a lot," the cab driver said; then, as Ernie flung himself out the door, missed his footing, and nearly went sprawling, he shouted, "Hey, you all right?"

"Yeah, I'm fine. I just misjudged the curb," Ernie said, watching his grandfather turn and disappear into the house. He had seen Ernie come reeling out of the cab, of course. He couldn't have missed that. Oh, hell, Ernie thought.

"You sure, now? I don't want you breaking your neck coming out of my cab."

"I'm sure. Don't worry, I'm fine."

"Okay. Take it easy, now, buddy."

"Yeah," Ernie said dully, and turned to trudge in to a squalid confrontation scene.

Grandfather's voice was keening through the house like a high-speed drill. It went up a full octave when Ernie walked into the kitchen.

"Look at himself," Grandfather hooted, joyously outraged, "falling out of a dirty lousy taxicab at four o'clock in the afternoon! Reeking with booze, that's what he is! Look at him, smirking away like a dirty duke! Smell his breath, Mary, go on, smell it," he ordered, plucking eagerly at his daughter-in-law's elbow, "it'll knock you down, it will!" He darted forward, shook his finger at Ernie, and skipped back to resume his elbow-plucking. "You should have seen him, Mary. It would have broken your heart. You would have died of shame right in front of the house, to see your own son come flopping out of a taxicab and roll around in the gutter like a dirty drunken bum!" He glared at Ernie and delivered the traditional interdict. "You're no Quinn!"

"All right, I'm no Quinn!" Ernie said desperately. "I'm a Mao Tse-tung. Are you happy, now?"

"Listen to that! Did you hear that, Mary, did you hear the way he came back at his own grandfather?" the old man howled, almost levitating in the sheer ecstasy of peevish righteousness.

"Have some respect, lad," Ernie's mother sighed.

"But he's wrong, Mom! In the first place, it's not four o'clock, it's ten to five—"

"It's a quarter to five," Grandfather snapped, pouncing on the error. "Do you hear that, Mary? He's so drunk he doesn't remember that the clock is fast. Oh, you can't fool me, lad."

"All right, it's a quarter to five," Ernie admitted. "Big deal. Is there a law against riding in cabs before five o'clock? And why are all the clocks around here five minutes fast, anyway?" he riposted.

"So we can tell when you come home drunk, that's why!" Grandfather said triumphantly.

Ask a stupid question, Ernie thought, and Grandfather always had the right answer.

"Well, it's not four o'clock, and I'm not drunk, and I didn't fall out of the taxi, so what's all the fuss about?" Ernie said, trying to appear calm and slightly miffed by the pettiness of it all.

"That's it, lie to your mother and your old grandfather. Do you hear the lies, Mary?"

"Why don't you go in and turn the television on, Dad? You don't want to miss your program, and it's nearly time," Mrs. Quinn said placatingly. "It comes on at five, and you want to get the set all warmed up and fixed before it comes on. I'll talk to Ernie."

"Hah! Thought you'd make me miss my program, didn't you, lad? Well, you're not so smart. Hah!" Grandfather made his exit, muttering and ejaculating to himself.

"What's it all about, lad?" Ernie's mother asked, after a cautious pause.

Ernie shrugged. "I saw someone off at the station after school, so I took the cab the rest of the way home, and I tripped when I got out. I didn't fall down or anything, Mom, I just misjudged the curb. It was really the driver's fault."

"Were you drinking, lad?"

"I had a drink before we left for the train. I don't *look* drunk, do I?"

"It's not good, drinking in the afternoons. That's the way you start. Have a cup of tea."

"Okay," Ernie said. He was willing to let it drop.

"And when you're finished, go in and sit with your grandfather for a few minutes. It'll quiet him down, and do you no harm. He's an old man, Ernie. It's not good to get him excited."

"The excitement was all his idea."

"All right, just go in and sit with him for a while. Bring him a cup of tea. It won't hurt you, and it makes him happy."

"Okay, I'll go in as soon as I finish," Ernie said, glad to accept the compromise at this stage.

"And don't just stick your nose in the room and then run off to your schoolbooks. You never spend any time with the family any more. That gets the old man upset, too, you know. It's Friday, so you shouldn't have to stay up all night with your books and your papers and your other paraphernalia."

"I'm going to a party tonight. Doris' father is throwing a party and he asked me to come."

"It's the father invites you to parties now, is it? You'd do well to watch your step. They'll have you married before you know what happened."

"They're not like that, Mom."

"Oh, don't listen to your mother," Mrs. Quinn said in fine martyred tones. "We sent you to college, so now you know everything, and we can't even give you a little good advice. Ah, that's the way it is today. Here, drink your tea. At least you'll be sober for the professor and his daughter."

Ernie accepted the tea in silence. His mother's last remark had established the fact that regardless of all evidence he could offer, including sworn statements from the cab driver and twelve neighbors, this would go down in the unwritten annals of Clan Quinn as "The Day Ernie Came Home Roaring Drunk at Four O'Clock in the Afternoon and Fell Out of the Taxi." It was going to be touch and go all weekend, with a beginning like this. The thought of broaching the subject of his departure from Glen Park High School reared its nasty little head, and was hurriedly stuffed into one of the cluttered bottom drawers of his mind. Maybe next week would be better. Hell, he thought, *any* time will be better than this afternoon.

On top of everything else, the tea was too strong.

The commerical was just coming on as Ernie entered the living room. He watched in fascinated horror as a swarm of shrieking toddlers worked themselves into a manic state over some sticky, offensive new candy bar, yapping its short, catchy, repellent name at every opportunity. His grandfather turned and looked suspiciously at him.

"What is it, lad?"

"I brought you a cup of tea."

"Good. Put it right here on the table."

"Okay. Look, I didn't mean—"

"Shh! The program's coming back on now. This is the good part, with the bears," Grandfather said, abandoning Ernie and fixing his eyes on the tiny screen.

Ernie settled on the couch and tried to work up interest in his grandfather's daily passion, the Kiddie Kartoon Klub. They were old cartoons, and they weren't very good even when they were new, but to his grandfather, they were The Garden of Delights. Ernie looked at him, leaning forward in his chair and gumming away in innocent merriment at the antics of Bumpy Bear, and he suddenly felt an awful surge of sympathy for the old man.

Grandfather was eighty-two years old, seventeen years retired, and his only interests in life were Bumpy Bear, the I.R.A. (to which he had never belonged), and the devoted nursing of a universal grudge. He had no hobbies and no friends. He spent his time sitting on his bony old behind, stirring up resentments and grievances like eyes of newt and toes of frog in a bubbling cauldron, sprinkling the scalding brew that resulted on anyone who crossed his path. It was simply Ernie's misfortune to cross his path more often than anyone else; there was nothing personal in Grandfather's jeremiads.

Ernie tried to understand, but Grandfather took a hell of a lot of understanding. Ernie tried to make himself feel how it would be to know that you were the very last one left; to realize, whenever you heard an old friend's name, that the last time you saw it, it was cut into a headstone; to open your eyes every morning not to the thought of a new day but to the consolation of one more night safely and irretrievably set down in the record book. He began to feel as sorry for himself, prospectively, as he did for Grandfather, until he thought of Doris. That perked him up.

When he was eighty-two, Doris would be seventy-eight. Doris at seventy-eight might not be much, but she'd still be a big improvement over Bumpy Bear and a cup of tea. He realized, with a start, that he was beginning to think along the lines of a Donne sermon. There was no time to think about the implications of this, though, because Grandfather began to talk.

"So you're spending a little time with your own family now, are you?" Grandfather snapped as Bumpy Bear gave way to a shrill commercial.

"I just thought I'd come in and sit here for a while."

"Precious little while it will be, too. You're always off somewheres."

"Come on, now—I bet you didn't sit around the house when you were my age," Ernie said, trying to be mildly jovial.

Grandfather mulled over that for a few seconds, then came up with a cool, logical observation. "I didn't spend my time running around with the daughter of some atheist professor!"

"He's no atheist," Ernie said patiently.

"They're all atheists!" Grandfather said, his eyes ablaze.

Ernie shrugged his shoulders, rose off the couch, and stretched. "All right, have it your way." He knew what would come if he stayed any longer, and he didn't want it. He made one last conciliatory gesture. "Can I get you anything?"

"Bring my cup out with you," Grandfather said, thrusting the empty cup at him. "It'll do you good to do some work around here."

"Right. Keep smiling, sport," Ernie said, and moved out fast.

Ernie arrived at the Fleckers' house just before nine. Voices could be heard through the open windows, and a piano somewhere in the background, but the party seemed to be still in its early and more controlled stages. Mrs. Flecker opened the door, looking like an academic Auntie Mame; she was flourishing a half empty cocktail glass with just the right combination of caution and gay abandon.

"Ernest!" she said warmly, presenting her cheek for his quick social kiss, "it's so good to see you. I *must* tell Doris you're here. She's been running to the door every two minutes to—*there* she is!" She flung up an arm and waved it vigorously, still, miraculously, not spilling a drop. "Doris! Doris, dear!"

Doris appeared at the end of the hall, smiled brightly, and hurried to them.

"Hi!"

"Hi, Doris. I just—"

"You must excuse me, my dears. I have to see about the canapés," Mrs. Flecker said, swooping off.

"Doris, you look great," Ernie said. "I like your hair that way."

"And the dress?" Doris asked, turning around slowly.

"Terrific. And just the right color."

"I remembered what you said about blue. I had to try three shops before I got this kind of dress in blue," she said, smiling.

"It was worth it. You look absolutely great. You'd look great to me in a gunny sack and Army shoes. But I guess you'd feel a lot better in a new dress."

"Well, considering the occasion . . ." she said solemnly, then laughed.

Ernie smiled down at her, proud and possessive, and took her hands in his.

"Doris, can we go someplace and talk for a few minutes?" he asked. He wasn't exactly sure what he wanted to say, but he felt it might be wise to break the news about Glen Park before Doris started introducing him to people under false colors.

"The whole house is overflowing with people, Ernie. Is it really private and personal?"

"Well, it's not something I want to announce in public. I quit Glen Park High School today, effective as of the end of the semester."

"Oh, Ernie! Did you really have to? I was hoping . . . Oh, I thought things might not turn out to be so bad. . . ."

"It was that or be fired. It seems that things were a lot worse than I thought yesterday. More complicated, and worse. Now I feel kind of funny being here."

"Why should you feel funny? We want you here, Ernie."

"But doesn't it look a little odd? Here's your father, just promoted to chairman, and here's a clown who can't even last a year as a teacher, going out with his daughter. I don't know what I'm going to do, Doris. It's going to be tough getting another job now."

"You'll get something, Ernie. I know you will."

"But what about tonight? If I start talking to people and they ask me about my work—"

"You can tell them you're leaving Glen Park. It's none of their business why."

Ernie looked at her, thoughtfully. "You're right. Sometimes you're so sensible it's terrifying. Go on, terrify me some more."

"If anybody asks you what you do, you can just tell them you teach at Glen Park High School. You still *do*, so that's honest. And I bet everybody you meet will be so busy telling you all about themselves that they won't ask you *anything*."

"Doris, you're great. You're absolutely great," Ernie said, drawing her close. They parted quickly at the sound of footsteps; it was Mrs. Flecker.

"I hate to sound like the harassed hostess, dear, but could you help me to get the younger people to *do* something? Ernest, you could probably save the day, if you'd help her," she went on, distracted but poised. "All the young people are standing around drinking like mad, and half of them will be absolutely *stinking* by eleven o'clock if we can't get them singing, or dancing, or *something*."

"All right, Mother. Can you handle the Professor's friends?"

"Oh, they're no problem. *They* won't be stinking until one o'clock, and then we can start easing them out. It's the young people I'm worried about."

"We'll fix it. Come on, Ernie, let's get to work," Doris said.

"Oh—and Doris: watch out for Professor Northrup. He has that gleam in his eye."

"Don't worry. I brought my hatpin," Ernie assured her.

"You're darling, both of you," Mrs. Flecker said, with a cheerful wave of farewell.

"Ernie, will you stay after the others go?" Doris asked as they made their way into the house.

"Did you think I was going to leave? Come on."

Most of the student contingent was located in the family room. As Ernie and Doris entered from the hall, Ernie glanced over at the piano, where a young man was seated, playing something harmless and social, the sort of tune that was probably being played at that very moment in cocktail lounges all across America from Lexington Avenue to Market Street, and being heard by no one. He looked up and nodded to Ernie, and Ernie raised a hand in greeting, surprised that the fellow had remembered him from the two or three parties they had attended in common. This fellow—Garrett was his name, but whether it was Garrett Something or Something Garrett Ernie had never bothered to determine—had always been at the piano, while Ernie had always been prowling around, drink in hand, looking for Doris, or, before Doris, for anyone attractive and unattached. Ernie had never paid much attention to Garrett, but apparently he had a good memory for faces.

Garrett didn't seem to be a bad sort, but Ernie felt no desire to go over and slap him on the back in mid-trill. He presented an odd appearance, a kind of clean-cut youthful sleaziness; he looked like something painstakingly assembled by a Nuremberg toymaker, using nothing but old school ties, patent leather, and mustache wax. Garrett was a pretty good piano player, as far as Ernie could tell—which wasn't very far—but he had a trick of making everything he played, from Handel's "Largo" to "High Above Cayuga's Waters," resemble late Cole Porter. After a half-hour or so, Garrett began to sound like live Muzak.

"You go mingle with those people by the window, Ernie," Doris said, after a quick survey of the room. "I'll get the others."

"Do I have to get them to *sing*, Doris?" Ernie said queasily.

"I'll take care of the singing. I'll get a bunch together at the piano. You try to get some of them to dance."

"Okay. What shall I say, 'Put down the booze and start dancing'?"

"That might be a little bit too subtle."

"You're right. I'll play it by ear."

Ernie sauntered over casually and drifted into the fringes of an animated discussion.

". . . a true-false exam with about twenty million crazy questions. A real Jap. I bet half the class flunked. I went into it with an A, and I'm lucky if I wind up with a C."

"That's why I like Hoffman. He always gives essay exams."

"They can be rough."

"Yes, but at least you can say *some*thing. I mean, if you know anything about anything you can put it down and hope he's tired when he marks it."

"I suppose so," the first speaker said, sounding unconvinced. Noticing Ernie, he switched the subject. "Say, you're Quinn, aren't you? Ernie Quinn?"

"That's right. I don't seem to recall . . ."

"Tom Bolender. I think we met at one of the plays. You were with Doris."

"Oh, yes, I remember. Somebody said Columbine was overacting and we both jumped on him at the same time."

"That's right," Bolender said happily. "By the way, this is Columbine."

A tall, slim redhead standing next to Bolender favored Ernie with a radiant, practiced smile. "Thanks for defending me," she said throatily.

"Oh, you were good. I'd offer you a macaroon, but I don't seem to have—"

She struck a taut, pleading pose and delivered, "But Pierrot, I cannot *live* without a macaroon!" then threw her head back and laughed a rich, full laugh.

"Her real name is Heather," Bolender said. "Do you know everybody, Ernie?"

"No, I don't. Would you mind, Tom?"

"Well, that's Phil and Doreen—"

"Hi!"

"Glad to meet you, Ernie."

Ernie nodded and began shaking hands all around.

"—Cara, Jack, Diane—"

"Glad to meet you."

"I've heard a lot about you."

"Oh, Doris has mentioned you *so* often!"

"—Paul, Barbara, Sandy—"

Ernie made his way clockwise around the little circle, nodding and smiling like a happy marionette, forgetting names as fast as they were thrown at him.

"Listen to what Garrett's playing!" one of the girls suddenly squealed as a fast, loud beat began to issue from the piano. "Come on, let's Squidge!"

"Do you Squidge, Ernie?"

"Well, I really . . . I'm not sure. . . ."

"It's just like the Flam, with a little more hip action and hardly any shoulders. Come on," Heather said, snatching Ernie's hand and towing him out to the center of the floor.

They Squidged, and then they Flammed, and then, as the dance floor became more crowded, they switched to something with more vertical and less horizontal movement, which some called the Geronimo and others the Cannibal. Heather drifted away with Tom, Ernie did a few gymnastic turns with two of the other girls, then, satisfied that he had done well by Mrs. Flecker, he eased toward the kitchen for a drink.

The shortest way to the kitchen was through the living room, and as Ernie passed through the hall and entered this room, to which the Professor's friends and colleagues had gravitated, he was aware of a definite change of atmosphere. It was like the intermission on the opening night of an avant-garde play: people clustered in threes and fours, talking in low, well-modulated but intense voices, not about personal crises but about things that were significant or very, very *in*. At least they sounded that way to Ernie, who was only able to pick up random scraps, even though he slowed down and listened carefully.

". . . understand that cryptic reference to the *Zeitgeist* is the kind of thing one expects from a pretentious undergraduate, not a respected . . ."

". . . a music critic? He goes to the opera because he enjoys the plot!"

". . . got off the plane, and this strange little man with an enormous green cigar in his mouth came up to me and said, 'Prof, baby, don't worry about a thing. You provide the brains and we'll provide . . .' "

". . . opens a whole new field of interpretation when you realize that Buddy is actually a John the Baptist figure, and Boo Boo . . ."

". . . noticed that world leaders just don't seem as *charismatic* as they did five years ago?"

". . . can explain it best by paraphrasing Shakespeare: some men are born petty, some achieve pettiness, and some have pettiness thrust upon them. We have splendid examples of all three types right in the English Department. First, there's . . ."

Ernie, always willing to listen to nasty remarks about English teachers—you could never tell when they might come in handy—paused within earshot of the speaker of these words, a young man with a round boyish face, pug-nosed and pink-cheeked, and the beginnings of a blond beard bristling from the lower half of his face. He was smoking a calabash that looked big enough to be used as a kennel for an Irish setter. As Ernie caught a whiff of the smoke issuing from it, he got the distinct impression that the young fellow had done just that, and apparently forgotten to remove the dog before lighting up. He moved on.

". . . doesn't really matter, does it? I mean Sartre calls him a *saint*, and if . . ."

". . . getting a Negro in the Speech Department next year. Now, God knows, I'm not prejudiced, but it seems to me . . ."

". . . writer-in-residence for nearly seven months, and then one day the Dean asked him what he had written. Well, it turned out . . ."

". . . didn't *say* 'statement of a non-idea,' I said 'non-statement of an idea,' which means something entirely . . ."

". . . intelligent enough, but I can't bear to listen to him speak. He's full of wise saws and clever instances, and they all sound like the sort of thing you find on a plumbing-supply calendar. He speaks in mottoes, if you follow me. Just yesterday, he asked me . . ."

". . . has a manner that seems to bring out the natural reticence in everybody."

Ernie was almost to the kitchen now, and he noticed, with some annoyance, that the doorway was blocked by two men whom he knew and did not, at the moment, feel like talking to. One was Doctor Abbott, who had taught one of the dullest and most pointless courses Ernie had ever endured, a course that was a perfect reflection of the instructor. Abbott was a prig; was, in fact, a *prig's* prig. He was convinced that the mere fact of his presence in the front of a classroom was enough to strike sparks of intellectual fire from his students, so he wasted no time on such trivia as familiarizing himself with the course material, instead devoting the period to whimsey, bombast, and self-praise. His companion, Doctor Porteus, was the exact opposite; his trouble was that he knew too much, perhaps everything. Ernie had had Porteus for something called "Introduction to Mathematics," and in the course of the academic year had heard lectures full of valuable and interesting information on art counterfeiting, etymology, dress designing, smuggling, Zen, the elder Edda, baroque music, bookbinding, and dozens of other obscure, fascinating topics, but had never really been properly introduced to mathematics. And Porteus was a sprayer. Talking to him was like standing at the prow of a four-master in a high wind. Porteus let his spray fall on listeners and passers-by, students and faculty, the just and the unjust, with Godlike impartiality. To increase his efficiency, he had taken to smoking a pipe, which he employed as an aspergill to besprinkle everyone within a three-yard radius. But when Porteus was in top form, listening to him was worth a spraying.

". . . *another* identity crisis?" Porteus was saying, amazed. "That's her third this year!"

"She has no identity. That's her crisis," Abbott said, with a smug little smile.

"Ah, no," Porteus responded, flourishing his pipe. "She has crises. That's her identity."

Game, set, and match to Porteus, Ernie thought comfortably. Porteus always came through.

Someone emerged from the kitchen, forcing Abbott and Porteus aside, and Ernie took the opportunity to slip in past them. Doris was busy at the table, and a slim, goaty little man was hovering about her, practically salivating. This had to be Professor Northrup.

"Hi, Doris," Ernie said, neatly cutting in between them, "can I give you a hand?"

"Oh, Ernie, would you mix some manhattans? They're almost gone, and I have to get back to the kids, and I can't mix good ones anyway. Would you mind?"

"Not at all," Ernie said, removing his jacket and surveying the bar equipment.

"Do you know Professor Northrup?"

"No, we've never met. I've heard a lot about you, though, Professor," Ernie said, extending a hand and glancing quickly at Doris, who gave him a quick, horrified "Don't say a word!" grimace and fled from the kitchen.

"Are you with the students or the faculty, Mr. . . . ?"

"Quinn. Ernie Quinn. Actually, Professor, I'm a sort of liaison man. Maybe 'schizophrenic' is a better word. Part teacher, part student. Even part bartender."

"Yes, yes," Northrup nodded eagerly. "Tell me, are many of the students here?"

"There must be twenty or thirty of them in the family room."

"Oh? I must try to see them. I enjoy seeing my students socially."

"It must be fun," Ernie said, measuring out some vermouth.

"Oh, yes, yes. As a matter of fact, I think I'll just drop in on them now. In the family room, you said?"

"Through the living room, down the hall."

"Yes. Thank you, Mr. . . ."

"Quinn."

But Northrup was gone, little cloven hoofs, oaten pipe, and all. Ernie returned to his task, and having mixed the batch he tasted it and found it good. He filled all the empty glasses he could find, then donned his jacket, picked up two manhattans, and returned to the living room for more eavesdropping.

As the evening wore on, the talk turned more to professional matters, with an occasional petty observation on the Professor's good fortune intruding itself. Ernie tried to divert himself by counting beards (seven), then pipes (twelve), and then he tried counting useful words, words like "alienation," "heuristic," "ambivalence," "image," "relationship," "engagé," "absurd," "commitment," "escalation," "anti-novel," "existential," and "anxiety," which were flying around the room like snowflakes before the blast.

He noticed the Professor, moving from group to group and shaking hands, exchanging smiles, and accepting congratulations, and he decided to be nice to him if he got the chance. After all it was his party—his and Mrs. Flecker's—and his night. It wouldn't hurt.

The Professor saw him, waved, and started across the room toward him. Ernie looked around fast, but there was no one else close by; the Professor wanted him. Maybe they need some more manhattans, Ernie thought quickly.

"Ernest, I've been trying to find you," the Professor greeted him. "Do you have a few minutes?"

"Sure. What's up?"

"Let's go up to my study. I'd rather keep it private."

The Professor was friendly enough, but a bit too businesslike for Ernie's peace of mind. Faint warnings went off, and Ernie began to wonder what he had done. He hadn't insulted anyone that he was aware of, and he certainly wasn't drunk. His intentions toward Doris, though a bit vague, were honorable enough; as honorable as the circumstances permitted, anyway. What the hell was going on? Could it be something good? No. But what?

The Professor switched on the light and waved Ernie to a big leather wing chair. Ernie settled in it comfortably while the Professor poured two drinks. Looking around him at the close-packed bookshelves lining two entire walls, the good prints, the massive, paper-cluttered desk in an alcove by the window, the ship model on the mantelpiece and the crossed foils above it, Ernie felt a grudging admiration for his host. He may have been playing a role, but the son of a gun was playing it to perfection. The only thing missing was a roaring fire and a big Weimaraner sprawled beside his master's chair. Ernie thought for a moment on that detail, then decided against it; a Weimaraner would be too outdoorsy for the Professor's study. A cat would fit in better; a fat, peevish black cat, the kind you were always supposed to see in Parisian grocery stores. Or maybe a pair of Siamese.

"Here we are, Ernest," the Professor said, interrupting Ernie's appraisal. He sat down on the top step of a small library ladder facing Ernie, and pointed to the table beside the chair. "Just pile those papers on top of the typewriter, and you'll have a place to put your drink."

"Thanks."

It was good Scotch. Ernie had slight misgivings at the thought of pouring it down on top of two generous manhattans, but he forced himself. It was easy.

"I'm sorry to take you away from the party, Ernest, but I wanted to talk to you."

"That's all right. I usually wander off somewhere at a party, anyway. Having too much fun depresses me." He paused, thoughtfully. "I like parties," he explained, "but I don't want too much all at once."

"I know what you mean. I used to do the same thing."

"You did?"

The Professor nodded. "In fact, I once had a rule that I had to spend a half-hour all by myself at every party I went to. I'd walk around the block, or sit on the porch, or something of that sort, just to restore my perspective. It impressed my wife enormously when we first met," he went on, with a faint retrospective smile. "She thought I was terribly Byronic. Except for my face."

The Professor wasn't really such a bad guy, Ernie thought. You just had to get to know him.

"To get back to what I wanted to say . . . first of all, if you feel that I'm butting in, just say so."

"Okay."

The Professor leaned forward, his forearms resting on his knees. "Last night, when I got home, Doris asked me a few questions that puzzled me. She seemed to have become interested in school policy all of a sudden—suspension procedure, disciplinary rulings, that sort of thing. I didn't think much of it, but she did the same thing at breakfast. After she left for school, I mentioned it to my wife. She said that Doris seemed a bit worried after you left last night."

The Professor paused. As if by mutual agreement, they each took a long drink. Ernie groped for his cigarettes.

"I asked Doris what the problem was when I saw her this afternoon, but she was evasive. She admitted that she was worried about you, but she told me she had promised not to say anything."

Doris was as loyal as they come, Ernie thought warmly, loving her more than ever.

"Are you in any trouble, Ernest?"

Ernie took a deep breath, nodded, and sighed. "Yes. I'm sorry I got Doris upset, Professor. I didn't mean to. I had to talk to somebody, and she's the only one. I asked her not to say anything, because . . . oh, I just don't like to drag other people into my problems. Anyway, it's pretty much a closed issue now."

"You needn't feel that way. If I can help you, I will."

He wasn't bad at all, Ernie realized. At least he was offering to help, not just waiting around for the kill, as everybody else seemed to be.

"To tell you the truth, Professor, I don't think there's much you can do. It's one of those situations where everything is intangible, and it's going to boil down to my word against someone else's."

"Who's the other party?"

"A student of mine. I hit him the other day, and he thought he'd use that to try to pressure me into passing him."

"That doesn't sound so bad," the Professor said encouragingly.

"His father is on the Board of Education."

"Oh." The Professor nodded gravely. "That sounds bad. I'm beginning to see."

"That's not all. Even before this happened, my chairman practically—"

"Wait a minute," the Professor cut in, rising and taking Ernie's glass. "It sounds to me as if you've got a long, dry story to tell."

With a fresh drink in his hand, Ernie launched into his tale. He tried his best to keep it clear and orderly, to avoid editorializing, and make it as objective as possible. It was difficult to be objective when talking about Mikropoulous and Steve Hirsch, but Ernie tried hard. The Professor provided an attentive and sympathetic audience, but Ernie felt less and less confident as he proceeded. He knew he was getting a terrible shafting, but there was nothing tangible to fight, no proof to offer, only his own positive convictions. How could anyone believe him unless they knew Mikropoulous and the way he worked; and the way pressures were exerted, subtly but inexorably, from the unseen powers in distant offices upon the principal, the assistant principal, the chairman, and finally upon their goal and destination, the teacher? It was like the Army all over again, where injustice and absurdity showered down upon the helpless heads of the lowly with the magnificent impartiality and impersonality of rain; and the officers had all the umbrellas. Ernie felt a sudden seizure of the old inarticulate, directionless rage at being bullied and used by unknown people who didn't even know he existed, and didn't care, but just wanted him to keep in his place. Wherever you go, whatever you do, he thought, you play the game, and it's always their game, and you don't have a chance unless you switch to their team, the dirty bastards. There were rules to cover everything, but you never knew about them until they were used against you. In fact, *that* was the first rule of all.

"Nice bunch of people you work with," the Professor said when Ernie finished his account. "I bet they'll go places."

"Offhand, I can only think of one place I'd like to see them go."

"I can guess. How about another drink?"

"Yes, please."

"You're in a tough spot, Ernest, and right now I don't see any way I can help you out of it. Supposing I can't, what will you do?" the Professor said as he poured, with a generous hand, two shots of Scotch.

"I'm not sure." Ernie paused, then decided to plunge ahead and unburden his soul all the way. "You know, for years now, I've had a crazy kind of ambition. I kept telling myself I'd be a book bum someday." He looked over at the Professor and grinned sheepishly.

"Book bum?"

"Like a ski bum, or a tennis bum, only with books. I thought I'd pack up a satchelful of books and take off for Europe. Just travel, and read, and pick up odd jobs when I run out of money."

"It sounds good. Here's your drink."

"Thanks. Yes, it always seemed like a good idea to me, but now that I have the chance . . . well, now I want other things a lot more." He thought of Doris, now so hopelessly unattainable. How could he ask her to marry a dropout teacher? Or a book bum? Or whatever kind of bum he was going to be?

"There's no reason to give up on the idea, Ernest. You can be a teacher, and still have all summer to be a book bum."

"What makes you think I can be a teacher? After the Glen Park Mafia get through with me I probably won't be able to get within a mile of a school without being stoned."

"Glen Park High School isn't the world, Ernest, it's just one school of thousands. Don't lose your perspective."

"Well, that's right," Ernie agreed hesitantly, "but still, when I think of the tale of horror that will come from Glen Park if anyone ever asks about my references, I'm not too hopeful about getting another job."

"Do you want to teach?"

"Yes. I wasn't too sure when I started, but now—now, of all times—I really want to stick with it. I like teaching, I guess. Even after all this."

The Professor nodded. He rose and went to his desk, returning to his seat with a sheaf of papers.

"I can't do very much about the spot you're in at Glen Park, Ernest, but maybe we can help each other."

"How?"

"For the past few years, I've been trying to inaugurate a new course in the Education Department. Now that I'm chairman I can do it, but there are other problems. The big one is getting the right teacher."

"What's the course all about?" Ernie asked cautiously.

"I visualize it as a kind of workshop. We'd take the most promising seniors—a small group of them—and have them work closely with an experienced teacher. Ideally, each student would have the opportunity to teach a full schedule for two weeks under close supervision. There'd be conferences and group discussions and special problems to handle. I think that after a semester of this kind of training, the kids would be a lot more confident and capable in their first assignment. They'd know the ropes from the beginning, instead of having to pick things up as they went along, the way most of us did."

"It sounds good. I wish I'd had something like that," Ernie said.

"That's what everyone says. I think this kind of a course could be the most valuable one in our department," the Professor said, beaming.

Hell, let him beam, Ernie thought. Let him twinkle, if he feels like it. He's all right. We need more men like him, the old fox. He sipped his Scotch.

"But I'm having trouble getting the right teacher. I had hoped to get someone with about ten years' experience, but I can't offer a competitive salary. I've interviewed half a dozen teachers' college graduates, but they're too young and they have no classroom experience." The Professor paused to take a drink. Then, putting down his glass and rising, he pointed at Ernie. He looked, for an instant, like Uncle Sam on the recruiting posters, only beardless. "So I want you for the job."

Ernie was caught off guard by the Professor's offer. He had expected something like this, but he had never thought that he would be so pleased when it happened.

"Me? Why me?"

"A lot of reasons. That talk we had the other night, for one. I didn't agree with everything you said, but at least you showed that you have ideas, and are concerned. I want a man like that for this course."

"It's awfully nice of you to make the offer, Professor, but do you really—"

"Nice, hell," the Professor cut him off. "It's just sensible. I think you're the best available man for the job. The fact that you have enough professional integrity not to cave in under all this pressure proves it, as far as I'm concerned. Don't sell yourself short. I think you're the man I need."

"You do?" Ernie asked, unbelieving. The Professor had opened up a whole new prospect of this lousy mess, and it was a good prospect.

"Yes, I do. I would have offered you the job Monday, but the course didn't have final approval until last night. That's what the mysterious meeting was all about. I'm not being sympathetic, I'm being practical."

"Then you're not offering me the job just to help me out? It's not charity or anything like that?"

"Certainly not. I think you can do the job. If you can't," he added, "I'll have to let you go. You understand that."

"Sure. What would I be doing, exactly?"

"It's all here," the Professor said, handing him the papers he had taken from his desk. "That's the tentative syllabus, and some notes I put together. Take it home and look it over, and don't be afraid to suggest any changes you think necessary. If you think you can handle the course, let me know before Monday. I'll take care of the rest."

Ernie folded the papers carefully and slipped them into his pocket. He sipped his drink, then leaned forward. "You really think I can do it, then? All the trouble at Glen Park doesn't bother you?" he asked, sounding rather doubtful.

"You're not in trouble because of bad teaching, are you?"

"No. No, my teaching has nothing to do with it," Ernie said, vaguely recalling those words from another context. Aaron? No, Millard, that was it.

"Well, that's all that concerns me."

"I might get an awful reference, you know," Ernie warned, still not entirely ready to trust Lynn's estimate of Miss Grimm. "It will look as though you're hiring a sadist."

"If I thought you were a sadist I wouldn't be too happy about your going out with my daughter, would I?"

"No, I guess not," Ernie said thoughtfully. That raised another question, but Ernie thought it best to handle one thing at a time.

"Can you think of any other questions?"

"No," Ernie shrugged.

"You don't care about salary, then?" the Professor asked, twinkling ever so slightly.

"As a matter of fact, I do. What's the salary?"

"I can't tell you exactly, but I know it will be more than you're making now. If you have your Master's degree by September, I may be able to get you seven thousand. Seven thousand to start. Incredible," the Professor said, half to himself. "Things have certainly changed. I have students working part-time and making more than I made as an instructor. That's progress, I guess. Brave new world. You're lucky, Ernest."

"Brave new worlds don't impress me any more, Professor," Ernie said. "They always turn out to be the same old world under new management. The only thing that changes is the price. It always goes up, one way or another."

"You're quite bitter."

"I sure am," Ernie cheerfully agreed.

"Well, I can't blame you," the Professor said, draining his nearly empty glass. "Not after the deal you got at Glen Park. However . . ."

"Yes," Ernie said, closing that topic.

"Is there anything else you'd like to ask me? If you can't think of any questions now, I'll let you get back to the party. You can call me, or drop over, if you think of anything."

"That's fine, Professor," Ernie said, rising. "I'll let you know what I decide by tomorrow; or Sunday, at the latest."

"Good. Have fun tonight."

At the door, Ernie paused. There *was* another question he wanted to ask, the biggest question of all, but the thought of actually doing it terrified him. This was the perfect time; but tomorrow, or Sunday, he told himself, would be almost as good. It would give him time to think. He grabbed at the knob, opened the door, then stopped again. What the hell is there to think about? You love her, don't you? he demanded of himself. The job was all that was worrying you, and now you've got a job. He shut the door and turned back to the Professor.

"Professor, there's one more thing."

"Let's hear it."

"Well, it's . . . kind of indirect. It's about the job, but it's not *really* about the job, it's about. . . . Look," he blurted out desperately, "I want to marry Doris. I love her. I think she's great. Would that make any difference to you? How would you feel?"

"Greatly relieved," the Professor answered, leaning back against his desk and smiling broadly.

"You would?" Ernie said, taken aback.

"I would. She thinks a lot of you, Ernest. I don't believe I've heard anyone else's name mentioned as often as I've heard yours in the past few months. And when she brought you here for the first time, we liked you right away. I don't know if you realized it, but she's been showing you off to us every chance she gets. You must be pretty sick of the sight of Mrs. Flecker and me."

"Oh, gee, Professor," Ernie said lamely, realizing painfully that the Professor was not quite so dumb as he had liked to think.

"I've always wanted a son, and now I'm going to get one. Well . . . that's enough of *that*. We'll both be in tears soon, at this rate. Best of luck, Ernest."

"Thanks, Professor," Ernie said, taking the extended hand and clasping it firmly. "Thanks a lot."

"Let's have a drink to celebrate. Just a short one."

"All right. Fine."

The Professor moved carefully toward the bottles—hell of a nice guy, Ernie thought, observing him, but not too good at holding his booze—and poured two shots of Scotch with intense precision. Ernie recalled another facet of his future life with Doris, one that he thought might interest the Professor, and decided to clear it up now.

"There's another thing, Professor: about the job."

"Anything at all, son. Shoot," the Professor said, lifting the two glasses side by side, comparing their contents, and then presenting one to Ernie. Not even a splash of water this time, Ernie thought, with some slight apprehension.

"Well, do you think it might make things a little awkward, my being married to your daughter and working in your department?"

"Not for *me*, it won't. It might make life a hell on earth for *you*, if some of your bitchier colleagues decide that you got the job by marrying the boss' daughter, but you can take that, can't you?"

"I can take anything, as long as I've got Doris," Ernie said; a bit dramatically, thanks to the cumulative effect of two manhattans and three generous Scotches.

"Good boy," the Professor said, clapping a hand on Ernie's shoulder. "You know, Ernest, you'll be on your own; I won't be able to help you very much, and I definitely won't interfere —with your job or your private life. And if you make a mistake, I'll have to be twice as critical with you as I would be with anyone else. You realize that, don't you?"

"I'll do a great job—for you, and for Doris," Ernie said, ignoring the inner voice that said jeeringly, "Thou ham!"

"Let's drink to that."

They drank to that. The Scotch went down with surprising smoothness, and Ernie realized, in a vague and foggy way, that this was one of the danger signals. He resolved to splash cold water on his face at the first opportunity. Tonight, of all the nights in his life, he did not want to ruin everything by belching out of context, brawling with the guests, throwing up, or collapsing, sodden and helpless, behind some large piece of furniture. He knew from bitter experience that these actions could cause a severe strain in his relations with a host and hostess. By some miracle, the Fleckers had gotten a good impression of him. It was important not to spoil it.

"Have you asked Doris yet?" the Professor asked abruptly.

"No. No, I haven't. I guess I should."

"You're damn' right you should," the Professor said, steering Ernie to the door, "and right away. 'Faint heart ne'er won . . . ne'er won . . .' " He halted, puzzled.

"Fair lady," Ernie finished for him. "You're right. I'll find her now and ask her. And thanks again, Professor, for everything."

"My pleasure. Now go, and don't come back until you're betrothed. You know," the Professor said with a loose, well-I'll-be-damned grin—he's showing his booze, Ernie thought smugly —"You know, I thought you'd never ask Doris to marry you. Go on, hurry up and ask her, so I can get some rest."

Ernie started out the door, but as he gripped the doorknob, the Professor clapped a hand on his shoulder.

"You know, Ernie—can I call you Ernie? Doris always call you Ernie."

"Sure, Professor. Call me Ernie."

"You know, Ernie, I've had a hell of a lot to drink," the Professor began, then paused and drained the last drops from his glass. "I'm glad my daughter is marrying a man with guts. I like you, Ernie."

"Thanks, Professor. I'd better find her now, don't you think?"

"Sure, Ernie. Best of luck. Oh—one thing more."

Ernie flinched at the echo of Mikropoulous' Portia line. If the Professor cut him down now, he would run amok.

"Yes?" he asked cautiously.

"Will you please call me John, or Jack, or Daddy-o, or something? Anything, as long as it's not 'Professor.' I'm sick of that damn' name. It makes me feel like something out of a German comic strip."

"I thought you liked it," Ernie said, amazed.

"Hell, no. It started as a joke, years ago when Doris was a baby, and it just stuck. Maybe with your help, I can kick it. Will you, Ernie?"

"You bet, Jack," Ernie said with enthusiasm. He left his host with a great deal of beaming on both sides.

Ernie closed the door softly behind him, feeling wonderful in a slightly uneasy way. All of a sudden, things were looking good, and that was usually a bad sign. The Professor thought that he had guts. He was giving him a good job, and he was even giving him Doris. He's all right, Ernie thought, suddenly feeling like a mean hypocritical bastard at the memory of what he had once thought of the Professor. Jack. Well, live and learn.

He steered toward the festive sounds coming from downstairs, trying to squash his guilty feelings by firm resolutions to be a fine husband and a great teacher; mainly a fine husband. Find Doris, he ordered himself tersely. You can feel guilty later.

The party had apparently progressed nicely without the help of Ernie and the Professor. Of *Jack*, damn it. Ernie handled the stairs well, coming down slowly and maintaining close touch with the banister. He decided, before seeking out Doris, to try another drink—a mild one—just to settle his nerves.

The kitchen was busy, crowded, and smoky. Ernie maneuvered his way through a cluster of intense conversationalists to the table where the bottles stood. There were not very many left; the Fleckers had underestimated the capacity of their guests. A cute little brunette was perched on the edge of the table, and rather than struggle around her wordlessly, like a compulsive lush, Ernie was sociable.

"Hello, there. Mind if I pour myself a drink?"

"Hi!" she said brightly, shifting a little. "Would you freshen mine up, too? Scotch and a little water."

"Sure."

As Ernie began to pour, she slipped off the table and stood next to him, looking on intently, as if he were performing some obscure rite.

"Are you from the college?" she asked.

"No, I'm a . . . friend of the family."

"Oh. Do you know many of the people here?"

"Just Doris and her parents, really. Ice?"

"Yes, please." She took the drink and sipped it as Ernie worked on his own glass. "Just right," she announced. "Hey! I never even asked you your name!"

"Ernie Quinn. What's yours?"

"Betty. You're Ernie! Doris has said so much about you."

"She has?" Ernie brightened.

"Oh, you bet she has." Betty took a step back and looked Ernie over appraisingly. "But she's wrong. You don't look a bit like Jason Robards, Junior."

"Sometimes I look a lot like Jason Robards, Senior," Ernie volunteered. "Tomorrow morning the resemblance should be quite striking."

Betty laughed at that. It was a nice, warm laugh, not the kind he expected from her at all. She looked intellectual, and intellectual girls usually laughed in some odd way. Betty was damned cute for an intellectual, too; she managed to avoid the pallid, smothered look affected by so many of them and to wear glasses without giving the impression that she was hiding behind them. She wasn't the sort of girl who'd melt in your embrace, look up with soft, half closed, yielding eyes, and whisper, "Tell me of Shelley's struggle to move from Godwinian necessitarianism to Platonic idealism." Not Betty.

Of course, neither was Doris. And Doris was just a little bit taller, and just a little bit better arranged, and just generally great in so many ways. Ernie felt ready to ask her, now, as soon as he could find her.

"Do you know where Doris is, Betty?"

"Gee, no." Betty frowned thoughtfully for a moment. "She was with Ted the last time I saw her."

"Ted?"

"He's one of the graduate assistants at the college. Ernie, he's a riot. You'll love him."

"I bet," Ernie said, smiling, through clenched teeth. He immediately and permanently rejected anyone described to him as "a riot." Maybe Betty was an intellectual, but that didn't make her smart.

"Let's see if we can find them," Betty suggested, taking Ernie's hand and guiding him through the thicket of leaning, perching, squatting, pipe-puffing, finger-thrusting, palm-pounding, head-nodding, eyebrow-raising conversationalists placed about the Flecker house like potted palms at a reception.

Betty paused at a group of four young people, two of whom looked vaguely familiar to Ernie, probably from some collegiate bacchanal they had attended in common. Three of them were standing languidly, the two men with their arms folded, the girl in a chic, angular, *Harper's Bazaar* pose, one hand on her hip and the other fooling with a long, loose, clattery wooden necklace, while the fourth member of the group was talking with great animation. The speaker was a stocky fellow with tiny, delicate features cushioned in a large square face that seemed to be oozing over them and trying to absorb them. His eyes looked like peas dropped in quicksand. He was going full blast, waving his pudgy little hands in great sweeping arcs and tossing in an occasional bit of body English to reinforce a key argument.

"Of course he's difficult to grasp. He's working with an entirely new concept, motion in stasis," the square-faced boy said with an enigmatic gesture, intended, apparently, to convey the idea of motion in stasis.

"You make him sound like Calder," one of the others said thoughtfully.

"He's not at all like Calder, George. He's progressed so far beyond Calder there's no comparison."

"Excuse me, people," Betty broke in, "we're looking for Doris. Have you seen her?"

"No. We're discussing the art show," the girl answered.

"You're Quinn, aren't you?" the square-faced fellow asked Ernie. "Know anything about art?"

"I know a lot about art, but I don't know what I like," Ernie told him innocently. Fred Millard had used that line on a girl from the Art Department, and Ernie had been waiting for months for an opportunity to try it out. Betty giggled and George laughed appreciatively, but the others received it in cold silence. Oh, well, Ernie thought, three out of six isn't bad.

"We'll check the other room," Betty informed the group, tugging Ernie along. "'Bye now."

Ernie waved a farewell and followed Betty down the hall into the family room.

"Ardsley is going to hate you, Ernie. You caught him so beautifully."

"Is Ardsley the fat one who was doing all the talking?"

"Uh-huh."

"He sounded like an awful phony."

"Well, he *is*, but everyone—"

The rest of Betty's remark was drowned out by a sudden rush of voices that greeted them—more accurately, assaulted them—as they entered the family room. There was a mixed group of about a dozen loosely clustered around the piano, and at that moment they were bellowing forth the opening words of the "Drinking Song" from *The Student Prince*. Oh hell, Ernie thought with peevish disgust, it's going to wind up being one of those damned parties where everyone gathers around the piano and sings. He caught Garrett's eye, and there seemed to be a plea there—"Shout 'Fire!'" or "Smash my fingers! Do anything! Just get me out of here!" Ernie smiled and nodded, and decided to let Garrett suffer. It served him right.

There would be, he knew, about an hour of boisterous, boyish, collegiate drinking songs, then one or two dreary comic songs delivered, after a great show of reluctance, by members of the Glee Club, and then an endless series of old-time favorites, all of which Ernie hated with fanatic vehemence. In Ernie's view, anyone who went to a party just to hang around a piano and sing was out of his mind. He could understand it if you were stuck at a party where there were no pretty girls and no booze, but here at the Fleckers' it was ridiculous.

Ernie scanned the group quickly and was relieved to find that Doris was not among them. Much as he wanted to see her, he did not want to see her *there*. It would be a bad note on which to start their engagement.

"There she is, Ernie. Over there," Betty said, pointing to a group in the corner of the room. Ernie looked quickly and saw Doris disappear into the midst of the cluster with someone's arm around her. Something primitive stirred deep inside him; ominous Wagnerian chords began to reverberate in his subconscious and he heard the sound of a distant trumpet, calling him to battle, amplified by the quantity of manhattans and Scotch he had been downing for the past few hours. And this afternoon's martinis probably didn't hurt the cause.

"Wait here," he said, dropping Betty's hand and striding over to the corner.

He squeezed through the loose circle of tweedy folk gathered around a chair on which a straw-haired young man had perched one foot, and was now busily fooling with a guitar, meanwhile feasting his bright, All-American blue eyes lecherously on Doris. This, Ernie thought, has to be Ted. There's one at every party. Sooner or later, some shaggy-haired son of a bitch in his Levis and fruit boots thinks he'll step into the spotlight, twang out a few lousy social protest songs, and grab any girl he feels like grabbing. Not this time, buster, he said to himself.

"Doris, I'd like to see you for a minute," he said.

"Hey, now, friend, you don't want to take this pretty little gal away from us, do you?" Ted drawled, flashing a grin to the adoring world. He sounded like a talentless Princeton freshman trying to do Gary Cooper. Ernie countered in kind; he looked him up and down and gave him a cold, scornful, Bogart half smile, showing a trace of upper teeth, then turned to Doris once more.

"Do you mind, Doris?" he asked, taking her hand.

"You don't want to leave us now, honey," Ted said, grinning cutely and placing an affectionate hand on Doris' shoulder. Ernie reached up, lifted the hand delicately, as if he were picking a cinder or a piece of lint off Doris' dress, and let the hand drop.

"Don't paw the girl. Stick to your guitar."

Ernie could sense the sudden tension around him. It was like the showdown in the saloon at the end of an old John Wayne movie. He loved it. For years, he had been aching to do something positive about the Teds of this world, and tonight, for the first time, he believed that he actually could.

"Ernie, don't!" Doris said, her voice strained but low enough not to carry beyond the group.

"Maybe the little lady doesn't feel like talking to you, friend," Ted said, laying his guitar on the chair.

"Maybe it's none of your business."

"Now, listen here, friend—"

"Ernie! Ted!" Doris said desperately. "What's wrong with the two of you?"

"I can't stand around and let you get pawed, Doris," Ernie said angrily.

"What the hell do you mean, pawed?" Ted blurted, his face reddening. "You bust in here—"

"Don't push it, minstrel boy," Ernie snapped, in a cool, menacing voice that amazed him when he realized it was his own, "You'll wind up with that guitar wrapped around your head."

"Stop it, both of you!" Doris said, sounding frightened and close to tears. "Oh, Ernie!"

When he heard her say his name that way, as if he were on the pier and she was calling from the deck of a steamer that was taking her away forever, Ernie felt everything inside him slump. He was only half aware of the sudden flow of people that eased him away from the group, of a muted background of patronizing phrases such as, "All right, now, everybody," "Let's all take it easy," and "Calm down, calm down, folks." Someone had a firm grip on his arm and was steering him toward the kitchen. He looked around, interested in his surroundings once more, and saw—was it George?

"George, isn't it?" Ernie asked feebly.

"Right, Ernie. Betty asked me to come over and try to get you away. She thought there was going to be some trouble."

"There damn well was. And there will be, if that hairy bastard tries to—"

"Relax, relax. He's nothing, Ernie," George said loftily. "Not worth starting a brawl over, anyway. Doris wouldn't waste her time on that slob."

"I guess you're right," Ernie said listlessly. "Still, the whole thing bothers the hell out of me." He became intense and quite angry once again, as he thought about it. "Some creepy son of a bitch like that goes out and gets a guitar and learns a couple of lousy songs, and he thinks—"

"You don't like folk singers very much, do you?" George said, grinning broadly.

"I like *good* ones," Ernie explained, "but that clown is no Bob Dylan."

"Well, you're right about that. Shouldn't let it bother you, though. Come on, have a drink. Loosen up."

That sounded good. Ernie felt the need for some loosening up before facing Doris again; he was dying to explain himself, but it would have to be good, and that would take planning.

George led Ernie into the kitchen, empty now, perhaps because all the loungers had rushed out to see the brawl and had not yet drifted back; or perhaps because almost all the liquor was gone. George began poking about in the forest of empty bottles on the table and the floor, trying to keep Ernie amused by chanting a *sotto voce* litany of meaningless sociable kapok, highlighted with "Let's see, now . . ." and "What have we *here?*" with an occasional "Ahah!" or "Hmmm." As a bartender, George was an eclectic, probably through circumstance rather than conviction. Finding no bottle containing enough to provide two decent drinks, he began to compile a fearsome amalgam of his own by emptying the dregs of assorted gin, rye, vodka, bourbon, and Scotch bottles into a single glass. Ernie lit a cigarette, straddled a chair, and looked on, fascinated. It was better than brooding.

"We're not supposed to *drink* that, are we?"

"Why not?" George said briskly. "It's all booze, isn't it?"

"Well, yes. But isn't mixing it like that supposed to make you sick?"

"Superstition," George scowled and shook his head.

"Oh." What the hell, Ernie thought, maybe he knows something I don't know. Maybe he's a scientist.

"Are you a scientist or something?"

"No. It's just reasonable."

"Oh," Ernie said dubiously.

"You see, what gets you sick, Ernie, is mixing different *kinds* of drinks," George explained, hoisting the result of his ingenious efforts, a glass half full of an unappetizing tea-colored fluid. "Now, all of this is booze, so it won't hurt you. But if you were to drink this and then switch to *wine* . . . oh, boy!"

"Yes," Ernie said weakly, his stomach suddenly active and threatening rebellion. "I see." He wet his lips.

"Well." George paled a little as his own words sank in, but he set manfully to work, dividing his elixir equally—despite Ernie's selfless protests—into two highball glasses, adding, for some insane reason, a dash of grenadine, and splashing soda generously into each glass. There was no more ice in the refrigerator, so he stirred the drinks and handed one of the warm concoctions to Ernie.

"Cheers, Ernie," he said with a weak smile, wetting his lips.

Ernie nodded and took a sip. He shuddered and made an awful face. "It tastes like Old Specimen, George," he gasped. "We really need ice."

"Yes," George said faintly, turning a nice chartreuse around the temples, looking a bit like a fever victim in a movie about British colonials. "I'll bring some back," he said quickly, as he set the glass down and bolted, covering his mouth with both hands.

"So long, George," Ernie called after him; but there was no reply.

Ernie stood in the center of the kitchen, undecided, for a minute or so. He thought of splashing cold water on his face, but there was no towel in sight, so that was out. There were a few tiny ice-cube remnants lying at the bottom of empty glasses. He rinsed them off and dropped them in his drink. He really wanted to find Doris, but going in to the party again might mean another clash with Ted, and George wouldn't be there to stop him this time, and there would be a brawl. Much as he wanted to punch Ted in the nose, Ernie realized that a drunken brawl in the midst of Professor Flecker's promotion party would have lasting effects on his future. Of course, people were starting to get sick now—judging from George's case—so maybe the party wouldn't last too much longer. Ted would go, and his friends, and the singers, and Ernie would be able to talk to Doris without interference.

Assuming that she would talk to him.

He wandered out the door on to the Fleckers' rear patio, savoring all the unpleasant ramifications of this new possibility. Suppose Doris decided that he was boorish, possessive, hot-tempered, sarcastic, and belligerent, and decided to break off with him? It was too awful to think about. He decided to switch back to feeling guilty about the Professor. To Ernie, Doris' father would always be the Professor.

There was a single chaise longue, with a thick, soft-looking pad on it, standing close to the door. Ernie moved it to one side of the patio, turning the back toward the doorway. Proper brooding required privacy, and he was ready for some pure, classical-style brooding of a kind seldom seen since the heyday of the German Romantics. He settled himself, took a deep breath of the cool night air, and sighed.

The Professor.

He was all right, the old son of a gun. Ernie had been wrong about him, dead wrong, about as wrong as one man can be in his estimate of another. Sure, he had his ways, and they weren't Ernie's ways, and Ernie didn't like them; but what right did that give him to make the Professor into a fool, a poseur, an egomaniac who was trying to manipulate Ernie's life? The Professor's mannerisms might not be the greatest ones in the world, but at least he wore them proudly, not like Ernie with his Agent C21 and his crazy Kafka fantasies that everybody in the world sat up nights scheming about new ways to screw up his life. Nobody cared about screwing up Ernie's life, he realized; nobody had to—he was doing a great job of it all by himself. He saw himself, for the first time, as he really was, a terrified resident of a scared, cramped, selfish little soul lined with distorting mirrors that he manipulated to squeeze the whole world into the wrong shape, minimizing everything good and exaggerating everything bad, or inconvenient, or even mildly irritating, making himself a shabby, half-assed Hamlet who didn't have the guts to look his problems in the face. It was time to start breaking those mirrors, to push his way out of the mean little world he had made for himself and put both feet down solidly in the real world. It was time right now, tonight.

Right after this drink.

He leaned back in the chaise and downed a hesitant sip of the explosive mixture George had thrown together in the kitchen. He shuddered and let out a long, agonized gasp as it slammed home deep in his vitals and began gnawing away. A few of these and he wouldn't have to worry about tomorrow; or next week, either. He reached for his cigarettes.

The first deep drag burned furiously in his throat, tasting like something plucked out of a burning flophouse mattress. Ernie felt an unpleasant foreknowledge of the way his mouth would taste in the morning: as if it had been the scene of a gypsy encampment, or had been sandblasted with Coney Island sand and then had each tooth encased in its own tiny individual sweatsock, much-used and seldom-washed. But right now, Saturday morning's mouth was the least of his worries. He closed his eyes, relaxed, and took another drag . . .

Agent C21 exhaled a deep cloud of blue smoke from his El Kibir and reached for his drink, a curiously smooth mixture of three parts Jack Daniels Green Label and two parts Remy Martin V.V.S.O.P., with just a dash of grenadine. There was a soft footfall behind him. He sat motionless, his eyes intent on the surface of the glass in his hand, on which he could see reflected—

But he couldn't see a damned thing; the glass was wet and frosted. Maybe this stuff worked for Agent C21, but it didn't work for Ernie. Everything worked for Agent C21, damn it, and nothing worked for Ernie, but that was over now. C21 was out of business, finished, through. Maybe it was the booze, but something was pushing Ernie, and pushing hard. It was time to start breaking those mirrors. He rose out of the chair, grim and determined.

"Ernie?" said a soft, familiar voice.

"Doris?"

"Oh, Ernie, why did you act like that? You insulted Ted terribly."

"He was looking for it, the way he was pawing you," Ernie said, looking down on her, hard-eyed.

"Ernie, you were awful!"

Ernie took her by the shoulders, affectionately, but firmly. "Doris, if I thought there was reason for it I'd go in there right now and flatten every man who's looked at you, or talked to you, or brought you a drink. I'd start the biggest chair-throwing, bottle-breaking, glass-smashing brawl you ever saw, and it wouldn't be awful at all because you're my girl and I love you."

"Oh, Ernie," she said softly, seeming almost frightened; she sounded halfway between amazement and tears.

"Well, I do. I love you and I want to marry you. And soon. No more of this waiting around. It's no good for us."

"Ernie, you do love me!" She was crying now, he could see, but it looked like a happy crying. She was trying to smile and sniff back the tears at the same time, and she looked so cute, so perfectly feminine, that he had to pull her close to him and kiss her; and then he could feel the wetness of the tears on her cheek against his, and feel her shaking, and hear her sniffling and saying his name. It was so great he kissed her again, repeatedly.

He stepped back, then, and taking out his handkerchief—thank God, a clean one—he began to wipe away her tears, looking down at her and loving her so much it made him ache.

"Doris, I've always loved you. Didn't you know?"

"I could never be sure. I thought you thought I was just nice to go out with, and . . . you told me I had nice legs, and you said I had a great sense of humor, and a cute smile. You even told me I had cute *ears!* But you never said you loved me." She sniffed.

"I do, Doris. I loved you the minute I saw you. Before I even knew your name, I knew I wanted to marry you. But things kept . . . getting in the way. But that's all over now."

"Ernie," Doris said softly, leaning her cheek against his shoulder. "Oh, Ernie, I love you so much."

"Enough to marry me? Soon?"

"Tomorrow, if you like."

"It's a date."

The chaise longue was big enough to seat one person comfortably, and two cozily. After a long, pleasant interval of coziness, Doris suddenly sat up.

"Ernie, it's awfully quiet. I bet everyone's left!"

"Good. Very considerate of them," Ernie said happily, pulling her close to him again.

"We ought to tell my father and mother, Ernie," she murmured, settling into place.

"I think they may have figured it out by now. I had a long talk with your father just before I came looking for you."

"About us?"

"About us and a few other things. I told him all about Glen Park and Mikropoulous, and he seemed to think I did the right thing. He offered me a job at the college."

"He did?" Doris bounced up. "Are you taking it?"

"I'm going to let him know. I wanted to talk it over with you first, before I decided. I'm not just making decisions about *my* life any more; now it's going to be *our* life."

Doris snuggled close to him. "That sounds so nice. Say it again, Ernie."

"It's not my life any more. It's ours." He paused. "It *does* sound nice."

Doris purred agreement.

"You know, Doris, your father is okay. I had him all wrong. Ye gods, I had *him* wrong and everything *else* wrong. But all that is over now. It's been a busy week, but I learned a lot."

"It's been a wonderful week."

"Well, tonight has been a wonderful night, but the rest of the week—the best I can say is that it was busy."

He kissed her once more, emphatically, then rose and took her hands. "Come on, my wife-to-be," he said. "Let's go in and tell everybody the good news."

Waiting for the bus, Ernie had plenty of time to think. But it was a new, non-furtive type of thinking; the tall policeman of his mind was off duty, and he could think without turning up the lapels of his conscience and looking over his shoulder.

You can't eat your cake and have it, too, he admitted—but who wants to? If you keep cake around long enough, it just gets stale. Sometimes the only way to get the thing you want most is to give up the thing you want second most. That's the way it is, and there's no point in bitching and whimpering about it. It's Doris and no Europe, or it's Europe and no Doris; so that means it's Doris. Take your choice and be glad you have one, he told himself, because Europe and no Doris would be nothing at all.

He worked on it for a while, and it began coming out better. Once you made your choice and got the best thing, then you had it. Then the second best thing moved up a notch, and you could work on getting that, too. The system could be beaten.

Things looked good. He had Doris, and now they could work together on getting to Europe. It would mean making a few changes in the great dream, but they would all be improvements. He had a good job, if he wanted it. And he still had himself. He hadn't sold out, or given up, or broken down, or knuckled under, or caved in, or surrendered in any other direction. He had even managed to show that bastard Ted.

He took a last deep drag on his cigarette, flicked the butt into the gutter with a defiant Bogart gesture, and looked up the street. The bus was on its way. Tonight, he knew, he could take the bus and there would be no backtalk. He was Ernie Quinn, strong, victorious, unbeatable. Ernie Quinn, winner and new champion. He had it all, and he wasn't going to give it up. Not even on Monday.

Things looked good. For once in his life, Ernie could think of nothing to say and spoil it.